THE POWERS THAT BE

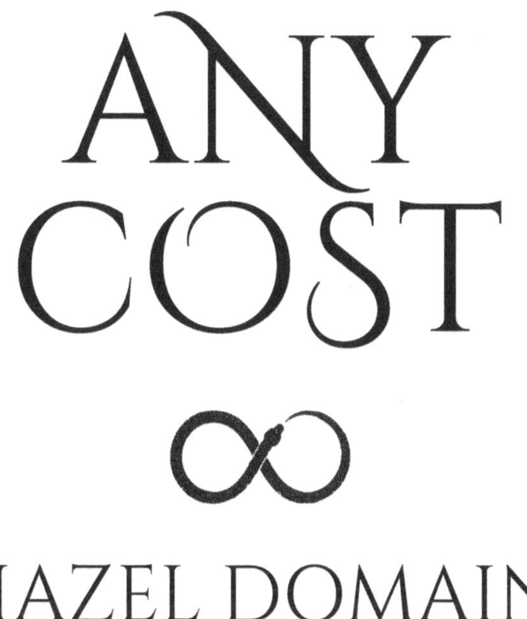

HAZEL DOMAIN

Riptide Publishing
PO Box 1537
Burnsville, NC 28714
www.riptidepublishing.com

Any Cost

Cover art: Simoné
Editor: Rachel Haimowitz
Layout: L.C. Chase

ISBN: 978-1-963773-03-3

First edition
September, 2024

Also available in ebook:
ISBN: 978-1-963773-08-8

THE POWERS THAT BE

ANY COST

HAZEL DOMAIN

For Gertie, the beta who stayed.

TABLE OF CONTENTS

CHAPTER ONE

There were bad jobs, and then there were *bad jobs*.

There were jobs where you weren't fast enough, where you missed something, where you couldn't do anything, where you just plain fucked up. Those were bad.

And then there were jobs where you did everything right, and everything went to shit anyway. Where you spent the drive home looking for options that weren't there, trying to fix what couldn't be fixed.

In some ways, Dominic thought, those were the worst.

His dad had always known what to say. Knew how to talk *around* the problem, letting Dominic know it was okay. Or, at least, that it would be. It was a skill that Dominic had never really appreciated, until now.

Behind him, Gestalt shifted his wings.

"You okay back there?" Dom asked, not really expecting an answer and not getting one.

"I think he's asleep," Micah said without moving. He'd been driving in silence for the last hour, eyes never straying from the pavement ahead.

"How about you? Are you . . . okay?" Dominic couldn't think of anything good to say because his brain was too busy coming up with *terrible* things like, *That sure was a nightmarish amount of blood*, or maybe *Did you notice they used two silver bullets for everything? Even the slaves?*

"I'm all right," Micah said quietly, and Dom didn't say, *That's good 'cause* I'm *unhinging a little*, like his brain suggested.

"It's okay to *not* be okay," he said instead.

"I know." Micah's smile tried for reassuring and didn't quite get there. "It's been a long day."

"Yeah," Dominic said. He didn't ask, *Did you know that's three thousand dollars just in silver?*

Micah didn't want to know that, he was pretty sure.

"How are *you* doing?" Micah asked before Dominic could come up with some other useless comment. "Any more side effects from the mana drain?"

"Nope, fit as a fiddle." He gave Micah a winning grin, which Micah didn't see. "Don't worry too much. Getting your mana snacked on by a feral birdman is just part of the job for us controllers."

Micah laughed, once, humoring him.

"You want to pick some music?" Dominic asked, because otherwise he was going to ask, *And those were the people who held* your *contract?*

Micah hummed noncommittally, and Dominic brought up the music app on his phone, selecting the first playlist and putting it on shuffle. "A Kind of Magic" came through the speakers, too low to hear clearly over the sound of the road. Neither of them turned it up.

"What do you think he eats?" Dominic asked.

"Who? Gestalt?"

Yes, because this was awkward and Dominic was going to fix it the same way he fixed everything awkward: by throwing food at it.

"Yeah, 'cause we're gonna have to feed him and that's gonna be a problem if he eats like, snails or metal shavings or Neosporin or something."

"His body's human," Micah said, glancing behind him. "Wow, he's really out."

"His body's human?" Dominic raised an eyebrow. "How do you know?"

"He's what they were trying to summon, that time." Micah's affected nonchalance didn't fool Dom for a second. "Pretty sure. On his wings, there's these circles that look like the ones I saw . . . before."

"Oh." Dominic didn't ask about before. Didn't ask, *Could that have been* you *down there?*

He wasn't sure he could handle the answer.

Gestalt didn't wake up for the whole trip, not even when they stopped for gas. Not when they pulled onto Dominic's gravel driveway and hit a pothole. Not when Dominic said, "Home sweet home," and Micah said, "Hey, wake up."

Gestalt didn't stir until Micah climbed into the back seat with him and shook him by the shoulders.

Even then, all Micah got was a groan and a brief glimpse of eyes so washed out they looked gray. Gestalt reached for him, pressing his fingertips to Micah's face, and Micah saw that light again.

The purple was barely a glow now, ashy and pale. The bright ribbon of *Dominic* was fraying at the edges, broken in places, and dulling even as he watched.

"What's wrong with you?" Micah whispered.

Tell him I'm sorry, the angel replied. Without being told, Micah knew that speaking aloud was beyond him. *I took too much and it still wasn't enough.*

"Micah?" Dominic said from outside the car. His voice was alarmed. "Is he okay?"

Micah stared at the creature. Beyond the fading light, his skin was turning pale and his lips had a tinge of blue. His wings were folded awkwardly on the seat behind him, and the tips of the feathers were turning a dull, chalky black.

He shook Gestalt again.

"Hey. No. No you don't. Don't you dare die on me." Micah glanced back to Dom, then to Gestalt. "I'll help you."

Micah's head was filled with Gestalt's confusion, too nebulous to even register as words. A protest that Micah didn't trust him. Micah didn't *like* him. Micah didn't want him there. Micah was angry for what he had done to Dominic. Dominic needed *someone* to survive that massacre. Dominic would help him.

"No, fuck you," Micah snarled. "Stay away from him. You need something? You take it from me. Not him. Hear me? *Take it from me.*"

A bolt of alarm, and then the collar flashed blue. Micah felt himself dissolving.

CHAPTER TWO

∞

Dominic considered dragging them into the house, but they were big and heavy, and they'd be just as unconscious inside, so it wouldn't really help anyway.

Gestalt was spread out across the back seat, his wings bunched up against the passenger door in a way that would probably leave them tingling when he woke up. And Micah, who had climbed in to try to wake him, had instead passed out on top of him. Micah's head was lying on Gestalt's bare chest, and one of the daiyura's arms was lying over his shoulders. Their legs were tangled together, and Micah was beginning to drool.

Dominic took a photo.

He should be way more concerned. He knew that. Two people had been rendered unconscious during a supernatural lightshow in the back of his car; it was the sort of thing that should worry a guy.

But, somehow, he wasn't. Kneeling on the front seat, his arms crossed on the seatback, he could see they were fine. Or rather, *feel* they were fine. He didn't know how to explain it. Back at the manor, he'd felt he could trust Gestalt. And now, looking at the two of them, he *felt* they weren't in danger.

It was like waking up and knowing he wasn't alone. Even when Micah wasn't touching him, Dominic could still feel him there—through body heat, or the sound of breathing, or some undefined sixth sense.

He felt that now.

Gestalt shifted, groaning softly, and blinked at Dominic in the light.

"Welcome back to the world of the living," Dominic said softly. Micah was still out.

"He made me," Gestalt protested, his hand tightening on Micah's still shoulders. "I have his mark. He made me."

Micah groaned. "Fuck, my head hurts," he mumbled against Gestalt's bare chest.

And then he must've realized he was mumbling against Gestalt's bare chest, because he sat up fast enough to bang his head on the roof of the car.

"The fuck? *Ow*," he complained, rubbing his scalp.

"You're alive," Gestalt breathed. The amazement on his face was reassuring to no one. "I tried not to— Do you have any idea what you almost *did*?"

Micah raised an eyebrow. "Uh, saved your life? You're welcome?"

"You told me to *take your mana,* you *imbecile*," Gestalt snapped. "Do you have any idea how *many* of you I could absorb and still not be back to full strength?"

"I figured you'd know I didn't mean *all* of it," Micah grumbled, trying to extricate himself from the tiny space.

"*I* knew," Gestalt hissed. "The *cuffs* didn't."

"The wha— Oh. I forgot about that. Did that come across as an order?"

Gestalt gaped at him. "*Yes.*"

Dominic clapped his hands together, grinning. "Well, good on you for not sucking Micah's soul out. And good on you for not letting the daiyura die in my car. Pats on the back all around. Who wants dinner?"

Micah kept his hand on the doorframe to steady himself as he stood. "How long were we out?"

"About twenty minutes. I figured I'd give it an hour and then start trying to wake you up for real."

Micah rubbed his head. "Yeah, when you passed out back at the manor, it was about twenty minutes then too."

Dominic went and hauled the duffel bags out of the trunk, slamming it with his elbow. Gestalt was having some trouble maneuvering his wings out of the car. Micah opened the door, catching him by the shoulders and hauling him to his feet before he could fall.

"Is that normal?" Dom asked. "Twenty minutes for an energy transfer?"

"I don't know. I've never actually seen the bond used that way before."

"So we were your *guinea pigs*?" Micah asked.

"Dominic was my guinea pig. *You* were acting as my captor," Gestalt reminded him. He was stretching his wings out one at a time, giving them little shakes like he was trying to wake them up.

Micah scowled. "Yeah, thanks, glad to know you only gambled with *his* life."

"I would think your distrust would mellow somewhat," Gestalt said, "considering that I didn't kill you even when you *ordered* me to."

Dominic fumbled with his keys, passing the bags off to Micah as he picked the right key off the ring. "Casa Blackburn," he announced, pushing the door open.

Gestalt looked around. "Micah led me to believe it was brighter," he said after a moment.

"Not at dusk," Dominic said cheerfully, kicking his boots off and honing in on the kitchen. "Gestalt, that door over there is your room, we're down the hall. Are you guys not starving? I'm making burgers. With cheese."

Gestalt curtly informed them that he didn't eat and retreated into the guest room. Unlike Micah, he didn't sit in the doorway. He shut the door and sat on the bed and stared angrily at the cuffs around his wrists.

Micah turned the stove burner on while Dominic made patties. He added oil and set the heat to medium so the oil wouldn't splatter, and then he went into the room they shared. He came back out with a pair of Dominic's pants and one of his own shirts. Dominic had just been thinking that the wider shoulders on Micah's shirts might help accommodate the wings better.

"We'll probably have to cut this or something to make it fit," Micah said, crossing the room. "The pants should be okay though."

Gestalt opened the door before Micah could even knock, surveying the man's offering with a wrinkled nose.

"The blanket is insufficient?"

Micah looked taken aback. "I dunno, I just figured you might want pants."

Gestalt narrowed his eyes, tilting his head at Micah. "Oh," he said, realization dawning. "Yes. Because that's what Dominic did for you. Yes. I accept." He took the bundle of clothes and shut the door without further discussion.

Micah rolled his eyes toward Dominic. "How long do you think he's gonna be staying here?"

"Have a little sympathy, Micah. He's been through some fucked-up shit. You were weird too, when you first came here."

Micah huffed and walked back into the kitchen. There were tomatoes and mushrooms in the fridge, and he began slicing them without being asked. Dominic dropped a patty onto a plate.

"You of all people know what Slate's capable of. Can you blame him for not trusting us? For being desperate?"

"I can blame him for bleeding off your mana like a vampire."

"Is that money still in the bathroom?"

Micah blinked. "What?"

"The four dollars and some-odd cents you said you hid in the bathroom. Is it still there?"

"I guess. I haven't moved it." Micah pushed the vegetables to the side and set to browning the buns. The oil in the pan was popping, and Micah added a shake of cumin.

"I think you should go get it," Dominic said, sliding the rounded patties onto the pan.

Micah replaced the glass lid and vanished into the hallway. He was back a minute later, the money held tight in his hand.

It was obvious Micah was embarrassed about it. He held it out to Dominic like he was expecting the man to hit him, and Dominic sighed. "Keep it, Micah. It's not about the money. It's about trusting me. Do you?"

Micah nodded.

"But you didn't then, and that's why you took it."

Micah nodded again, not looking up.

"So the two of you aren't really that different."

Micah wrinkled his nose at that, and Dominic sighed.

"Give him time. And hold on to that. Maybe look at it now and then."

"It's not the same thing," Micah protested. "What I took and what he took."

"Doesn't matter. It's the—what's it called—the *principle* of the thing."

"Yeah, well, in *principle*, it's not the same thing."

Dominic rolled his eyes and turned his attention back to the food, flipping the burgers once more and then sliding them onto buns. He added a full set of toppings to his, finishing it off with a glob of mustard. Micah did the same.

"I thought you didn't like mushrooms?"

Micah blinked at his plate. "I dunno, felt like a change."

After dinner, Micah put the food away and Dominic did the dishes. Gestalt didn't come out of his room. Occasionally, one of them would shoot a glance at the locked door, but neither of them said anything.

"Want to help me do a spell?" Dominic asked when the kitchen was clean. Micah nodded. Dominic gave him a thumbs-up and went to get his kit.

Dominic's spellcasting equipment, such as it was, lived in a plastic tote under his bed. He dragged it out and popped it open, looking over the assembled gear. A better magician might be able to pull this off with nothing but the circle, with maybe an incantation, but Dominic needed the energies mapped out in physical space. He had a neat set of tackle boxes filled with feathers and bones and fossils and, yeah, a couple of crystals—they were useful sometimes. A leather satchel held a collection of essential oils, and he had a spice rack full of jars of various plants. Velvet bags kept the sun off three different spheres, plain glass balls picked up at a shop two states over where *definitely* no one would recognize him.

Dominic still felt a little dumb about his particular flavor of magic sometimes.

He grabbed what he needed and headed back out to the living room.

Micah had already pushed the couch out of the way, clearing a space in the middle of the room. With the carpet rolled up, the symbols on the floor were clearly visible. The circle itself was a permanent mark, put there by Dominic's dad back when Dominic was a teenager and it'd become evident that spells were going to be a semi-regular part of their process. Drawing circles was painstaking and error-prone, and the elder Blackburn had finally thrown up his hands and done it in white paint.

Micah set out the candles while Dominic chalked in crosshatches and ikons. Each of the candles was joined by a sprig of sage and a dab of lavender oil.

Dominic rapped on Gestalt's door. "You up? I've got an idea for a spell, if you want to come give it a try."

The door swung open. "I don't sleep. I am always 'up,'" Gestalt grumbled, glaring. He'd ditched the blanket in favor of jeans, slung low over his bare hips.

"Good to know. Come on, you're over here."

Gestalt regarded the spell circle dubiously.

Dominic pointed to the floor. "Just sit in the middle and try to feel hopeful, will you? You're going to throw the whole thing off with your shitty attitude."

"This is extremely primitive magic," Gestalt said, but he sat in the circle anyway.

"Yeah, well, I didn't go to school for it or anything." Dominic gestured to a bottle. "I need to put some of this on you. Is it okay if I touch you?"

"Your soul is holding mine together; we are joined as intimately as it is possible for two creatures to be."

Dominic blinked. Gestalt sighed.

"Yes, human. You may touch me."

"Okay. This is a weird combination of smells, but bear with me and it'll be over soon."

Dominic twisted open a small dark bottle, and the room filled with the scent of roses. He tipped the oil onto the middle finger of his right hand, leaving a sheen. This he used to make small marks on Gestalt's forehead, lower lip, throat, sternum, and navel.

Orange blossom was next, anointing the insides of Gestalt's wrists, elbows, and knees. After a moment of consideration, Dominic also decided to add the oil to the inside of the largest joint in each wing. The feathers fluffed when he reached for them.

"I'm just gonna put a dab of oil there."

Slowly, Gestalt spread his wing out to give Dominic access. Dominic could tell he was trying hard not to flinch away from the touch.

In the light, it was obvious that some of the feathers were missing.

"Did they take them?" Micah asked, gesturing to the holes in the plumage.

"They thought they were good luck," Gestalt said stiffly.

"They're beautiful," Dominic said. Up close, the shafts caught the light like St. Elmo's fire, and he could see a pattern of spots and swirls in the black vanes.

Gestalt pulled them back, holding them tight behind him. "They turn pale when they're pulled out. There's no magic in them," he said hastily, turning to try to keep them both in sight.

Dominic felt suddenly uneasy, like something was about to go wrong but he didn't know what.

"We're not going to try to take them," Micah said. Very slowly, he made his way around the outside of the circle, coming to stand near Dominic.

The uneasiness faded somewhat, and Dominic thought he should try to stand near Micah more often.

"They'd do you no good if you did," Gestalt reiterated, still holding his wings tight behind his back.

There was a growing knot of fear in Dominic's stomach, and it was making his hair stand on end because he didn't know where it was coming from. He and Micah were both trying to reassure Gestalt, but the daiyura looked defensive, not dangerous.

"Do we seem like them?" Micah asked. "I mean, you were with them for a while. I know that look. So you know what they're like. Their methods. Do we seem like them?"

Gestalt's eyes narrowed. "Creatures of the dirt all seem the same to me. You're not as different as you like to think."

"No, cut the shit. We've seen inside you, and that means you've seen inside us. You *know* that I know."

"You don't know *anything*," Gestalt hissed. "You can *die*, human. What you saw is a *caress* compared to the things they did to the immortals in their possession. You were a sexual favor and a *pet*; I was a medical curiosity." He gritted his teeth, swallowing hard before he went on. "They wanted to see how I worked, so they *took me apart*."

Dominic's stomach rolled, but Micah's expression didn't change. "I know," he said softly. "In the car. You showed it to me. All of it." Micah's hand settled gently over his belly, his fingers splayed. His eyes didn't leave Gestalt's face.

Gestalt paled. "That shouldn't— I didn't—"

"I saw you, and you saw me. So I'll ask you again. Do we seem like them?"

Gestalt slumped, his wings relaxing somewhat.

"No," he said at last.

Micah nodded. "Good. Now let Dominic finish his voodoo."

"It's not voodoo," Dominic muttered. He wasn't sure exactly what had just passed between the two of them, but the fear in his belly was easing. He'd ask Micah about it later.

There was a proud sort of affection associated with the thought of talking to Micah, maybe tonight, while they were curled up in bed. Hopefully it would be one of Micah's good days, and they'd be able to sleep close, limbs all entangled and Micah's breath warm on his skin.

He shook his head.

Focus.

That warm little bud of affection was still there. He pushed it aside. He had work to do.

"This is ginger," he told Gestalt, holding up another dark bottle. "I need to rub it into the metal of the cuffs, and it's going to take a couple minutes because I need to say an orison while I do it. It kind of focuses the spell on the cuffs."

Gestalt nodded, and Dominic felt a sense of grim determination that didn't really match the severity of the incantation he was preparing. It was just a general relinquishment spell, and here he was, steeling himself like he was about to do something dangerous.

He must be tired.

For a few minutes they were all quiet, letting Dominic do the orison. He started with the ankle cuffs, making sure to work the oil into the full circumference of each bangle. His fingers slowed as he imbued the spell with the power it would need. He did the wrists next, careful not to disturb the dots of oil already on Gestalt's skin. The smell of ginger was getting uncomfortably strong, and Micah opened the door, propping it ajar to let a little air in.

The collar was last, and Gestalt hesitated before lifting his chin and granting Dominic access to his throat. Dominic spun the band slowly, rubbing the oil into the silver and trying to ignore the pounding of his heart. The daiyura wasn't making any overtly threatening gestures, wasn't even *looking* at Dominic, so he was completely at a loss for why his heart was beating so fast.

"Okay. I think that should do it," Dominic said at last. "I've just gotta do one last invocation to pull everything together, and we'll see if it worked."

This one he didn't know by heart, so he had to consult one of his books while Micah lit the candles. It didn't take him long to find the page, and he dutifully read the prayer—in Latin, of course, because all the old academics used Latin. The spells worked just as well in English, but Dominic could read Latin and it wasn't worth the effort of translating them all. He felt slightly self-conscious with Gestalt and Micah both staring expectantly at him. The mild embarrassment was joined by a discordant sense of anticipation and excitement, like he was doing something much more serious than a relinquishment.

He finished the prayer and closed the book.

Nothing happened.

The candles sputtered, but that might have been the draft from the open door.

"Did it work?" Gestalt asked.

"Bark like a dog," Micah said.

The cuffs sparked blue, and Gestalt made a guttural noise in the back of his throat.

Dominic tried not to laugh, even as a spike of irritation went through him. "Micah, that's a dick move."

"I agree," Gestalt said, glaring at Micah.

Dominic couldn't help grinning. Micah's smile was contagious, because who could look at that face and not feel happy?

Gestalt, apparently. He looked away, scowling but not exactly angry. "May I remove the anointings now? They're quite pungent," he said, wrinkling his nose.

"Yeah, shower's down the hall on the—" But Dominic didn't get to finish the statement because Gestalt's body did a little shiver, his feathers puffing and then settling, and the scent of oil began to fade.

"I'm more than capable of cleaning myself, thank you."

Dominic felt a twinge of irritation. He ran his hand through his hair. Gods, what a day. "I've got a couple ideas for things we can try tomorrow, but I think I'm done for tonight. Gestalt, if you need anything in the next eight hours, you're on your own."

Dominic was out before his head hit the pillow. He dreamed of a party where everyone wore masks.

Micah settled in beside him, pillowing his head on his shoulder. Micah dreamed he was a child, running through the halls of a now-familiar house.

Gestalt didn't sleep. When he felt the other two drift off, he slipped out the door. The moon hung bright over the forest, making the birch trees glow like ghosts. He ventured into the trees, eventually settling down onto the top of a large, flat rock.

He was still watching the stream when the sun came up.

CHAPTER THREE

The early morning sunlight was catching in Dominic's hair, making it gleam gold.

Micah's dreams had been confusing and fragmented, unfamiliar people and places that he'd pictured as though he'd known them all his life. He'd woken up vaguely distressed, and the first thing he saw was Dominic.

And that made it all okay.

Micah reached out, fingers hesitating over the skin of Dominic's bare shoulder. He could imagine touching—warm and solid, soft skin layered over hard muscle, the faint thrum of heartbeat beneath the surface. He knew exactly how Dominic would feel, and feeling it again wasn't worth waking him up.

Dominic's other arm was burrowed under the pillows, and Micah's mood darkened when he remembered the fingerprints that had marred the skin. Gestalt's fingerprints.

The memory replayed in his mind as clearly as though he were watching it happen all over. Dominic's frantic attempts to free the angel from his bindings, and then Gestalt, coming to life all at once and gripping Dominic with an intensity that made them both burn. The light had been too bright to look at, and so Micah had gone toward them blind, reaching for Dominic and praying, *praying* there was something left to grab.

The angel could have destroyed them both, easy as breathing, but Micah hadn't cared about that. He would get Dominic away from the creature, or go down with him. There wasn't another option. He hadn't even needed to think about it. He didn't remember making a decision. He only remembered the terror of his center dropping out from under him and the *need* to get it back.

Dominic was a constant, a fixed point in a world that wouldn't stop spinning. Micah knew he was clinging too hard to his former owner, but in moments like this, he couldn't bring himself to care. Dominic felt safe, comfortable, in a way Micah had never felt with another person. Dominic didn't have expectations of him, didn't want things from him, he just . . . *was*.

Dom's brow was furrowing in his sleep, and Micah reached out, smoothing his hair back in what he hoped was a calming gesture. Dominic's hair was fine and light and soft. Micah found himself running his fingers through it and drew back. He didn't want to pull away. He wanted to comb his hands through it until he knew every whorl and cowlick. He wanted to go over every inch of Dominic's body, looking and touching and caressing and, at the same time, he wanted to pull Dominic close and bury his face in Dominic's shoulder and never let go. He wanted to feel Dominic above him, that familiar weight, all their limbs tangled together. He wanted to hold him down and kiss him until he begged and then ride him until those blue eyes clouded with ecstasy.

He *wanted* all of these things, he realized, and then he realized that Dominic was waking up, blinking sleepily at him, already smiling as he stretched and murmured, "*Hey*."

Oh thank god, Micah had time to think, and then he was rolling half on top of Dominic, kissing him deep.

"Good morning to you too," Dominic laughed when Micah let him up for air. He cupped the side of Micah's jaw, and Micah felt like he was going to break. He pushed into the contact, nuzzling against Dominic's palm, but the touch wasn't enough. He needed to do something, anything, *everything*, but he didn't know where to start. Every nerve in his body was wound tight, and it had something to do with Dominic, but there was no direction, no goal, just a persistent, growing *energy*.

He leaned in, kissing hard and frantic, the stud in his tongue clicking against Dominic's teeth as Micah delved into his mouth. Dominic's hands were on his sides, holding him tight and steady, and Micah ground down against the solid warmth of Dominic's body.

There was no finesse to this. No strategy. Arabelle would be disgusted, but Micah didn't care. His body was thrumming with desperation, pounding through him like a second heartbeat, one that said *want, want, want.*

"Please," he murmured, lips brushing over Dominic's mouth. "Please, I don't—"

Dominic hummed in reply, rolling Micah onto his back and covering him with his body. Micah's hips bucked, pressing up against Dominic's and the friction was like molten gold, flowing up his spine and pooling in his belly. Dominic's cock was a hard, thick line along his hip, and Micah was elated to find that *excited* him.

Finally.

Dominic dipped to mouth at the hollow of Micah's throat. Stubble ran rough across his skin, and Micah thought there would probably be bruises there, afterward, and that excited him too.

His dick was driving him crazy, begging for attention with a single-mindedness he hadn't been able to feel since the early days of his training. He arched his back, sliding their bodies together, grinding against Dominic with a groan.

Dominic pulled back, considering him carefully. "What do you want me to do, Micah?"

"Anything," Micah begged.

Dominic was too far away, and Micah rose up onto his elbows, pressing his lips to Dominic's mouth. The angle was weird but the contact was glorious. "Anything you want, just *please*, Dominic."

"You sure?"

"Yes!"

Dominic laid him back onto the bed, kissing him all the way down. His hands brushed over Micah's bare sides, catching on the waistband of his pants with a hesitation that felt like a question. Micah answered with a moan, and Dominic pulled back, sliding the loose sleep pants over his hips.

Dominic's mouth was fire on his skin, leaving a line of wet heat up his thigh and over his hip. Micah made impatient noises that turned desperate when Dominic's rough cheek slid along the edge of his cock.

It wasn't that Micah had never gotten a blowjob before. Far from it. He'd gotten them from other slaves during training and during the various performances he'd participated in over the years. He'd even gotten them from owners who got off on being degraded, reduced to the level of sucking off a slave. Micah was well-accustomed to the feeling of mouths on him.

But not like this.

Dominic gave head like he kissed, all leisurely enjoyment and aimless exploration. His rhythm was nonexistent, and he made detours across Micah's hips and up his belly and down his thighs. He kept his weight on one elbow, his arm under Micah's leg, stroking the side of his ass almost absently.

Micah kept his arms above his head, crossed at the wrists the way he'd been taught, his fingers brushing against the headboard. He felt like he was falling, or floating down some torrid river. His stomach was twisting like he was excited or afraid or both, but every time it threatened to spike into something painful, Dominic was there, keeping him centered like always.

Dominic's free hand traveled up his side, past his belly and over his ribs, nails scratching lightly against Micah's skin.

Micah hesitated, then reached for him. Their fingers laced together, and Dominic held him tight.

Micah didn't know if he was supposed to come, and he didn't think he had the words to ask. The river was cresting, a hot wave pushing him forward, faster and faster. Something crashed out in the kitchen, and he felt a momentary burst of confusion but quickly smothered it. He was falling. He managed a weak "*Dominic*," but all Dom did was squeeze his hand and take him deeper as the wave crashed down.

There were spots on the ceiling, twisting lazily across the chipped plaster in a reassuring rainbow of colors. The tips of Micah's fingers were tingling, and he found one hand was still gripping the headboard. His other hand was still entwined with Dominic's, and with a guilty jolt, he realized he hadn't done anything for Dom at all.

Dominic didn't seem too upset about it. He was lying between Micah's legs, his head pillowed on one of Micah's thighs, distractedly playing with the hair leading down from Micah's navel.

He saw Micah worrying, and smiled. "Hey."

"Hey." Micah wasn't sure what else to say. "You want me to . . .?"

Dominic shook his head. "Weirdly enough, it's going down. I feel . . . I dunno, I feel good." Dominic's brow creased. "You good? I know you said, before, but . . ."

Micah nodded with a little grin. He was confused, but not too worried about it. "I'm good. Maybe it's just the shock from yesterday. Made me wonder what I'd do without you and I guess something . . . triggered."

"You'd do just fine." Dominic gave Micah's thigh one last kiss, then got up, stretching out and rolling his shoulders. "Whatever it was," he said, pulling on yesterday's shirt, "I'm not complaining. You wake me up like that *whenever* you want."

"You didn't even come," Micah protested.

Dominic tipped his head. "That's true." He was interrupted by another crash from the kitchen. "Oh yeah, our angel."

Micah scrambled into his pants and followed Dom out into the hallway.

Gestalt was standing in the middle of the kitchen, surrounded by the shards of what appeared to be half a vase. The other half, oddly enough, was on the far side of the room, piled against the far wall.

"What gives?" Dom asked, gesturing to the situation as a whole.

"Your vessels are too fragile," Gestalt groused.

"They're *glass*," Micah said sourly, picking a path to the broom closet. "What were you doing with a vase?"

"Moving water, obviously," Gestalt replied, rolling his eyes. His tone was dismissive but his posture was defensive, shoulders back and wings flaring to the side.

"Why?" Dominic asked with genuine interest. "Do you drink?"

"No. I don't. I just needed to move some water."

"Why? Where to?"

Gestalt gestured helplessly.

"Is that what you've been doing all night?" Micah asked, fishing out the dustpan. "Carrying water around?"

"*No*," Gestalt snapped. "I've been outside. I came in for this one thing and got distracted by all the—" he waved his hand dismissively "—fornicating."

Dominic made a little choking sound. "Could you hear us?"

"No, I could feel it," Gestalt said slowly, like he was explaining something simple. "Micah experiences things very clearly."

Micah's stomach lurched. "You were *feeling* me having sex? What the hell is wrong with you?"

Gestalt rounded on him. "It's not my fault the two of you were resonating so strongly other *humans* could probably pick it up. I couldn't *not* feel it."

Micah thought he could sense the beginnings of a headache coming on. And the day had started so well.

Fucking angel.

Gestalt rubbed his temples.

"So . . . what happened to my jug?" Dominic asked, when it became obvious Gestalt wasn't going to volunteer any more information.

"I got startled and dropped it." Gestalt paused. "It was somewhat . . . overwhelming."

"What, you've never been around sex before?"

"Not between people I was bonded to."

Gestalt said it casually, a little *too* casually, which would have been a red flag in Micah's book even if the words themselves hadn't been so obviously weird.

"Back the fuck up, *what* now?" Dominic asked. Apparently it was a red flag in his book too.

"Yesterday?" Gestalt prompted. "The transfer of mana? It's a bond, it goes two ways." He looked from Micah to Dominic and back. "You don't know about this?"

"*How* would we know—"

"So you can see into our thoughts now?" Micah asked, aghast.

Gestalt frowned at him, tipping his head. "Haven't you noticed? You've been feeling the minds of three people for almost a full day and you haven't noticed at *all*?" Gestalt paused, taking in their blank stares. "I knew your minds were chaotic, but I had no idea it was so bad."

"Bullshit," Dominic announced emphatically. "Maybe it's different for angels, but I, for one, can say there's *no way* I can read minds. I'm not getting anything off either of you. Micah, what am I thinking?"

Dom furrowed his brow, apparently thinking something very hard in Micah's general direction.

Micah shrugged his shoulders. "Probably something like 'This is bullshit, I want breakfast,'" he guessed.

"No!" said Dominic triumphantly, turning to Gestalt with a smugness that Micah realized he *could* feel.

"You were building a dam," he said suddenly.

Gestalt froze, and Dominic looked between the two of them with an expression of confused alarm. "What? He was what?"

"That's what you were doing with the vase. You were going back outside to mess with the creek."

Gestalt tried not to react, but the feathers along the edges of his wings fluttered slightly.

"Because you're in my head," Micah said slowly. "And that's what *I* do when I need to think."

"I think that means you're in *his* head," Dominic clarified, earning him twin glares.

"That explains this morning," Micah realized.

Dominic blinked. "What?"

"I woke up feeling . . . weird. I must have been getting it from you." The dreams and then, waking up *wanting*, wanting in a simple, uncomplicated way he'd been without almost too long to even miss.

Dominic shook his head. "I don't feel weird."

"Did you want to have sex?"

Dominic paused. "Well, I mean, as a general rule, yeah."

"Can you *not*?" Gestalt interrupted. "It was bad enough I had to be here for the actual event; please spare me the indignity of a *discussion*."

"Hey, *you're* the one who tricked us into getting all head-melded, so pardon me if the fallout is making you *uncomfortable*."

"I didn't *trick* you—"

"Why is half the jug over there?" Dominic interrupted, tipping his head toward the far wall.

Gestalt rolled his eyes hard enough that his shoulders moved. "It doesn't matter. I'll clean it up."

"No, I want to know," Dominic said, and Micah realized tendrils of curiosity and exasperation and embarrassment were creeping into the sides of his thoughts. And a little sadness, maybe?

"Dominic, do you feel sad?" Dominic paused.

"Huh. A little? That's weird."

"Gestalt, why are you sad?"

"It doesn't matter," Gestalt repeated, and the sadness disappeared under a wave of irritation.

"Because you broke the vase?" Micah mused, but no, that didn't make sense.

Gestalt hesitated. "Because I couldn't *fix* it."

"It's just a jar, man," Dom said after a second. "It's not a big deal."

"It's not about the jar," Gestalt hissed, but the fight was already leaking out of him. "I want to fix it, that's all."

"It's glass," Micah said. "It generally can't be fixed."

Gestalt sighed, then crouched down, making an odd little twisting motion with his hand. The shards under his fingers spun, floating up as though caught in a whirlpool. Four or five of them fit together, fusing into the rough shape of the vase rim. Gestalt caught it in his hand, holding it up for inspection. It was a little jagged. The pieces hadn't fit back exactly the way they should, and as Micah watched, it cracked. Part of it fell to the floor with a tinkling noise.

Gestalt hurled the remaining fragment at the wall, where it shattered into pieces that joined their brethren on the floor.

"Well," said Dominic, "That solves that mystery."

Micah stared at the shattered glass, wide-eyed. "That's amazing."

Gestalt fixed him with a cold stare. "Yes, I managed to make a few fragments stick together momentarily. The mind boggles."

Micah's head was filling with loss, huge and unimaginable. "Gestalt . . ." he said quietly. He wasn't sure what else to say.

Dominic stepped up. "Look, if you want the jug fixed, I can probably put it back together. Just gather up the pieces into a silver bowl—"

"It is *not*," Gestalt repeated slowly, "*about the jug.*"

"*Should* you be able to fix it?" Micah asked. "Under normal circumstances?"

Gestalt stared at the floor. "This is a pointless topic of conversation, and I'm tired of discussing it."

"Tell me."

It wasn't a request. The collar sparked, and Gestalt made a sound like he was trying to inhale and cough at the same time. "I should be able to fix it," he ground out.

Dominic looked sharply at Micah. "Not cool, man."

Micah was getting twin feelings of irritation and anger, but he ignored them. "Tell me why you can't do it now."

Gestalt was glaring daggers at him. Micah had seen this before. Slaves whose bitterness poisoned them against even their allies.

"I'm running on what could be termed 'emergency reserves' and I have been for quite some time. The power isn't there."

"Why?"

"Fuck off."

"*Tell me* why," Micah amended. The collar was glowing now, blue sparks winding along the metal, growing increasingly faster and brighter.

"Because I haven't been home," Gestalt said, forcing each word out through clenched teeth.

"Where's—"

"That's *enough*, Micah." Dominic crossed his arms, meeting Micah's exasperated look.

"What?"

"He doesn't want to tell you; you can't just force him."

Micah frowned. "Why not?"

Dominic paused. "Because he doesn't want you to."

"But he's not acting in his best interests."

"And you are?"

"Sure." Micah turned back to Gestalt. "Tell us how to help you."

"*Micah*!" Dominic shouted, at the same time Gestalt said, "Mana. Another dozen transfers, at least."

"See?" said Micah, shrugging off the pointed jabs of exasperation and anger. "We can do that."

"I didn't ask you to," Gestalt snapped, drawing back from him. His wings were tucked tight behind his back.

"I know you didn't, and you wouldn't," Micah explained. "But you needed to, and that's why I made you."

"That's not your decision, Micah," Dominic said in a low voice.

Micah realized he could feel Dominic there, at the edges of his mind, roiling like storm clouds. "Why? If he's going to be all sullen and defensive instead of letting us help him, then maybe it shouldn't be his decision." Dom's storm stilled, replaced with a subtle confusion. Micah pushed on. "It's probably harder for you to understand because you've never been owned."

Dominic's jaw dropped.

"Ah," said Gestalt, nodding. "You were trained. I'd forgotten." He tilted his head toward Dominic. "Micah has made his share of 'sullen and defensive' decisions. He learned a lot of things about the transfer of control."

He said all this evenly, calmly, as though discussing the weather. There was nothing to betray his intentions, leaving Micah all the more shocked when the angel slammed into him a moment later. Gestalt's momentum sent the two of them crashing to the floor, knocking the air out of Micah's lungs as Gestalt landed atop him. Gestalt's hands were fisted in his shirt, and the sparking collar matched the dark fire of his eyes as he leaned in close.

"I am not a pet, human. I will not be trained. Do not test me."

Micah hooked one long leg around his assailant, flipping them over and pinning him to the floor. "Don't act like a fucking idiot and I won't have to."

"You are a *child*," Gestalt hissed, struggling, his wings trapped awkwardly beneath him. "I was already ancient when your species crawled out of the sea. Don't you ever *dare* to presume—"

"That's *enough*!" Dominic shouted, grabbing Micah by the shirt and hauling him off the angel. "He's right, Micah. It's not your decision to make." He turned his attention to Gestalt. "He does have a point, though. If you're hurting and we can help, all you've gotta do is ask."

"And be in your debt?" Gestalt wrinkled his nose.

"We already saved your life once, what's another bit of mana between friends?"

"We're not friends."

"Yeah, you've made that pretty clear," Micah said, dusting himself off. "Are all angels assholes, or are you special?"

"We weren't the ones—" Gestalt started, then stopped short, his eyes flashing.

"Don't antagonize him, Micah," Dominic said, rubbing his temples. "Gods, are you two going to be like this all day? I already feel like I need a nap."

"I'm going back outside," Gestalt said shortly, pulling his wings high.

Micah watched him go with more than a bit of satisfaction.

"We really do need to know more about him," Micah said when he was out of earshot.

Dominic sighed. "He's a grumpy dick, but he's not a threat. Whatever secrets he's keeping, they aren't putting us in danger, so they're not our business."

"We're not in danger *from him*," Micah clarified, flipping the laptop open. "What about other angels? Where did he come from? And why's his magic all broken? If we knew that, it might help us figure out what magic was used to bind him, and we could get him freed all the sooner."

"He's the one who's bound. If he wants to be stuck that way, why do you care?"

Micah huffed. Before he could answer, Dominic's phone warbled. Dominic swiped it off the counter and punched the button.

"This isn't over," he said to Micah, before answering in an entirely more pleasant voice.

Some lady in Garden City had dug up a pair of spectacles with a tendency to burn people's eyes out. The cops wanted Dominic to come get the things contained, which was fine. Dominic wanted Micah to stay behind and watch Gestalt, which was less fine.

"You heard him, he's like a billion years old, I think he can handle himself for two days," Micah groused. Dominic rolled his eyes and went back to burning ikons into the side of the wooden containment box.

"Hey, Ges, what happens if you stick a knife blade in an outlet?"

The angel blinked at him from the corner of the couch, where he'd retreated to after it had begun to rain. His feathers ruffled slightly. "Why would I do that?"

Dominic turned back to Micah. "He's hedging because he doesn't know. And that's why he can't stay here by himself."

"So, I have to stay and babysit him." Micah frowned. "What happens if something happens to you? I'm supposed to be helping you."

"You are helping me. By watching Ges."

"Can't we just take him with us?"

"Yeah, 'cause you two are so much fun, I can't *wait* to spend two days stuck in a car with you." Dominic shook his head. "Anyway, for three people I'd want two hotel rooms, and I'm not doing it. Stay here and talk to each other. Make popcorn and bond over *V for Vendetta*."

"I don't eat," Gestalt reminded him.

"See?" Dominic said, grinning. "He's easy to take care of, just make sure he's in his jammies by eight."

Dominic's easygoing humor pushed gently at Micah, and he let it in, feeling it soothe the deep irritation that permeated his own . . . whatever it was. Whatever Gestalt was feeling, he kept it to himself. His side of the bond was oddly closed off, which worked fine for Micah.

"We don't have a phone," he said suddenly. "You've got your cell."

"I'll get you a prepaid while I'm out so you'll have one for next time."

"Next time?"

Dominic finished the runes and brushed the box clean. "Yeah, Micah, next time. We don't know how long he's going to be here, and I can't just put everything on hold. I have a job to do."

Micah set his jaw.

CHAPTER FOUR

Dominic left a little before noon, the sound of the car's engine fading into the distance and leaving the house weirdly quiet.

It took less than an hour for Micah to realize that Gestalt was afraid of him.

Gestalt wouldn't turn his back on him, shifting to always keep Micah in sight. He moved slowly, silently, as if trying not to draw Micah's attention, trying to be small. He spread his weight out onto his hands, making sure the furniture wouldn't creak. Micah knew all these tricks because he had used them himself, tucking quietly into the corners of back seats and motel rooms when he knew his father was going to take his anger out on *something*.

Micah dropped onto the couch, facing him. "You know how to work the sink. What else?"

Gestalt blinked. "What?"

Micah gestured around the main room. "I'm not going to be stuck on babysitting duty forever. Dominic doesn't think you can handle yourself here, so I'm teaching you. You know how to work the sink. What else?"

"What's an outlet and why would I put a knife blade in one?"

Micah located a receptacle and pointed it out. "You plug stuff in there, and the electricity powers it. If you stick a knife in there, the electricity goes through your body and you start a fire or die or something."

Gestalt crouched down, fingers tracing over the plastic cover. "There isn't enough energy here to kill me."

"And hopefully a breaker would trip first, but you get the idea."

"Would this kill you?"

Micah eyed him carefully. "Probably. Why?"

"Your avatars are fragile."

"Yeah. Well. We're only human. And electrocuting me falls under the category of things the collar won't let you do, so you can quit that right now."

Gestalt gave him a dark sneer. "I wasn't thinking to harm you."

Micah looked away. The angel had already tackled him once today. It wasn't like he didn't have good reason to keep his guard up.

"If the electricity is so dangerous," Gestalt asked, "why are there so many outlets?"

"We use it for a lot of stuff. The lights, the TV, the stove, the fridge . . . pretty much everything runs off it."

"Why not just use magic?"

"What, to run *everything*?" Micah considered a moment. "I don't think it would work."

"It's a flow of energy. It doesn't seem that complex."

"But it's constant. You'd have to keep the spell running continuously. It would take a lot of energy and concentration."

Gestalt glanced around. "This constitutes 'a lot' for you?"

"It doesn't for you?"

Gestalt chuckled. "I've done more powerful spells by accident."

The smile dropped off his face, and Micah felt that same crushing loss echo through the bond. He bit his lip. "You can get it back, right? The power you had?"

"It doesn't matter," Gestalt said evenly. His wings spread slightly, the primary feathers flaring, like he was preparing to bolt.

"Why is this such a secret? You already did a transfer with me and Dominic both. If a couple more will fix you up, then what's the big deal?"

"I still have some parts of myself that are *mine*," Gestalt snapped. "Though I don't expect you to know what that's like."

Micah wanted to be angry, to protest, but all he felt from Gestalt was pain. The barb hurt, but attacking back felt wrong. Like kicking him while he was down.

"Fine. Whatever. Come here, I'll show you how to work the stove."

"I don't eat."

"Yeah, you've said. Got anything better to do?"

Gestalt raised an eyebrow. "Off the top of my head I can think of several dozen more intellectually stimulating tasks."

Micah gestured around the room. "Like what?"

Over the next few hours, Micah gave him a crash course in twenty-first-century living. They went through the various kitchen appliances, the thermostat, the woodstove, and the DVD player. The latter was of interest to Gestalt because it was the only device whose function could not be performed faster and more efficiently with magic.

He still wouldn't turn his back on Micah.

Micah could live with that.

He showed Gestalt how to flip a breaker and change a light bulb and make the smoke alarm shut off. Gestalt told him how remarkably unnecessary all these tasks were, but he learned them anyway.

Micah offered to cut up one of his shirts to fit around Gestalt's wings, but Gestalt showed a marked disinclination to let Micah anywhere near him, particularly with scissors. Shirts were a human invention, in any case. He was fine without one.

Socks and shoes were similarly dismissed as unnecessary, though Micah thought he might change his mind if he spent more time outside.

Around six it started to get dark. Micah checked the computer and saw he had a message from Dominic. After assuring Dominic that he and Gestalt were both still alive, he opened his inbox and found emails from Ian and Mia.

Mia's proudly announced that she'd closed two more suits. They'd gone better than she'd hoped, and the message was less a notification and more a chance to brag.

Ian had forwarded him a collection of photographs. Some were mugshots, others looked like family photos. He wanted Micah and Gestalt to look over them and see if there was anyone they recognized.

Micah opened the first photo.

It hit him in the center of the chest like a mallet, and for a second he couldn't breathe. He'd seen the man before, twisting a silk blindfold between his fingers as another man laid out a line of shiny sterile needles. He'd been leering at Micah with a predatory grin that made Micah's stomach drop.

Micah clicked his barbell absently against his teeth, remembering the man's voice in the darkness, his breath warm on Micah's ear as rough fingers pulled his arms back and pried his jaw open—

"Micah?"

He snapped back into the present, blinking. "Yeah?"

Gestalt's wings were held high, the primary joint two full feet above his head. They curved forward, hiding his shoulders behind feathers long enough to reach his hips. He was looking at Micah like he couldn't decide whether to come closer or run. "You were afraid," he said hesitantly.

"Yeah," Micah said, rubbing absently at his temples. "Yeah, I just remembered something. I'm fine."

He should open the rest of the photos. He and Gestalt should sit down with a notepad and start making a record of who they remembered. What had happened. Who had been there.

Micah shut the laptop.

CHAPTER FIVE

Gestalt watched the human cautiously. Micah wasn't doing anything overtly threatening at the moment, but as long as the spell kept Gestalt bound, he was at the human's mercy. And Micah knew it. And Gestalt knew that Micah knew it.

It was pointless staying on guard against such a threat, keeping him always in sight and staying out of reach. Why brace for flight that the man could arrest with a word?

Humans had a knack for exploiting the absurd, Gestalt had found. It wasn't enough to cut him or beat him or rape him; they wanted him to bring them the instruments they'd use to do it. They wanted him to beg for it. They wanted him to lock the restraints around his own wrists and spread for them. They wanted him to count off the strokes and ask for more and thank them for all of it afterward.

Gestalt had resisted until the silver bands had glowed hot, blistering his skin. It hadn't mattered. He'd eventually obeyed anyway, the pain of disobedience accentuating the shame and pain and fear of compliance.

Micah knew all about these behaviors. Gestalt had seen it in his mind. The sweat and skin and heat and exhaustion and pain, the obedience and the games. Micah was only human, so while the physical reality of his experiences was comparably mild, it had still left him with scars too deep for Gestalt to heal. He'd wiped Micah's skin clean, but the human's mind was fractured.

He'd been broken a long time. He'd been ordered to endure the same indignities as Gestalt, but Micah hadn't needed magic to make him comply. And there were darker scars than that. Micah *understood* his masters. His mind was clouded with reservations, but behind them, Micah knew how to inflict those horrors on others.

Gestalt couldn't help but flinch when Micah spoke up. He braced for a simple order, like *Take your clothes off* or *Get me hard.* That was how it usually started. There was no point in pretending Micah wasn't interested in sex. Not after what Gestalt had heard this morning.

But, instead, Micah told him about electricity and climate control and microwaves and refrigerators and light bulbs and bathtubs and shoes and couches and garbage disposals and dishwashers and fire extinguishers, and Gestalt began to understand.

Even in his ridiculously limited corporeal form, Gestalt could stand stationary long enough for stone to erode, without getting hungry or cold or even uncomfortable.

Humans, he realized, had to manipulate their environment in a hundred tiny ways every minute just to keep themselves alive. No wonder they'd never learned to do proper magic. No wonder they felt the need to keep beings like Gestalt under such rigid control. He'd go insane too if he were like them, floating through life in bodies as fragile as soap bubbles, cowering at any stray breeze.

Gestalt contemplated this while Micah checked the computer. The machine was a way for humans to communicate, Gestalt knew that much. Humans couldn't sense each other, couldn't talk to each other across distances except by sending their voices as electronic signals or transferring written messages. It was so limited, so confining, that Gestalt felt a crushing sense of loneliness on their behalf, suddenly grateful for—

He clenched his eyes shut, cutting off the line of thought. No sense thinking about it now.

The discomfort wouldn't subside, and Gestalt shoved at it, pushing it down, willing it to disappear. It built inside him, an acid-sour ball of fear that grew and grew until he realized it wasn't coming from him. It was coming from Micah.

Gestalt frowned, taking stock of their surroundings. He couldn't sense any immediate threat. "Micah?"

The man started, breaking his gaze away from the laptop and looking at Gestalt. "Sorry," he muttered. "Lost in thought."

Gestalt probed gently at the dwindling fear, and like before, Micah's mind scrabbled at the bond, circling it and crashing against Gestalt's mind like a flood. It was almost possible to forget how much the human hated him.

"Why do your memories frighten you?"

Micah's look was sharp. "You should know. You were there."

"I fought them," Gestalt said, tipping his head. "As hard as I could. Every day. But you sought to please them and were proud when you did."

"I can work through pain. That doesn't mean it doesn't hurt."

"Why would you want to please people who hurt you?"

"What's with the twenty questions all of a sudden? Don't pretend you care."

Gestalt conceded the point. "I admit curiosity. You're very multifaceted creatures. You have such complex minds, like you're trying to fit a whole lifetime of thought into your abrupt lifespans. There are contradictions. It's . . . interesting."

"Thanks, Ges," Micah said drily, and Gestalt wondered if he had made a mistake. "Speaking of our tiny little lifespans, how long until we can do another transfer?"

Gestalt scowled.

Micah set the laptop aside. "Don't be like that. You need it, right? And I'm offering."

The collar sparked. Right. Because it was pointless to argue against Micah. If he wanted Gestalt to make a connection, then Gestalt would eventually have to. Micah would force him open, penetrating into his core and there would be nothing he could do to—

"Figure of speech," Micah amended. "Be like that if you want. But I'd like for you to accept my help."

"Don't pretend *you* care," Gestalt snapped. "You don't want me here and you don't trust me."

Micah nodded. "True. But the sooner you're healthy, the sooner you can fuck off back to being grouchy wherever it is you came from."

Gestalt couldn't contain it this time, and he could *see* the reaction as the wave of loss spilled out of him and into Micah: Micah gasped, his mouth falling open.

"Holy *shit*," Micah breathed. "What did I *say*?"

Gestalt didn't answer. Micah pawed at the bond, and Gestalt shoved against the human's mind, pushing him away. "Stop it!"

Micah looked confused. "I didn't do anything."

"Leave the bond alone."

"I didn't do anything! You're the one sending tsunamis of grief at me!"

Grief.

Was that what it was? Gestalt supposed it was as good a term as any. Micah was nudging at him again, pressed against the bond in a way Gestalt wasn't used to, but at least the human wasn't picking at it anymore.

"I want to go home too," Gestalt said. His voice was low. He wasn't sure the human could even hear him. He brought one hand up, twisting at the silver bangle wrapped around his wrist. "Believe me."

"Then let me help you."

The collar flashed, and Gestalt heard Micah swear. He grit his teeth, resisting the magic seizing through his body.

"*Figure of speech*!" Micah shouted, and the collar dropped its assault. "Fuck, that's a pain in the ass."

"So quit playing with it! Give me the damn order and get it over with!" Gestalt was shaking, ready to fight the onslaught when it came. He met Micah's gaze, clenching his jaw, daring the human to make his move.

"It was an accident. I won't make you open a bond."

"*Again*," Gestalt spat.

Micah nodded. "Fair enough. If you want to sit over there feeling sorry for yourself because you're burned out and won't ask for help, fine. But you get no sympathy from me."

"I didn't ask for your sympathy."

Micah groaned, rolling his eyes. "Why are you like this?"

"Because I wasn't raised in captivity, and have goals beyond the desire to please the being in closest proximity. You should take notes."

He shouldn't be antagonizing Micah. The human could hurt him, badly. In a way, Gestalt hoped he would. That Micah would finally do whatever it was he was going to do, so Gestalt could stop wondering. He'd been shot and stabbed and burned and a dozen worse violations.

He could take it. At least if it were happening, he could stop walking on eggshells and *fight*.

Micah was staring at him, a furrow between his brows. "What is that? Is that you? What are you doing?"

Gestalt realized he'd been shoring up the bond, protecting against an attack that Micah wasn't even close to being able to mount. He let the defenses collapse.

Something edged in from the side, questioning and hesitant.

"Dominic?" Micah asked, his eyes widening.

Gestalt sighed, rubbing his eyes, and sent the absent controller a reassurance.

"Is that Dominic?" Micah asked again, this time addressing Gestalt.

"Yes. I suppose this must be very confusing for him, lacking context."

"It's confusing for me *with* context. What was that?"

"Nothing. Leave it alone."

"Bullshit. You're telling me you can do stuff in my head from *across the state*?"

"Across the universe, probably."

Micah blinked. Gestalt could feel him worrying the bond again. Micah was concentrating, the little furrow between his eyebrows returning. He nudged into the bond, more directed, persistent, and then very clearly, Gestalt felt, *What is this?*

Back off! he shot back, and Micah twitched.

"That's you," he breathed. "That thing I can feel. It's you. And Dominic?"

"You might not be able to connect to him since you're both human and your minds are weak."

"How would I know? What's you and what's him?"

Gestalt tried not to be offended. "It would be obvious that he was different from me."

"So what were you doing before? It felt like someone was stuffing a wet towel in my ear. Were you trying to get inside my mind?"

Gestalt scoffed. "There's nothing in your mind that's of interest to me."

"Then what was it?"

"I was . . . shoring up a defense. Not that you'd be able to attack. It's a reflex."

"You expect me to attack you?"

"*Of course* I'm expecting an attack." He laid his hand across his chest, fingers tapping meaningfully against the scar. "I've known men who enjoy the anticipation, but you don't seem like one of them. It concerns me that you're waiting."

Micah's hands tightened. "I only marked you to help Dominic. And I've been giving you orders to help *you*. I saved your life, remember? You'd do the same if someone's life was on the line."

"I would rather *die* than force a bond on someone who didn't want it," Gestalt growled. "It wasn't your place to give me that order, and you have no comprehension of what you've done. What you feel as a 'wet towel,' I feel as a river of distrust and anger and resentment flowing into my head *constantly*. So you'll have to forgive me if I don't subscribe to your 'for your own good' bullshit."

Micah dropped his eyes, studying the white lines on the floor. Gestalt glared at him, daring him to defend himself.

"I didn't know," he said eventually. "That it was like that."

"Of course you didn't. You're drowning in a sea of things you don't know and that's why you don't get to *give me orders*."

"Is there a way to stop it? Undo the bond so you can't feel me anymore?"

"No."

"And every transfer makes it stronger?"

Micah still wouldn't look at him, so he hummed an affirmative. He assumed Micah could hear.

"I'm not going to attack you. I don't . . ." Micah ran a hand through his hair, pushing it out of his face, only to have it fall back a moment later. "Honestly, I shouldn't even be making decisions for myself. So it stands to reason that I'd fuck up making them for you."

Gestalt nodded. Micah was pressing into the bond again, grasping at it and holding tight, like he was trying to kink a garden hose. "It won't help," Gestalt said shortly.

Micah looked up. "What?"

"That thing you're doing. It won't help."

"I didn't realize I was doing anything."

Gestalt sighed. They weren't getting anywhere. He settled cross-legged in the center of the floor. "Come here."

Micah stared at him a moment and then obeyed, as Gestalt suspected he would, folding himself into the same position.

"Put your hands like this," Gestalt said, laying his palms over his knees. The silver bangles scratched on the denim when he moved.

It was a little disconcerting, being this close to the human. Micah wasn't like the other humans Gestalt had met, didn't seem to want the things they wanted. But sitting here, almost close enough to touch, it wasn't hard to imagine Micah leaning forward. He was bigger than Gestalt; he'd have no trouble pinning him to the floor. Micah would murmur in his ear, and the collar would burn, and eventually Gestalt would have no choice—

Micah pushed at the bond and Gestalt recoiled, wings flaring as he tried to recover his balance.

"What were you thinking about?" Micah asked, but Gestalt just shook his head.

"Palms on your knees," he said. "Straighten your arms a little more—put your shoulders back."

Micah did as he was told, mimicking Gestalt's pose.

"Good. Now you need to breathe slowly. Use your diaphragm, not your chest. Do you feel it?"

Micah took a couple of slow breaths. "No. What am I supposed to feel?"

"The bond. You've been worrying at it since it was formed. You can feel it, you just can't recognize it. Keep breathing."

"Where is it?"

"It's metaphysical. It doesn't have a location."

"Where do *you* feel it?"

Gestalt paused, circling the edges of the bond, trying to connect them to a place on his body. After a moment he raised his hand, letting his fingers rest above his breastbone. "Here, I suppose."

"Okay." Micah closed his eyes, drawing slow breaths in through his nose. The pose he held was unnaturally still, and Gestalt's mind went back to the memories of Micah's training.

"The pose is supposed to center your energy. It doesn't work any better if you're a statue."

Micah nodded, his eyes still closed. He didn't relax. But he didn't give up.

Outside, the sun went down and the darkness around the house deepened. Micah didn't move.

Gestalt sighed. It wasn't working. "Keep your eyes closed," he said, "and lean forward."

Micah did as he was told, his eyebrows furrowed and his jaw tight. Gestalt extended his wings, arching them up and around the two of them. His feathers rustled as the tips of his primaries crossed behind Micah's back. At the same time, he leaned forward, his forehead pressing lightly against Micah's.

He closed his eyes, berated himself for making such a terrible decision, and reached out through the bond.

Gestalt brushed against Micah's side of it, pressing hard enough for the human to feel.

Micah's eyes flew open. "Oh," he said softly. And then he attacked it, launching himself at the bond and clambering all over it, looking for a way in.

Gestalt shot back, slamming the bond closed as tight as he could, his wings splaying wide as he scrabbled across the floor.

"What? What?" Micah asked, his eyes wide as he watched Gestalt. He hadn't moved. "What did I do?"

Even as he said it, he was circling his side of the bond, sending little jabs at the link.

"I felt it," Micah said. "Whatever you did. I felt it. I could feel you. I think . . ."

The assault on the bond renewed, and Gestalt hissed, drawing his wings around himself.

"That's you," Micah breathed, staring. Gestalt kicked himself. He should have known this would end badly.

"Is it hurting you?" Micah asked. "Whatever I'm doing, does it hurt?"

Gestalt paused. How to describe . . . "No," he said after a moment. "It doesn't hurt. It's just . . . invasive."

"I'm not trying to," Micah said, and Gestalt nodded.

"You don't know how to control yourself. It's to be expected."

Micah narrowed his eyes. "I can control myself fine. I just have to figure out what the hell I'm supposed to be controlling."

Gestalt rolled his eyes. "You think holding still is the same as self-control." He made a dismissive gesture. "Your mind is like a child's, running amok and latching on to anything new and shiny."

"So *teach* me how to control it."

Gestalt paused. "I'm not sure you can learn."

Micah laughed at that. "Only one way to find out, right? You would have to show me what I'm doing. Or what I *should* be doing."

Gestalt frowned. "The bond is like . . . It cannot exist as a physical object. It is a passageway and an entity simultaneously. On your side, it is a point containing all of me, and on my side, it is a point containing all of you. We contain each other. Do you understand?"

Micah gave him a blank look. Gestalt sighed. Very slowly, he moved closer to Micah, settling into the same cross-legged position from earlier. He kept his wings back, suddenly unwilling to put them within Micah's reach.

Micah leaned forward, like he had before, and Gestalt flinched back.

"Sorry," Micah said, retreating.

"No. You— It's difficult being this close to one of you. You're very . . . present." He didn't know how else to explain it. Even when Micah was sitting still, he was in constant motion. His muscles were perpetually tensing and adjusting, keeping his blood flowing and his temperature steady. Even his slowed breathing kept his whole body thrumming with energy.

When Gestalt held still, his body was solid as marble. A bloodhound could pass within five feet without detecting his presence. But humans, humans seemed to be always in the process of dissolving into their environment. From this close, it was impossible to miss the heat and the scent and the motion of the man across from him.

It set him on edge.

Gestalt had felt breath on his skin, hot and sticky. The steady beat of a pulse when hands tightened on his throat. Flushed skin riding against him, slippery with sweat.

It was difficult being near them.

He forced himself to calm, to ignore the shiver up his back. He relaxed his wings, letting them settle naturally behind him. Micah was pressing at the bond, *again*, and Gestalt focused on the task at hand.

"Put your hands back," he instructed, nodding when Micah mirrored his pose. "I'm going to try to reach out again. When you feel it, try to leave it alone, understand? You try not to attack it and I'll try to withstand your pawing, and maybe we can find some middle ground."

"I'm pawing at it?"

"With some enthusiasm."

Micah frowned. "I didn't know I was doing that."

"I know."

"What does it feel like?"

Gestalt sighed. "I cannot describe it to you."

"Can you do it back to me? So I could feel?"

"No. You have no natural defenses, and certainly none strong enough to withstand one of my kind. It's hard enough not to harm you as it is."

Micah stilled at that. Gestalt spread his wings out, very slowly encircling the two of them. "Close your eyes and lean forward," Gestalt instructed, and pressed into the bond.

Micah appeared to him as a deep, burnished copper light. He knew that if he could see himself, he'd have wide threads of it running through his own indigo. Micah's mana was stitching him together; it shouldn't be so uncomfortable to feel him just *being* there.

In an instant, Micah was clamoring all over him again. Gestalt grit his teeth, trying his damnedest to ignore the intrusion. The human was probing at him, encircling him, pressing and pulling and exploring.

Gestalt tried to withdraw, but there was nowhere to go. He was no longer alone in his own mind.

Through all the tortures he'd endured, he'd always had this one singular holdout. One place he could be alone.

Waves of his anger crashed over Micah's light, swamping it, and he hauled back, separating himself.

Micah was staring at him, dumbstruck.

"You *hate* me," he breathed.

"Just returning the favor," Gestalt snapped. Even now, Micah wouldn't leave him alone. He could feel the human there, slotted up tight against the edges of his mind.

"No, I think you're an asshole and I resent you for what you did to Dominic, but you . . . you . . ."

Micah didn't have words. Good. "So now you know," Gestalt said. "You've watched your brothers take every piece of me but one, and now that last piece is all yours."

"You would have *died*," Micah growled, and Gestalt realized the human had the nerve to feel *indignant*. Then Micah's shoulders slumped, and he looked down. "I did the best I could," he said quietly.

And then, finally, he withdrew from the bond.

"There," Gestalt said. "That's what it feels like when you're not scrabbling at it."

Micah smiled a little, still looking down. "It feels like being alone."

"That's because you are."

"Yeah," Micah said. "Yeah, I know."

A moment later he was back again. Less frantic, less desperate, just . . . there. Like he was sitting with his back to a door between them.

Gestalt sighed.

Micah didn't look up. "I'm doing it again, aren't I."

It wasn't a question.

"Is Dominic doing the same thing?"

"No."

"Figures."

Gestalt reached out for the absent controller, coming back with nothing but some muddled memories. "He's sleeping."

"You can tell that?"

"Yes. Like I can tell that you're upset."

Micah snorted. "Yeah. Upset. That's what I am. Okay." He ran his hand through his hair. "Okay," he said again. "I can learn this. I can. I fucked up and now you're stuck with me, and I'm sorry. I can't fix it. But I can learn not to make it worse."

The words were paradoxically coupled with an increased pressure from the bond. "Leave it alone," Gestalt said. He was suddenly very tired.

"One more time. Let me try again."

The collar sparked and Micah pressed harder and Gestalt gave up. If he wanted in so badly? Fine. Let him look. Let him see the *immensity* of what he was up against.

Gestalt threw the bond wide open and surged through, all of his pain and fear and hate instantly overwhelming the human. The collar burned, but he didn't care.

Micah choked, clutching at his head. "*Stop*," he gasped weakly, and Gestalt didn't bother trying to fight the order. He slammed the bond shut again—

—and froze when he realized he couldn't close it completely.

Flickers of copper were seeping through, bright and strong.

"What are you doing?"

"I don't know!" Micah yelped. His eyes were wide, staring at Gestalt from somewhere far away. Gestalt scrambled back, but it didn't matter. The bond could reach him from across any distance.

The specks were becoming a stream, leaking slowly through the bond and creeping toward him. "Close it!" Micah's voice was urgent, but faint. "Close it off!"

"I can't!"

The copper light reached him and fractured. It wasn't like Dominic's, which had encircled him like a bandage. Micah wasn't pulling the pieces of Gestalt back together. He was seeping into the cracks, filling the empty places.

Gestalt couldn't breathe.

He had memories that weren't his.

People grabbing him. Hurting him. Some of the faces looked familiar.

The images dimmed, taking on a pale orange glow.

Don't.

He shook his head and shoved at Micah, twisting away, but the copper wisps reformed. He was trying to fight smoke.

An apple. He could taste an apple. Tart and crisp. A man smiled down at him.

I don't eat.

A girl glanced at him across a classroom. When she saw him looking, she blushed and ducked her head. There was silver in her smile. His stomach twisted.

Stop it.

Cold and wet. Outside the car, it was raining. The stranger in the front seat turned the heat up.

The copper wormed its way through him.

A girl in a park watched her balloon float into the sky.

Two men shared a cigarette in an alley.

A woman kissed him goodbye.

Micah!

The bond slammed shut, and the two of them were back in Dominic's living room, staring at each other.

"Is it over?" Micah asked cautiously.

Gestalt didn't answer. There were a hundred moments in his head, fitting into patterns and associations he didn't begin to know how to categorize. He had more of Micah's mana in him now, he could feel it.

"How did you do that?" he gasped.

"I don't even know what I did."

"Another transfer," Gestalt said slowly. He wasn't as angry as he felt like he should be. He was searching through the memories, looking for faces he knew. Looking for experiences he knew. Looking for feelings he knew.

Nothing.

Gestalt regarded the man in front of him. Opening the bond that wide should have left Micah a terrified mess. He'd looked better, but he wasn't traumatized. Not like he should have been.

"I think I know where it is now. I can feel it." Micah laid his hand on his stomach, above his belly button. "It's here, for me. I was looking higher, where you said yours was, but mine . . . I think it's here. I'll try to leave it alone."

Sure enough, the bond was quiet.

"I heard singing," Micah said. Gestalt looked up sharply. "Just like, a massive group of people singing."

Gestalt's throat tightened. His brothers and sisters. Micah had heard them. He'd shoved all his resentment and anger at the man, and Micah had heard their song instead.

"Is that what the bond should be like?" Micah asked. "All the time?"

"Yes," Gestalt said shortly. It seemed suddenly very quiet. The harmonies were long gone now. All he had left was Micah's hesitant scuffling and Dominic's distant dreams.

Micah opened his mouth, like he might say something, but then he stopped. His eyes lost focus, and Gestalt remembered the effect that the previous transfers had on the humans. He caught Micah as the man began to topple forward.

Micah's body didn't feel nearly as heavy as it should.

After more than a year of captivity and starvation, Gestalt was getting stronger. He could see it in the lines of his avatar.

He was still a long way from being able to *lift* Micah, but he could lay him on the floor so he didn't hurt himself.

Gestalt tried to do it quickly, touching him as little as possible. He was aware that human bodies got uncomfortable if they were compressed in certain ways but, since the stress positions had never worked on him, he hadn't paid much attention.

In any case, it would only be twenty minutes. They couldn't be so fragile that they could injure themselves in only twenty minutes.

Probably.

Gestalt felt a twinge of guilt and shoved it away. He hadn't asked for the transfer. Micah had done that on his own. So what if it was an accident? Even if it wasn't Micah's fault, it wasn't *his* fault, either.

Gestalt glanced over Micah's prone form. He looked fine. He was still breathing, and that was the most important thing about human physiology, he was pretty sure.

Gestalt fetched a blanket off the couch and laid it over the sleeping man. It only came up to mid-chest, but that was probably fine. He wasn't sure what the blanket was for, but he knew that humans slept under them, and Micah was sleeping, so. It followed. Logically.

Gestalt rolled his eyes at the empty room, and settled in to wait.

CHAPTER SIX

∞

Dominic got a call from Ian at 6 a.m. Normally it would have woken him up and pissed him off royally, but in this case it was actually a relief to hear a familiar voice.

"Hey, Ian. What's up?"

"You sound like shit," the detective informed him.

It made sense. He'd been sleeping in twenty-minute bursts all night, jerking awake from fever dreams of fireworks and Gregorian choirs and faceless horrors and who knew what the fuck else. Back at the house, Micah and Ges were either fighting to the death or doing some really fantastic drugs.

At least, he *hoped* it was something the two of them were doing. Otherwise he'd run afoul of a particularly nasty curse or possibly a witch.

"Did something happen? Or are you calling just to flirt?"

"Did Micah get those photos I sent him?"

"I don't know. I'm out on a case."

"Another one?"

"Yeah, Ian, another one."

"You know there's a feral angel in your custody, right?"

"No rest for the wicked," Dominic grumbled. He rolled out of bed and checked over the hex box he'd locked up the night before.

There was a heavy silence on the line.

"There's something else."

"Oh good, do share."

Ian paused. Dominic turned the box over, checking all six sides. No charring, that was good. The curse on the glasses wasn't breaking through.

"The guys we picked up at the manor. They've made bail."

Dominic's heart skipped a beat. "How many of them?"

"All of them. They even sprung the indents somehow. We've been fielding calls from lawyers all morning. Milgram's even worse. I've got a stack of complaint forms longer than my—"

"So a bunch of rich bastards didn't like getting caught with their hands in the cookie jar. We expected that. You've got a solid case."

"Well, no, I don't."

Dominic set the box gently back onto the table. "Run that by me again?"

"The case is solid," Ian said quickly. "But it's not mine. The facility we busted was just another domino in the chain. They've linked it to some outfit that got taken down in Oklahoma last month. There's evidence of another one in New Orleans, and they're connecting it to investigations in Ohio, South Carolina, and Vermont."

"Really? *Vermont*?"

"Turns out our wealthy sadists are snowbirds." Ian sighed. "Whatever's going on here, it's happening across the country. The feds have picked it up; it's their case now. You'll probably be getting a phone call from them once the sun's up. I thought it might sound better coming from me."

Dom rolled his eyes. He'd never had to turn a job over to the *feds*, but he knew the frustration of watching your case notes vanish into someone else's desk drawer. "So this place in Vermont; they have an angel?"

"No. As far as I've found, Gestalt is the only daiyura anyone's reported. Anywhere." Ian cleared his throat. "About that. The daiyura . . . he's a creature, Dominic. Obviously humanoid and intelligent, but legally, still just a creature. It's going to make his status complicated."

"I'll keep you appraised of any berserker rages or homicidal tendencies."

"I'm serious, Dominic."

"Me too. I know I can't prove it, but you just have to take my word on this. Ges is solid. And I don't think we'll need to spend too long figuring out what he is. Once he's unbound, I get the feeling he's going to flicker back to wherever he came from and we'll never see him again."

"In the meantime, keep an eye out. Attempting to kill him probably invalidates claims of ownership, but these guys have a lot of resources, and at least half of them are *really* fucked in the head."

"I saw the basement too." Dominic didn't want to think of those people going free. "Speaking of which, wasn't there some mention of a consultation fee?"

"Check's in the mail," Ian said, and hung up.

The mental fireworks weren't as bad now that Dominic was awake. He got almost all the way through a shower before an intense panic struck him and he tore the curtain while lunging for the knife by the sink.

The hotel room was empty.

Twice during breakfast he was hit with a vague sense of loss, followed by another, weaker burst of panic.

Around eight, he started to feel a low, simmering sort of confidence. It was good, and even better, it wasn't fading. It wasn't getting stronger, but it wasn't going away, either. Dom actually found himself whistling as he checked the hex box over again.

He winked at the clerk when he dropped off his room key. The sun was shining. The sky was blue.

He checked back at the house where he'd gotten the cursed glasses. No further disturbances. He left them his number, collected his fee, and cruised around town for a couple of hours to make sure nothing else gave him any weird vibes.

At noon, after four hours without an unexpected jolt of emotion, he decided it was safe to drive home.

He hoped Micah and Gestalt hadn't broken too much furniture. Actually, he hoped they hadn't broken *any* furniture, but if there was one thing Benjamin Blackburn had taught his son, it was to let go of unrealistic expectations.

It turned out he needn't have worried.

Dominic paused in the doorway, taking in the state of his living room.

Gestalt stared back at him, sullen and more than a little defiant. He and Micah were sitting across from each other, cross-legged, knees almost close enough to touch. Micah was blindfolded, which was . . . interesting.

"Do I want to know?"

Micah wriggled, raising his face toward Dominic. He couldn't do more than that with Gestalt still holding his knees down. His arms were pinioned behind his back, held in place with what Dominic assumed were handcuffs.

"I see you two made up, then," Dominic remarked, dropping his duffel and kicking his shoes off.

Gestalt scowled, retrieving the small silver keys from their place on the floor. "He's very large," he said defensively, and Dominic tried valiantly not to comment. Micah mumbled, pulling impatiently against the handcuffs Ges was attempting to unlock. "Settle!" Gestalt barked.

Micah immediately stilled until the cuffs clinked to the floor, then reached up to untie the T-shirt wrapped around his face. He blinked in the light. "Gestalt and I are working on the bond."

"Oh, yeah, I can see that," Dominic said, searching the fridge for cold cuts. "I don't judge; you keep doing you."

That vague sense of accomplishment and satisfaction was draining away, being replaced by a feeling of mild annoyance. Dominic switched tactics. "So I never finished the *Kama Sutra*, but that's not something I've seen before. What's the game plan?"

Gestalt frowned at him. Micah rolled his eyes. "We couldn't get a solid connection established. Gestalt kept getting spooked and dropping out."

"I had legitimate concerns." Gestalt had backed toward the hallway, and Dominic realized he was keeping both humans in his line of sight. "The bond is supposed to be a partnership. Micah has every advantage over me, because of the collar and in terms of brute strength. He does not have the ability to control his mind, and I don't currently have the power to force him."

Micah's face flushed. He wouldn't meet Dominic's eyes. "I did another transfer," he said quietly. "I didn't know I was doing it, and Ges couldn't stop me."

"How long ago was that?" Dominic asked.

"Last night."

"And you guys have been playing with it ever since then?"

The two of them exchanged glances, then nodded.

"Micah was rendered unconscious on several occasions, which slowed our progress somewhat."

"Yeah, I've had nights like that," Dominic quipped through a mouthful of sandwich.

"I'm getting better now," Micah carried on, ignoring the joke. "I can close the bond from my side, and I *think* . . ." He paused. "I think I can feel the difference between you and Ges."

"I'm taller," Dominic said. "And he's got wings. That should help."

Micah frowned at him, wrinkling his forehead, and suddenly Dominic felt some kind of jab. Right in the groin. "Fuck, what was that?"

"I tried to open the link between us, but it didn't work."

"You're trying too hard," Gestalt supplied. "You're trying to force it open instead of letting it happen naturally. Try again."

"Look, Ges, not that I don't want Micah having a direct link to my dick, but—"

Two things happened at once then: Dominic's phone rang, probably the FBI agent Ian had warned them about, and the front window shattered. A projectile thumped to the floor and rolled, a brick or rock, by the looks of it. What really had Dominic worried, though, was the little fabric bundle tied to it. It was crackling and leaking black smoke.

"Down!" he shouted, and then a flash of white obscured everything.

It turned out that the phone call *was* from the FBI. When Dominic called the number back, it was answered by a rather severe-sounding woman named Piper. He wasn't sure if that was her first name or her last name, and by the time he got a word in edgewise, he was afraid to ask.

She had complete copies of the case files regarding both Micah and Gestalt. It indicated some really efficient work on her part, seeing as Dominic had picked Gestalt up a day ago. She was particularly interested in whether or not the two of them had gotten around to checking Ian's photos. Dominic sent a questioning glance at Micah, who shook his head and went straight back to looking traumatized.

Piper wanted to know what the holdup was, and Dominic had to inform her that his house had just been hexed, drive-by style. That made her pause for a moment, like she wanted to be consolatory but couldn't remember the social conventions.

"It's cool," Dominic said when he realized she was struggling. "I had an angel fix my window."

Gestalt shot him a dirty look. He'd actually done a little bit more than that, but Dominic didn't really want to start spreading that around, especially to federal agents and especially over the phone.

"Mr. Blackburn, I don't mean to pry, but are you . . . *prone* to violent victimization?"

"Not usually, but my life's been a little weird lately. I actually got an interesting call from Ian this morning—you know Ian?"

"Detective Soulton, yes."

"Yeah. Well, *he* says you're cracking open a ring and that a lot of really important members made bail this morning. So I'm thinking this might be related to that. Since we're, you know, witnesses and all."

"It's possible. Would you like us to send someone out to watch the house?"

"Nah, I think we've got it covered."

To say the least.

She didn't ask for more details, and he didn't offer. She told him to be careful and to set the angel on the photos, and hung up without further small talk. Dominic tossed the phone onto the couch, then realized he'd meant to pick up another one while he was out. Shit.

"Are we going to talk about this?" Micah asked.

Klaxons started going off in Dominic's head because *good* conversations never started that way.

The brick was still sitting in the middle of the living room, smoking gently where the remains of the bag were still attached. Normally, Dominic would have kept it intact, checked it over to try to figure out what he was dealing with, but. Well. Gestalt hadn't really stopped to ask about Dominic's standard operating procedure.

"Do we have to?" Dominic asked, and Micah fixed him with a gaze that indicated, yes, they had to.

Dominic dug out potholders, intent on taking care of the brick.

"Someone tried to kill you," Gestalt said, watching the brick disposal process nonchalantly.

Dominic picked the brick up with two potholders, chucking it out through the open door. "I'm pretty used to that, just, generally, you know. Not in the house."

Actually, *never* in the house. Dominic had killed a lot of shit in his life, but none of it had ever followed him home. It was giving him a weird fluttery feeling in his stomach that he was set on ignoring.

"It's because of us," Micah said hollowly, and the little flutteries ramped up their activity. "They tried to kill *us*," he said, gesturing to himself and Gestalt.

"Well, they suck at it. We're fine."

Micah stared up at Dominic. "They screwed up *this* time. Dominic, we have to leave."

"No way. We're not gonna hide."

"No. Me and Ges. We have to go. We're the evidence, not you."

"Hey, I'm a witness too," Dominic said defensively, and then backtracked when he realized what Micah was saying. "You're not talking about going *without* me?"

"We have to. Once they realize they failed, they'll be back. And you don't . . . you don't understand the kind of people they are."

Gestalt was watching Micah talk with an expression Dominic couldn't decipher. Micah's voice was getting faster.

"You saw the kinds of things they did for fun. Imagine the things they'd do for *revenge*. This is way too big. They can't be fought. Best-case scenario, we don't drag you down with us."

"*I* intend to fight," Ges said. He was calm enough that Micah was temporarily derailed. "It can be done, if you aren't determined to sacrifice yourself for your master."

"I'm not his master," Dominic interjected, but Ges waved him off. Then the daiyura looked back at him, scrutinizing, and Dominic felt something in his chest *yank*—

The phone rang and glass shattered and the spell rolled across the floor. The moment Gestalt saw it, he knew it meant death for the humans who had taken him in. He could tell Dominic knew it too, and Micah . . . well. Micah didn't know magic, but good tidings were rarely delivered via brick. Micah knew who it was from, and why it was there, and what he needed to do.

But Micah was too far away, too insubstantial. This wasn't a bullet he could dive in front of. The room brightened in slow motion, the magic spilling its bonds, and Dominic raised his arm to block the light. Micah was moving, but he was too slow and wouldn't make a difference. But the intent was there anyway. Overpowering and compelling and surrounding and omnipresent.

Gestalt spread his wings, throwing half the room into shadow. The magic hit him like a wave, roaring and falling back, harmless as dew on a flower petal.

In the end, it didn't really matter. The poison rushing out of the hex bag would have killed most people in seconds, but then again, most people didn't have fresh curse-dispersal circles painted on their living room floors.

What escaped the circle might have given the humans, at worst, a migraine and some persistent nausea, but Micah didn't know that.

Micah didn't know it, so the thoughts he shoved into Gestalt reflected all the seriousness he believed the situation to have.

—and Dominic staggered back. "He *made* you protect us?"

Gestalt frowned. "No. The bond isn't mind control. He simply expressed a sincere desire that I do what I could to shield you."

"Wait," Micah said, "I did what?"

"*Just* me?" Dominic asked slowly.

Gestalt nodded. "But my wings work better in pairs and I've grown somewhat fond of Micah, so I shielded him as well."

Dominic watched Micah closely. Once, on a job, a ghost had reached into his father's chest cavity and twisted his actual literal heart. That was the expression Micah had now. "I did *what?*" he asked again.

"You asked me to save your master," Gestalt explained. "Quite eloquently, I'd say, given the time you had to work with."

Dominic raised a finger. "Not his master."

"Not up to you," Ges answered.

Dominic thought it was possible Gestalt didn't understand how indenturement worked, and filed the topic away for discussion at a later date.

"This just proves my point, though," Micah said. "Apparently I'm bringing killers down on your head and I'm shoving Gestalt into the way. Neither of you is safe."

Gestalt's eyes narrowed. "You *compelled* me to do nothing, human. Do not overestimate your abilities."

"All right, all right," Dom interrupted. "You're very superior, thanks for saving our lives. Micah, the weight of the world does not rest on your shoulders. Cool it."

Micah looked pained.

The way Dominic saw it, they needed a game plan. They were outgunned, sure, but he was playing on home field and that gave him the advantage. Whoever was out to kill them probably wouldn't risk coming back until the sun was back up, so they had that going for them, at least.

Ges *had* actually managed to fix the window, and the smoldering remains of the curse brick were cooling in the front yard, so those were another couple of pluses. For now, the house was safe. They just needed to keep it that way.

For the next three hours, Dominic worked his way across the front of the house, carving sigils into the top sills of the windows and doors. It wouldn't keep out a projectile, but it would negate any magic riding shotgun.

Micah followed after him, comparing his sigils to the references in the manual, then using a small chisel to clean the edges of the marks and make sure they were legible. And Gestalt . . . Ges kept the sun up. Or at least, that was how it seemed to Dominic. Standing on a ladder in front of a plate glass window struck him as a particularly vulnerable situation, so Ges took up a position in the front yard keeping watch. And since he wasn't going to do it in the dark, the daiyura lit the woods up as bright as day. It actually hurt to look at him.

Micah's silence throughout all this was deafening.

"Where would you go?" Dominic asked eventually. "If you did leave."

Micah stayed focused on his work. "I don't know. I'd figure it out."

His whole body was tense, and Dominic could feel his fear seeping through the bond. "I'm not asking you to go."

"I know."

The nervous feeling retreated somewhat, and Dominic realized how impossible it was to lie to someone who was inside your own head.

Fucking weird.

He glanced back out at Ges, then blinked away the afterimage and resumed carving. "This isn't your fault, you know."

Micah rolled his eyes. "My former owners are smashing up your house trying to kill me because I went to the police about them; how is this not my fault?"

Dominic counted off on his fingers. "If you're gonna look at it that way? I bought an illegal slave. Then *I* went to the cops. Then I raided one of their hideouts and stole their angel. Plus, I'm the one keeping you here with my irresistible sex appeal. You have no choice, really."

He waggled his eyebrows and Micah looked away. "I guess not," he said quietly, a small smile playing at his lips.

"Yeah?" Dominic had been kidding about the sex appeal, but he'd be lying if he didn't notice the way Micah's arms flexed under his shirt as he chiseled.

Micah glanced over. "I can feel you doing that."

"Doing what?"

"Wanting me," Micah said simply. His voice was neutral.

Dominic flushed red. "It's not . . . I mean . . ."

"I like it," Micah said, not taking his eyes off his work.

"Oh." Dominic lost track of what he was supposed to be doing. "I'll . . . keep doing it, then?"

"All right."

It was past one in the morning when they finished the warding, and Dominic was so tired he'd be surprised if the last set was even any good. He called out to Ges, letting him know that they'd finished and it was safe to come back inside. Gestalt replied that he would rather stay outside, thank you very much, and since he didn't sleep, Dominic told him not to leave the area and figured that was probably fine.

Dominic brushed his teeth while Micah straightened the sheets, and then Micah stripped off his shirt while Dominic searched for his pillow. Micah was reaching for a sleep shirt but then Dominic got to staring, and Micah could *feel* him staring, and Dominic *knew* that he could feel him staring. He paused by the edge of the bed, not moving, letting Dominic look. Dominic thought maybe he'd like to put his mouth on the hollow of Micah's throat, and Micah thought he'd probably be amenable to that.

Micah thought it was unfair that Dominic was still wearing a shirt, and Dominic pulled it over his head, thinking that if they were being honest, their pants were probably going to get in the way too. So Micah popped the button on his fly, and Dominic remembered how the skin there had tasted, just two days ago. Dominic was sporting three-quarters of a hard-on by then, Micah noticed, which was probably fair since the two of them were sharing a thought process and Micah was *also* standing at half-mast. He thought maybe he'd like Dominic to suck him off again, or else he was just picking up on *Dominic* wanting to suck him off again, but at the end of the day it didn't really matter where the thoughts came from as long as they were acted on promptly, and that was how the two of them ended up falling into bed in a tangle of limbs.

They couldn't stay still, couldn't agree what they wanted to do, and they ended up rolling over and over and tangling in the sheets as they tried to adopt to ideas as fast as they were having them. Dominic's fingers were tangling in Micah's hair, one leg wrapped around his hip, both of them rutting together like teenagers, and Dominic wasn't completely certain whose desires he was feeling.

He felt like he was being pulled, some magnet behind his pubic bone yanking him along, against Micah and almost *through* him. He strained forward, desperate and needy, trying to connect in a way that no amount of grasping or pinning or sucking would ever come close to meeting.

"The fuck *is* that?" he groaned.

"Bond," Micah said simply, and then it opened, and Dominic *saw*.

Micah's body gleamed like burnished copper, eyes burning like twin suns, and when he drew Dominic toward him, his skin was impossibly hot. His lips pressed to Dominic's, and Dominic realized there wasn't actually a differentiation, not anymore, not here. Micah gripped his hips, fingers leaving divots and then sinking in, and Dominic saw what Gestalt had seen.

Dominic saw himself through Micah's eyes—saw the comfort and the stability that Micah felt in his presence, saw the foundation on which Micah was building his life. Gestalt had called him Micah's master, but it wasn't that—it was so much more than that. Micah belonged to him because Micah *loved* what he saw.

Dominic panicked, scrambling backward and slamming the bond closed.

It was suddenly very dark, Micah's wide eyes close to black in the moonlight.

"What? What happened?"

Micah thought he'd done something wrong, because of course he would, wouldn't he? He'd take it all onto himself. Whatever it took to make Dominic happy, keep Dominic safe.

It was too much. Dominic tried to stammer an apology or explanation, but nothing came. Micah had just used some psychic shit to tell him that Dominic owned his *soul*, and what the fuck could he even say to that?

It didn't help that the blood flow to his brain was still being efficiently diverted to the southern territories. Micah's skin was glowing in the pale light, all smooth planes and lithe muscles and—

"I need some air," Dominic stammered, casting around for a pair of boxers before—call it what it was—fleeing.

The humans assumed that their assailants wouldn't come back until morning, and they were partly right. The men who had attacked the house *were* waiting for sunrise before approaching again. From the conversation he'd picked up, Gestalt gathered they were standing by to see if the police arrived. If not, the hex had worked and the humans hadn't survived long enough to call them.

These assailants apparently assumed *Gestalt* would be vulnerable to the magic they'd sent through the window. Come morning, they were expecting to enter the house and find two dead humans and an incapacitated angel.

From his place atop the roof of their car, Gestalt listened and tried not to be insulted.

He wasn't sure why Coffey even *wanted* him back. Normally, Gestalt thought, slitting someone's throat indicated that your business with that someone had concluded. Evidently he was mistaken, because Coffey was here, sitting not-so-patiently and bickering with his companions.

"If they were still alive," he heard, "they'd have fled by now. There's only one road."

This voice was deep, belonging to the companion Gestalt had dubbed Sycophant Two. Sycophant One was mostly quiet, letting Coffey debate the pros and cons of their plan with his fellow lackey.

"The spell could take hours to dissipate; we've been over this."

"*Or* it could be long gone by now. I'll go check, report back, and we can be on our way hours early."

"If you're that desperate to stick your own neck out, then fine," Coffey snapped. "You go look, and if the spell hasn't dissipated, we'll throw your corpse in the trunk with the angel when we leave."

"At least I'd be out of these creepy fucking woods," Sycophant Two said, unlocking his door. He climbed out of the passenger seat, rolled his shoulders, slammed the door, and opened his mouth to shout when he saw Gestalt perched on top of the car.

Gestalt reached over, his fingertips brushing Two's temple, and the man was dead before he hit the ground.

"The fuck? Luke?"

Ah. So *that* had been his name.

Sycophant One struggled to simultaneously unbuckle his seat belt and unholster his weapon. He had time to do neither before Gestalt reached though his open window. The man fell back in his seat, a thin plume of smoke escaping his dead lips.

"That's very naughty of you, Gestalt," Coffey said dryly. He'd left the car while Gestalt was busy with the lackey, and now stood several meters out of reach. The blade in his hand glinted silver. "You'll be punished for that when we get you back home."

The sound of his voice sent a shiver down Gestalt's spine, and he curled his wings protectively around his body. It was weak, defensive, almost *submissive*, and Gestalt hated it, but he couldn't stop his body from reacting.

"You look different without all my little toys," Coffey remarked, giving him a slow once-over. "We'll have to put those back. Come along then, into the car with you."

Gestalt backed off quickly, hoping to cover the fact that the bangles weren't sparking. Dominic's mana had healed Coffey's mark, but there was no reason to broadcast that fact. Gestalt deflected. "You're on a fool's errand," he told him. "The passage is closed."

"We opened it once, we can do it again."

Gestalt's smile was sharp. "You were able to do it once because we weren't expecting an attack from *ants*. Our most rudimentary defenses can hold your species off for eons."

"Rudimentary, Gestalt, really? Does a rudimentary defense usually leave you stranded and bound?" Coffey's face held genuine curiosity. "Are you that weak? Or were the others that desperate to get rid of you?"

Gestalt didn't respond. His eyes were focused on the blade Coffey held. The human didn't know his mark was gone and still thought Gestalt was bound to his word. One nick of that blade, though, and he'd be right.

"I'd be lying if I said I wasn't interested in seeing how you measure up to others of your species."

"You'll die never knowing," Gestalt told him, and lunged.

His wings made him fast, flaring wide and pushing back, driving him forward before the human could react. He gathered up his magic, centering it in the palms of his hands, shoving it into Coffey's body when his fingers closed around the human's neck.

It wouldn't go.

Gestalt realized an instant too late that the power he had left wasn't enough—not even to burn out a shriveled little toad like Coffey.

The human swiped at him with the blade and Gestalt caught his wrist. Coffey was ready for it, driving his head forward into Gestalt's jaw, and it was all Gestalt could do not to bite his tongue. He staggered back, losing his balance and falling against the car when Coffey swiped at him again.

Options. He needed options.

He hadn't realized he was so drained. The magic centered inside him felt warm and full and solid, nothing like the cold wispy fog he'd come to associate with starvation.

Options.

He caught Coffey's arm again, yanking it high and trying not to jerk back in revulsion when the motion brought the human closer to him.

He remembered this feeling.

Options.

He twisted Coffey's wrist and the man dropped his knife. Gestalt twisted further and Coffey withdrew, turning to the side to try to relieve the pressure on his elbow. It only transferred the torsion to his shoulder, and Gestalt was able to bring a leg up and shove the man away. Coffey went tumbling to the ground and Gestalt scooped up the blade without taking his eyes off him.

Coffey was scrambling for something on the ground, a dark shape a few feet from his fallen comrade.

A gun, Gestalt realized, but it was too late to react.

Coffey turned and fired, the bullet passing cleanly through Gestalt's left wing. He hissed in pain, trying to draw the injured limb inward, but the pain only spiked when he moved it. Blood dripped from the wound, and the cuffs sparked as they reactivated.

"You wretched little brat," Coffey growled, rubbing at his injured shoulder. "You're going to pay for that. Drop it."

The collar sparked, and the blade seemed to grow hot in Gestalt's hand. He willed his muscles to tighten, to hold on, but he didn't have the magic to fight. The knife clattered to the ground. Coffey advanced toward him, gun held out for Gestalt to see.

"Get on your knees, Gestalt. You're going to suck the barrel clean and pray to your heathen gods that I decide not to kill you."

Gestalt sank to his knees, focused on keeping his jaw clenched shut because he *wouldn't.*

He would.

He'd have to.

He'd licked his own blood off knives before, what was *wrong* with these creatures—

His injured wing flared with agony when he shifted it against the ground. It settled, bent awkwardly, and he resolved to ignore it.

"Open, Gestalt."

The silver cuffs were alight now, his skin beginning to burn. He focused on keeping his mouth shut.

Coffey raised the gun so that Gestalt was staring down the barrel. "I do love it when you fight me. Hurting you is much more fun when you hurt yourself first."

The barrel jerked and the sound of a gunshot cracked through the air. Coffey looked confused for a moment, raising his hand to his chest.

When he pulled it away, it was red.

"Fuck," he growled, then unloaded his clip into Gestalt. The first three shots landed, but the rest went wide as the human toppled to the ground.

The collar grew cold.

"Gestalt? Fucking hell, *Ges*?"

Coffey's gunshot must have roused Dominic, then.

Gestalt pulled himself to his feet, slipping once when some muscle group in his core refused to pull its weight.

"I'm here," he called to the approaching figure, and Dominic shouted something unintelligible back. Gestalt took two steps toward him and then turned back, regarding the body on the ground.

"Back in the mud where you belong," he muttered, and spat.

His mouth tasted like blood.

"That was dumb, Ges."

Even with one of his arms slung around Dominic's shoulders, it was taking every ounce of Gestalt's concentration to stay upright. His avatar behaved unexpectedly on good days, but all torn up like this, it was damn near unmanageable.

He wanted to go home. Home, where things were predictable and people behaved in a civil manner.

"You should've told me they were back. I could have shot them just as easy with you *behind* me."

"I could handle it."

"Yeah, clearly."

His left wing was beginning to drag on the ground. He kept yanking it up and back, but it was slipping, and he wasn't sure how to make it stop. His magic was crackling around the edges of the wounds; they'd stopped bleeding by now, he was pretty sure. He had power enough for that, at least. Good to know that everything in this world was *utterly and completely unpredictable.*

They came around the corner and the house came into view, welcoming and bright. Gestalt didn't need to look to know Micah was waiting in the doorway. He'd been nosing around Gestalt's bond ever since Dominic's gunshots, questioning and worried despite Gestalt's repeated assurances that he was fine.

Micah was reaching out for Dominic too, encircling their bond and settling down over it like a hen on an egg. Dominic, though . . . Dominic was prickling at the contact and pulling back like he thought it was going to sting him.

Gestalt eyed the open doorway with distaste. The house was the humans' territory, thoroughly marked from floor to ceiling. It was vaguely unsettling for him to be inside, and being inside while wounded was going to be even worse.

His wing slipped again and he yanked it upward, wincing as a bolt of pain went through his shoulder. He could be wrong, but it felt like there was still a bullet in there, wedged between the twin scapulae.

That was going to be an issue.

"Why'd you stop? Come on, we'll get you patched up."

Bracing himself, Gestalt let Dominic lead him into the house.

Stepping through the door, the air was warmer, heavier, and the faint scent of humans permeated everything.

Micah had already laid out the first-aid kit, an impressive array of bandages and saline now covering the kitchen table. Light glinted off a hooked needle, sterile inside its plastic package, and Gestalt froze.

"No. I don't— You don't—"

Micah raised his hands slowly, leaving the tools on the table.

"Just thought you might need them," he said evenly, and Gestalt realized how easy it would be for Dominic to twist his arm back, hold him still while Micah—

He wrenched away from the human, ignoring the burst of pain from his shoulder. A second, muted wave bubbled up from his side, and he buckled, falling back and struggling to regain his balance. Dominic was reaching for him and he dodged away.

"No!" he said again. His back was to the wall now. He brought his arms up; he had no magic and no weapon, but humans were wary of hand-to-hand combat.

"Ges, hey—" Dominic started, but Micah was already there, pushing through the bond, soothing Gestalt's frayed nerves.

"Stay back," Gestalt hissed at him. He was calmer now, listening to Micah but keeping his eyes on Dominic. Dominic was closer and still showing every intention of approaching, his hands raised like he was calming a skittish animal. Gestalt bared his teeth.

"Dominic . . ." Micah said, warning him off.

Gestalt glanced at the larger man. He was still in the kitchen, leaning against a countertop with his hands in the pockets of his sweatpants. He was practically radiating calm. Gestalt's eyes flicked back to Dominic. There was nothing coming from him but confusion.

Which made sense, because he'd just half-carried Gestalt inside and had never done anything to hurt him. There was no reason for this reaction. On some level, Gestalt knew that. On another, deeper and more powerful level, he was hurting and surrounded in enemy territory, and his instinct said *fight*. It didn't help that Micah was worked up about the gunshots and Dominic was worked up about . . . something.

"I don't need help. I'll heal fine on my own."

Micah nodded and made no move to pack the bandages away. "Who shot you?"

"Coffey."

"Coffey's *here*?"

Panic.

"That was Coffey?" Dominic's eyes widened. "Like, Coffey from the basement massacre? That Coffey?"

Gestalt nodded slightly, keeping his eyes on Dominic.

"Fuck, if I'd known that I'd'a shot him in the gut instead of the chest."

"Coffey's dead?" The fear rolling off Micah turned into confusion and then relief.

Gestalt felt his own shoulders relax as the onslaught slowed. "Yes. And the two men he had with him."

There was silence for a long beat, and then Dominic said, "I should probably text Piper."

Dominic backed away at last, searching the living room for his phone, and Gestalt's shoulders relaxed the rest of the way. There was another vicious twinge, and his wing slipped.

There was definitely a bullet between the scapulae. He could feel it grinding.

"You're out of juice again, aren't you," Micah asked, and Gestalt shot him a glare.

"Striking the life from your bodies is harder than your constitutions would lead one to believe."

"That's a yes, then."

The edge of the bond thrummed as Micah circled it, and Gestalt sighed. No use pretending otherwise. "Yes."

"Is that why you and Coffey were slap fighting to the death?" Dominic had found his phone and was fiddling with it while he talked, presumably informing the authorities that there were corpses on his property that needed to be disposed of.

Gestalt gave up trying to hold his injured wing aloft, and it slumped against the floor with a final, tired surge of pain. "I resorted to physical combat because my attempt to use my magic failed. If that's what you're asking."

"Ges, you could have asked us for help," Micah said gently, and Gestalt sent a surge of anger at him through the bond.

"I shouldn't *need* your *help*," he hissed.

"Yeah, but you do, and that's why Coffey turned you into Swiss cheese. Speaking of which, you want me to stitch you up, or are you just going to stand there and bleed to death out of spite?"

"I'll heal. Give it time."

"We don't have time," Dominic said. "Cops are gonna be here in twenty, and we've gotta get our story straight by then."

Micah was tapped out. Gestalt took a cursory glance through the bond and refused to do another transfer.

Micah huffed and went to take a look around Coffey's car, leaving Dominic and Gestalt alone in the living room.

"So," Dominic asked, "like last time, then?"

Gestalt shook his head. "I can focus much more clearly now. You should sit down. Micah and I had the most luck on the floor."

"Yeah, Micah likes that."

Gestalt's brow furrowed, but he didn't comment. Instead he sat down in the same place as before, taking care to fold his wings behind him. Dominic sank down across from him, close enough that Gestalt could reach him if he leaned forward.

"You should be able to feel me when I do this."

He pushed against the bond, and Dominic's eyes widened slightly. He licked his lips. "Yeah. Yeah, I can feel that."

Ges looked at him carefully for a moment, and then eased the bond open. Dominic's eyes got wider, and he hesitantly approached it from his own side. Gestalt didn't rush him, and after a moment, he reached through.

Gestalt felt the same deep rich blue, encircling him like last time. Dominic's mana flowed in great wide ribbons, wrapping and swaddling and holding him in.

There was a faint cracking sound as Gestalt's forward scapula snapped back into place, the pieces of broken bone knitting back together. His flesh mended where three of the bullets had passed through, leaving nothing but a small puckered dot. The fourth bullet was still lodged in his shoulder, and he grimaced as his body worked to reject it.

The small projectile wormed its way to the surface. It forged a new path between the bones and up through the meat of his shoulder, finally piercing the skin and falling to the floor with a *clink*. A band of blue rolled its way across his shoulders, and the exit wound closed over.

Gestalt raised his arm, testing the movement. There was no more pain, and his shoulder was even a little rounder, the bone cushioned under muscle for the first time he could remember.

He looked up to thank Dominic, just in time to catch the man as he collapsed.

CHAPTER SEVEN

Dominic was the smooth talker of the three of them, but he was still out cold when the cops showed up. Micah had to manage on his own, based on what Dominic had told him.

Micah identified Coffey, but the other two he'd never seen before. Officers photographed the corpses, the burned remains of the brick and hex bag, the restraints and warding in the trunk of the dead men's car and, lastly, Gestalt. The angel crossed his arms, his wings tight behind his back, and narrowed his eyes at the photographer. The officer in charge was not amused.

"And he's a . . . *what* now?"

"A daiyura," Micah repeated. "He used to belong to Coffey—" (and here Gestalt's wings flared and a massive burst of indignation forced its way through the bond. Micah sent a silent apology back) "—but we're holding him, pending the results of an extensive abuse investigation."

"Never heard of a daiyura," the cop said.

"Us neither, but we're taking his word for it."

"Hmmm," the officer mused. He was watching the coroner shuffle the desiccated bodies into bags, and looking like he probably wouldn't take Gestalt's word for much at all. "You want us to take him in? You might be a little safer with him outta your hair."

Gestalt bristled, but he was frightened too.

Micah pushed more reassurances through the bond. "I think we'll manage fine here, Officer."

"You sure? There's a real good containment center in the penitentiary downstate; they can keep him locked right down until you need him. From what I'm seeing here, it looks like he's dangerous."

"Just following orders and protecting his keepers," Micah responded.

Gestalt huffed, turning and ascending into a nearby tree. He perched easily on an upper branch and did a very good impression of someone who was paying no attention to Micah at all.

"I can see he's trained real good," the officer said, staring up into the darkness at him.

Micah shrugged. "I won't deny he has an attitude. Anyway, if he starts making trouble, they're just gonna call a controller, and one of those already lives here."

"Right," the officer said, still peering into the tree. "And he's where, exactly?"

"Ahhh . . ." Micah turned his attention back down the drive, toward the house. "I think he's taking a call?"

"Must be an important call."

"I'm sure it is," Micah said with a thin smile. "Is there anything else I can help you with? It's very late . . ."

"No, this seems pretty open and shut. Give us a call if anything else comes up and, uh, keep an eye on the daiyura, will ya? Between you and me, I think you're nuts keeping him in the house. Those burned-out corpses give me the creeps."

Gestalt, who could hear him just fine, responded with a Cheshire cat smile. Fortunately, it was too dark for the officer to see.

Micah headed back up toward the house, leaving the others to their work. He rubbed his eyes. The sun would be up in a couple of hours, and he had every intention of shutting the bedroom door and ignoring it completely.

Gestalt alighted softly on the ground, falling into step beside him. "You lied to them."

"Yes. Try not to kill anyone else. I know you think you're the greatest thing since sliced bread, but here, you're a creature, and that does not put you high up on the totem pole."

"You presume I'm participating in your 'totem pole.'"

"Yeah, I do," Micah said. They'd rounded the bend and the house was coming into view. "Because Dominic and I are participating, and we've been put in charge of you. And you just got your ass kicked by one guy, so sorry if I don't see you toppling the system anytime soon."

Gestalt scowled, then paused and inclined his head toward the house, listening. "Dominic is awake."

"Hopefully not for long. God, I'm beat."

"Something's troubling him."

"He's probably just freaked out by the whole 'hexed in his own living room' thing."

"No, it's nothing so trivial. It's something to do with you."

Micah snorted. "Yeah, like I'm not trivial."

Gestalt gave him a strange look. Micah sighed.

He'd tried reaching out to Dominic through the bond, and Dominic had freaked. Pulled his clothes on and bolted. It had turned out to be for the best—it meant Dominic was outside when the shooting started—but still. Micah didn't want to think about what had bothered him so much.

Dominic didn't have a problem working with Gestalt; when the angel needed a transfer, Dominic had offered without hesitating. It was only his bond with Micah that was bothering him.

Gestalt had said that the bond wasn't a physical link, and he was right. But when Micah reached out, he could *feel* them there. Gestalt felt like walking through a fall rain, cool and beautiful in a way that made you grateful for your windbreaker. But Dominic . . .

When Micah was younger, they'd spent a few summer months living in a rented cabin. Micah had learned to swim and made friends with the ever-changing group of children staying in nearby campsites, but what he remembered most was the hammock. Just a standard polyester hammock, left behind by some prior occupant, strung up and forgotten. Micah had spent hours and hours in that hammock, reading borrowed novels in the dappled summer sunlight, eventually falling asleep and waking to sparkling water and the sound of cicadas.

That was what Dominic felt like.

Micah wondered what *he* felt like to other people. He wasn't optimistic.

Gestalt was still staring at him, like he was trying to puzzle out Micah's meaning.

"Never mind," Micah sighed. "Forget I said anything. I'm going to sleep. Do you need anything?"

"You opened the bond to him."

Micah felt a little twinge through the bond, like Gestalt had touched him. "Just ask, Ges, you don't have to go digging through my head."

"This is faster." Gestalt frowned. "You think he has rejected you."

Micah blinked. "No I don't."

"Yes you do."

The twinge got stronger, and Micah railed against it, trying to force the angel back. "Stop it, Ges!"

"You think he's rejected you for *me*," Gestalt said, wrinkling his nose.

Micah shoved him.

Gestalt caught himself easily, wings flaring as he regained his balance. Micah shoved again, this time through the bond, and this time Gestalt actually *smirked* as he waved off the attack.

"I don't want your master, Micah."

Micah's jaw set, his eyes narrowing. He turned and stalked toward the house. After a moment, he turned back to Gestalt.

"Just remember, if I told you to go fuck yourself, you'd have to do it."

Dominic was sitting at the kitchen table with a cup of coffee and a bottle of aspirin. He looked up when Micah came in. "Hey, I'll be out in a sec."

"Don't bother, they're gone."

Dominic rubbed his eyes. "I gather they bought it, then?"

"Yeah. I think Ian vouched for us. They wanted to take Ges in, but I talked them out of it."

"Fuckers would just call me if it went south, anyway."

"That's what I told them."

Dominic stared at the coffee as though blaming it for his chaotic night. When it refused to apologize, he cracked open the bottle of aspirin. "Where is our fallen angel, anyway?"

Micah shrugged. "Outside. I don't think he likes it in here. Fine by me."

"What, you guys all done playing leather and lace?"

"I was trying to help him," Micah snapped. "It's not my fault he's scared of me."

Then again, maybe it *was* his fault. Gestalt could barely stand being within a couple feet of him. He would open the connection and then yank back like it had burned him. Gestalt watched Micah the way Micah had watched Slate. It would be easy to blame it on Ges, say he was just paranoid, but . . .

But he wasn't afraid of *Dominic.*

Micah wondered again what the others felt when he reached out to them.

He had a bad feeling he knew. And he had a bad feeling he knew *why*.

Micah crossed the room slowly, the darkened doorway of the bedroom beckoning. He glanced over his shoulder, back at Dominic. Fuck the bond. He'd fix this himself. Whatever he looked like on the inside, Dominic was still attracted to his body. It was something he could work with.

"Come to bed."

Dominic shook his head. "It's almost morning; I'm gonna try to push through."

"Dominic." His voice was soft, feminine, the way Arabelle had taught him. "Come to bed."

Dominic raised an eyebrow. Micah tilted his chin toward the door, beckoning Dominic with bedroom eyes. When Dominic hesitated, Micah shrugged, turning away with practiced nonchalance.

"Suit yourself," he said casually, pulling his shirt off and discarding it. He'd gotten halfway across their bedroom before he heard the kitchen chair scraping across the floor. A small smile touched his lips. He could still do this, at least. His hands were steady, unbuckling his belt and dropping his clothes to the floor. When Dominic's shadow fell across the doorway, Micah was ready for him, turning to draw him into a kiss.

Dominic hesitated, probably remembering the way this scenario had already played out once today. Micah's hands rested on his hips, fingers skimming under the band of his jeans, and Dominic relaxed. His mouth fit to Micah's perfectly, fingers running through his long hair.

"I want you so bad."

Dominic's breath caught, but before he could respond, Micah was gripping the hem of his shirt, teasing it up over his body. Dom raised his arms, letting Micah undress him, but Micah only got it as far as Dominic's elbows before twisting the shirt around his wrist. Dominic was left trapped, the shirt holding his arms up and back, the collar pressed tight over his eyes.

"Micah—" he started, but Micah cut him off, kissing him deep. Dominic gasped when he pulled away, then moaned when Micah worked his way down the side of his jaw and over his shoulder.

He released the shirt, and Dominic whipped it off, pushing Micah backward onto the bed and pinning him. One knee landed on the edge of the mattress, rough denim holding Micah's legs apart. Micah hooked a leg around Dominic's hips, pulling him down and grinding against him. Dom was hard as marble inside his jeans, and Micah made sure that Dominic's cock fit into the hollow of his hip as he rolled up.

Here, he had to improvise, because slaves never undressed their masters unless ordered to do so. They were supposed to wait, but Micah didn't think Dominic knew that. The next time the kiss broke, Micah slipped his hands between them and popped open the button on Dominic's pants. He worked the zipper down, stroking Dominic through the cotton of his boxers.

Dominic moaned softly, his mouth hot on the hollow of Micah's throat. His fingers skimmed over Micah's side, reaching between them. Micah was expecting this; Dominic was a textbook reciprocal lover.

Dominic drew back, watching him through hooded eyes, and Micah smiled. He remembered what it had felt like to experience this through Dominic's bond. The desperate *energy* of it. He wanted Dom to have that. Even if he couldn't have it himself.

"God, look at you," Dominic murmured, and Micah leaned up and drew him back down into a kiss.

"I want you. Please," he said when they broke apart again. He knew how to beg for it. He knew how to take it and make it good and if that was how he could be close to Dominic, then that was what he would do.

Dominic looked at him with a question in his eyes, but Micah ignored it, instead focusing on divesting Dominic of his remaining clothing. He pulled Dominic down onto the bed, arching up against him.

Dominic was desperate for him—he could feel it even with the bond closed. And it *was* closed. He was holding it firmly shut, unwilling to open it even a crack for fear that whatever was inside him would leak out and scare Dominic off for good.

He let Dominic touch him, enjoying it but never losing focus on his own actions. Dominic moved slowly over his body, working with a care and attention that Micah wasn't used to. Dominic touched him like he was exploring, making a map of Micah's body and committing it to memory.

Micah wasn't used to being remembered. Something inside reached out for Dominic, before he smothered it, clamping it down before it could actually make contact.

Dominic asked him if he was sure, and Micah nodded, pleasantly surprised to find that it was true. He knew it couldn't last, it never had. Dominic was going to tire of him and move on, just like the others. But in this moment, this was exactly what he wanted. He was sure.

He lay back and let Dominic work him over, slow and easy. Dominic was far more careful than he needed to be, but Micah didn't hurry him. He was determined to let this last as long as Dominic wanted it to. Micah, for his part, thought that he could lie here forever, letting Dominic's body cover his.

He reached out, but Dom pushed him back, catching his wrists and pressing them gently to the mattress.

"Let me" was all Dominic said, and Micah let him. His fingers were hot on Micah's cock, stroking him in a slow, easy rhythm.

Micah started to lose focus a little. "Please, Dom, I want—" The words cut off with a hiss when Dominic moved down, licking across the head of his cock. Whatever he'd been about to say, it was lost. He moaned softly, rocking his hips against Dominic's hands. Heat was coiling in his belly, and it flared when he opened his eyes and saw Dominic looking up at him in the darkness.

He reached up (*don't do that, he put your hands down, he wants them down*) and cupped Dominic's face to pull him into a kiss. It was deep and insistent, Micah trying to tell Dominic everything this meant to him.

His breath was coming in gasps now, the muscles of his belly tensing, and he forced them to relax. He put his hands on Dominic's, holding him still.

"Not yet. I want you with me."

Dominic withdrew, going to the nightstand for a bottle of something slick. Dominic reached down, taking himself in hand, and Micah smiled. "C'mon already."

And then Dominic was covering him again, his cock alongside Micah's, the two of them sliding together. Dominic leaned in, nipping at Micah's throat.

Micah reached down, his hand wrapping around both of them.

"Ah, *fuck*, Micah," Dominic groaned, grinding into his grip. Micah adjusted, letting Dominic thrust into his fist, into the tight space between them. He could feel Dominic's skin against his, felt the head of Dom's cock with each stroke. Dom's side of the bond was bright with arousal, burning against the barrier that Micah held fast.

"Come for me," Dominic whispered, and Micah was gone.

Dominic fell asleep afterward, curled around Micah, their legs tangled together. One arm was thrown lazily over Micah's hip, their fingers entwined. Micah rubbed the pad of his thumb in slow circles over Dominic's knuckle, thinking.

For a moment there, he'd been worried he'd irrecoverably screwed up. Never in his life—*never*—had a lover abandoned him midsession. But he'd clearly recovered. He just needed to make sure not to make the same mistake again.

Ever.

He could keep the bond closed. The one time he'd opened it, it had felt incredible to reach out to Dominic, to feel him there. And being able to *feel* Dom's lust, without the rules and apprehension that bound Micah's own . . . it was indescribable. But if keeping it closed was what it took to keep Dominic with him, then that was what he'd do. And Ges . . .

Well, Gestalt wasn't planning on staying very long. That much was obvious. So there was no point worrying about the daiyura's opinion of him.

It was a *little* disappointing. Micah had thought they'd made progress while Dominic was gone. Ges was actually interesting and intelligent, underneath all that searing attitude and thorny sarcasm. Micah had been hoping to learn more about him, about the angels, about the bonds, about any of it, really.

He caught himself searching for Gestalt, wondering what he was up to, outside alone in the dark. Catching himself, he reeled the feeling back in and clamped the bond down tight.

He'd done enough damage.

CHAPTER EIGHT

More than three billion years ago, lightning hit a mud puddle and some amino acids fused sideways. It was utterly unremarkable, except for being a self-reproducing anomaly, and even *that* wasn't much to look at.

Every single living thing on this planet was a descendant of those self-replicating macromolecules, all of it the product of billions of years of shoving and jostling to make sure the carriers of their deoxyribonucleic acid were the ones that ate instead of being eaten. The drive to replicate was inherent in every living creature by the sheer nature of the struggle; anything lacking the single-mindedness required to reproduce had long since died off.

So, from a theoretical point of view, Gestalt could understand.

In practice, sex was confusing and maddening and occurring in his life with a frequency he found frankly unnecessary.

The bark on his branch scratched his belly when he stretched out, resting his chin on his forearms. He looked down at the stream, flowing underneath him perfectly contentedly without any biological fluid exchanges at all.

He didn't know how Micah could stand it.

It had taken Gestalt by surprise the first time his captors had raped him. His avatar was a close facsimile of human, but it was also *male.* Gestalt could have understood it if his avatar had appeared female—it still couldn't conceive with a human partner, but a casual observer might have suspected at least a *chance.*

Gestalt held his captors in nothing but the most bitter contempt, but he was hard-pressed to conclude that they were too stupid to understand their own reproductive systems. Stupidity could account for one or two, but there had been *so* many more than that, and they'd used him in ways that couldn't *possibly* result in offspring—

Up at the house, Dominic was approaching climax, and Gestalt halted his thought process to listen.

Micah, for some reason, was shuttered up inside his own mind like a hermit, refusing to let even a sliver of his light out into the bond. Gestalt found it vaguely perverse that they would interact so intimately with the bond closed. It was like singing a duet with your mouth shut, but maybe it was different for humans. Who knew.

It didn't seem to bother Dominic; he was broadcasting like a beacon, probably not even aware he was doing it. The sensations in his body were easily overpowering the tiny amount of control he had over the bond.

The more Gestalt listened, the more he was sure that Dominic wasn't paying attention at all. Dominic's mind was utterly focused on his present situation, on Micah and the way their bodies intertwined and interacted. Gestalt was a silent observer in all this, not reaching out to either partner. These actions were utterly foreign to him—he *knew* Micah and Dominic weren't stupid, they *had* to know their actions were biologically pointless, and yet here they were.

Dominic was reaching out to Micah, nudging uselessly around the edge of the bond, but Micah stayed locked down tight. Gestalt wondered if Micah was angry with his master, refusing to open up to him because of some argument, but Dominic didn't seem to sense anything of that sort. On the contrary, Micah seemed to be doing everything possible to make Dominic happy.

And Dominic *was* happy, Gestalt realized. Happier than was called for by the fulfillment of a simple biological imperative. He was still reaching out for Micah, and though he wasn't getting anything back, he kept doing it because it was the *reaching* that he drew pleasure from.

. . . *That* couldn't be right.

Inside the house, Dominic reached the pinnacle of his orgasm, and Gestalt had to brace himself against the branch as the waves of pleasure pulsed through the bond. It was . . . interesting. There was no outpouring of joy for other bodily fulfillments. Gestalt wasn't pounded with waves of pleasure when the humans ate, or urinated, or awoke from sleep. Only this. This one thing, which they did seemingly without purpose.

He couldn't settle comfortably back onto his branch, and he belatedly realized that his avatar was aroused. He rolled his eyes and wished he had been summoned to a female avatar, one which wouldn't need to deal with these indignities.

Back at the house, Micah and Dominic were pulling the blankets up, still tangled together. Dominic was radiating contentment and satisfaction; Micah was barricaded inside himself. It was a wonder Dominic didn't notice his absence. Gestalt supposed if the humans went their whole lives alone inside their own minds, they were unlikely to miss each other after only a few days.

Not like daiyura missed each other. Not like Gestalt missed his brothers and sisters, the infinitely complex choir that served as the perpetual backdrop of home. He didn't regret what he'd done, the spells that had left him stranded here in this silent, backward world. But that didn't keep him from missing them.

He hummed, a low, lonely sound so removed from his memories that it actually made him feel worse.

Micah fluttered at the edge of the bond, and Gestalt grabbed at him like a lifeline, suddenly desperate not to be alone in his mind. But Micah had already retreated. The moment Micah was gone, Gestalt kicked himself. He didn't need dirt men to keep him company. They were barely better than nothing, really.

Yet being stranded in this world with them was the cost of closing the connection between realms. No more of his kind could be pulled through, and the humans couldn't get to his home.

He hadn't been lying to Coffey. The damage he'd done during his summoning *was* sufficient to disable the passageway. The humans didn't have the magic necessary to force it back open, not when a daiyura had been the one to close it. He'd rather die than fix what he'd done, and for a while, it had looked like he'd get the chance.

They'd wanted an explanation, and the collar had sparked and burned and he'd lied. They'd come with blades to demand the truth, and he'd given them vagaries and metaphors and language barriers it would take them eons to overcome. He buried relevant truths in irrelevant ones, flavored heartily with speculation that couldn't be falsified, and when his tricks had been discovered, *oh, they'd been angry—*

Gestalt realized he was reaching out for Dominic, using the human's calm, contented slumber as a counterpoint to the horrors in his own mind. He hesitated, plucking a leaf off the branch and shredding it while he contemplated. It probably wasn't good to get in the habit of bonding with humans. They were simplistic and feral, and most likely they'd never be able to communicate a fraction of the way the daiyura could.

But there weren't daiyura here. Gestalt was alone, and what he had was Dominic.

Sighing, he reached out to the sleeping man, leaving the bond open and meeting him halfway across. It wasn't like communicating with another daiyura. It was the intellectual equivalent of stroking a cat, but it was better than nothing.

It was past midday when the humans roused from their sleep. By then, Gestalt had reached a decision.

It was easier to enter the house when he wasn't wounded. The permeating feeling of *human* didn't set him on edge when he knew he had the ability to fight or flee.

Not that he would need to do either, by the looks of it. Dominic was barely mobile, hair mussed and shirt on backward. Micah was slightly better; at least he had the mental wherewithal to work the coffee maker. He still had the bond sewed up tight, and Gestalt took a moment to watch him. He didn't look angry or distressed. Gestalt was far from an expert on human body language, but Micah's hands had a way of trailing across Dominic's shoulders when he passed, and that would indicate affection. Or maybe there was another purpose; who knew with these two.

"The men who held me," Gestalt started. "They can be found?"

The humans both looked at him for a moment like they'd forgotten he could talk. He met their gaze.

Micah was the first to speak. "Yeah. Uh. There are some photographs we're supposed to check, actually."

Gestalt narrowed his eyes. "Why the delay?"

Micah's gaze darted to the floor before returning to Gestalt. "Been busy. Hold on, I'll get you the laptop."

He fetched the folding computer off the couch, setting it on the table and gesturing for Gestalt to come look.

There were dozens of them. The folder that Micah showed him was filled with faces, and already, Gestalt could see at least three that he knew.

"The filenames are unique numbers," Micah was saying. "So if you recognize the person in the photo, you mark down the number and where you saw them and what happened."

"What about names?"

Micah shook his head. "They're identified by numbers to try to avoid bias as much as possible. In case we've heard a name on the news or something."

"So then, how do we find them?"

Micah hesitated. "We don't," he said slowly. "We forward these back to Ian—"

"Piper," Dominic interrupted.

"—whoever, and then they're the ones who make the arrests."

Gestalt was incredulous. "And we trust them to mete out justice?"

"Yeah. They go to trial, and if there's enough evidence, they get convicted and punished."

Gestalt had ideas of his own on that process, but he kept them to himself. He might have to do some things behind the humans' backs, and the more he hid from them, the easier that would be.

"That one," he said, pointing to one of the photographs. "He was there when I was bound."

Micah double-clicked the icon, and the photo enlarged to fill the entire screen. The man was in the vicinity of forty-five, dressed in a suit and posed in front of a mottled gray background.

"*That* guy?" Dominic asked, crossing the room to peer over Gestalt's shoulder.

Gestalt stiffened, turning in his seat to try to keep the man in sight. "Yes, that guy. Do you recognize him?"

"Dude's a senator."

The word meant nothing to Gestalt, but Micah looked up sharply. "Seriously?"

"Yeah. He was on the news a couple weeks ago, actually. He was working to expand the list of offenses that could be punished with indenturement; bunch of people were pretty pissed."

"He broke three of my fingers," Gestalt said evenly. "When I first got here."

There had been a dozen of them, fascinated with the creature they'd caught. The body he'd found himself bound to was damaged far beyond the point of function, and he'd used up a huge amount of his limited power restoring it. The humans were amazed by the way he healed, and had immediately set to damaging his avatar to see how quickly he could repair it. Gestalt had been disoriented, bound by the silver cuffs and utterly unfamiliar with the sensation of being contained in a physical body. The pain (he later identified the sensation as pain) was all-encompassing, blocking every other thought from his mind and narrowing his focus to an unending litany of *stop stop stop stop stop—*

He was better at ignoring it now. He could shove it all down into a small corner of his mind and push through it. In those first few days, he'd had no such skills.

Dominic looked a little sick. "Why?" he asked weakly, and Micah's face mirrored Gestalt's.

"Because he could, I suppose," Gestalt said, shrugging. "Honestly, I have difficulty parsing the reasons for many of the things humans do. This man here," he said, pointing to another icon. "I think he's some sort of doctor. He and an assistant spent a lot of time stripping the skin and muscles off my back because they wanted to see how the wings connected."

He paused there, remembering. They'd originally been intending to remove the wings entirely, taking them out by the root for study elsewhere. They'd talked about it at length while they stood over him, marking his skin with felt-tip markers to remind themselves where to cut. Ultimately, they decided to leave the limbs in place. Gestalt had been in too much pain to be relieved.

"Coffey was there for that one," he added. "He came up with the idea of sewing my mouth shut to keep me from screaming. Apparently it was distracting."

"Gods," Dominic said hoarsely, but Gestalt shook his head.

"There were no gods there. Just humans. And I think maybe some . . ." he searched for the name of the other creatures that had been there that day. ". . . vampires?"

Micah's eyes had a faraway expression, and Gestalt thought that, behind his barriers, he was remembering things too.

They worked through the list one face at a time. Gestalt recognized a little over one in four. Micah recognized closer to one in eight, with some overlap. He could type, much faster than Gestalt, so he sat and listened while Gestalt told him what he remembered. Gestalt had a great memory for detail, or so Micah said.

Dominic sat with them for the first sixteen or seventeen stories, increasing amounts of disgust and anger seeping through the bond. It didn't affect Gestalt, but he could see it getting to Micah.

"Did any of them . . . I mean . . . With Micah, they were . . ."

The question was clear in Dominic's head, even if he couldn't make the words come.

"You want to know if I was raped."

Dominic's face turned ash white. "Yeah. Did any of them . . . ?"

"Yes." Gestalt looked to Micah. "Should I be including that? It seemed relatively minor compared to the rest."

"Probably. I can't guarantee anything will be done, but it's worth mentioning."

"Worth— *What*?" Dominic was getting worked up about this; it was spilling through the bond and setting Gestalt on edge. "What do you mean 'worth *mentioning*'?"

"I mean," Micah said evenly, "that Gestalt's classified as a creature, and creatures have limits on autonomy. Probably nothing will come of it."

"Don't lecture me on creatures, Micah, I'm a licensed controller. I know what the law is. Creatures aren't human, but that doesn't mean you can do . . . *this*!" He gestured at the laptop. "You can't vivisect them or torture them or fucking *rape* them—*fuck*!"

He stood, running his hands through his hair and looking around the room like the answer to this puzzle was hidden in the décor somewhere.

Gestalt and Micah regarded him calmly.

"The laws don't usually match up with the reality, Dominic," Micah said quietly. When Dominic turned on him, the impact on the bond was strong enough to make Micah flinch. Dominic was reaching out to him, looking to surround him and protect him and keep him safe. Micah's jaw clenched with the effort of keeping his barriers up.

Gestalt looked between the two of them with curiosity. "This upsets you."

"Of course it upsets me!" Dom exploded, turning away from Micah. "This stuff you're saying . . . I wouldn't do this shit to a *dog* and you're telling me that they did it to you—both of you—over and over and over and *nothing will come of it*?"

"We're not people, Dom," Micah said softly, and that was the wrong thing to say because something snapped inside Dominic and he got very quiet.

"I'm gonna . . . I'm gonna go see if I can figure out anything with the cuffs."

"Thank you," Gestalt said sincerely, and Dominic retreated into his room without responding.

Micah opened the next photo.

CHAPTER NINE

Dominic was not handling this well. Every time he closed his eyes, he saw it: The blood. The burns. The bruises. The nails through Gestalt's body, the lash marks on Micah.

Gestalt's voice, emotionless as he described his torture.

"We're not people."

Something was crawling up Dominic's throat, something like rage or sadness or panic. There was white noise at the edge of his vision as he dropped onto the bed, forcing himself to calm down.

Micah had been calm, he remembered. All those weeks ago at the police station, when he'd stripped off his clothes and let Ronnie photograph his scars, impassively jotting down his story in a notebook because his owner had taken his voice. If Micah could stay calm through that, then Dom could handle this.

Dominic saw Coffey again, standing over Gestalt with his gun raised. Dominic hadn't even hesitated, putting a bullet through him because Gestalt was angry and hurt and *afraid* and Dominic wasn't going to stand for that. Not for a minute.

Dominic didn't understand how his life had gotten here. How he'd gone out looking for some hired muscle and somehow ended up on the wrong side of some kind of sadistic kink party mafia. But this was his responsibility now, and hell if he was going to shirk it.

He shot up and slammed the door open, storming back into the living room and immediately regretting it when the men waiting there both flinched.

"You're people," he said, pointing. Micah's face was carefully blank, while Gestalt just looked amused. "*You're people*, and if I ever get my hands on the fucking..."

Words failed him. He ran his hand through his hair, trying to get some kind of hold on whatever it was that was wrapping itself around his lungs and squeezing.

"I'm not that bright," he said eventually. "But I know monsters when I see them. And what happened to you was done by monsters. And they're gonna pay for it if it's the last damn thing I ever do."

"Dominic . . ." Micah shook his head, like he was trying to clear out cobwebs. "Please, don't fixate on this."

Don't fixa— "How can I *not*? How can *you* not? How can you sit there and describe this and not be a fucking mess? I'm losing my shit just *listening* to it, and you're telling me you *lived* through all of it and came out the other side still alive and you're willing to let it *go*?"

"I'm not letting it go," Micah said quietly. "But there's no point exploding over it."

He was sitting on the couch instead of kneeling on the floor, but Dominic didn't miss the way his hands rested on his knees, perfectly still, waiting. Micah's face dropped into that blank expression, and Dominic realized he was gone. Dom took a deep breath. "Come back, Micah. I'm done yelling."

"He doesn't believe you," Gestalt supplied when a moment had passed.

"I probably wouldn't, either," Dominic admitted. He took another deep breath, resisting the urge to go out onto the front porch and scream his frustrations into the trees. The important thing—the *actually important thing right now*—was to not drive Micah back into his coping mechanisms.

"I'm okay, really," he said, calmer now. He took another breath. "Do you believe me?"

"Of course," Micah said immediately, giving him the answer he wanted, not caring that they both knew it was a lie. But what was Dominic going to do, order him to mean it?

"I'm not gonna let anything else happen to you," he said instead, and Micah's hands relaxed slightly. Ges's side of the bond felt like amusement, but the affectionate kind. "Either of you."

"I know," Micah said, and that, at least, sounded true.

Well, it was for *him*, anyway, Dom thought, glancing at Ges. Ges, who was positioned carefully to keep both of them in sight. Dom still couldn't do anything about the suppression bands keeping him prisoner, at least not until he figured out the ikons on the— Wait.

"Ges, can I see the collar again?"

Gestalt stared at him a moment and then tipped his head. There it was: a jagged diamond indentation in the silver. It wasn't a rune, and Dominic had mistaken it for decoration or damage.

He checked the wrist cuffs and, sure enough, the same jagged diamond.

"I'll be damned," he muttered, and then broke into a grin. "It's an ouroboros."

"Does that mean you can break it?" Micah asked, less tense now that Dominic wasn't yelling anymore.

"Not yet," Dominic admitted. He made an effort to keep his voice level. "But it's a start. It should at least give me a clue about how the binding works."

He twisted the cuff around in his hands, looking closer at the markings. "This diamond here, it's stylized but I'm pretty sure it's supposed to be a snake's mouth. See, here's an eye. So the band is an incarnation of the ouroboros, the snake eating its own tail."

"There are two of them," Gestalt said, rotating the bangle to expose an identical marking on the opposite side.

"Huh. Okay, so that's a little unusual. Two snakes, eating each other's tails."

Unusual worked. Clues were always more useful when they were specific. Dominic turned the bangle around again, searching the other markings but finding nothing inspirational. He tried to remember what he knew about the ouroboros: Witches used it as a symbol for eternity or for the cycle of death and rebirth. Two opposing snakes meant two *different* forces, continually feeding off and building from each other. One of the snakes probably represented the binding spell, so—

"Whatever the spell is, it's tied into something else. We just have to figure out what, and how they're connected. But if we can break the connection, then that should break the binding or at least weaken it."

Gestalt didn't respond, and when Dominic glanced up, he realized that Ges was staring at him. His wings were pulled high and tight, and his eyes were wide. He looked like he was a million miles away, not hearing a word Dominic said. Dominic realized he was still twisting the bangle idly around the daiyura's wrist.

He pulled back, dropping Gestalt's hand like it had burned him. "Sorry. So, okay. I'll see if I can find what the spell is tied to."

He glanced over at Micah, who was still sitting like he was waiting for orders, though he was looking at Dominic curiously. Which made sense because he'd been holding Gestalt's fucking hand and what the hell was *that*?

"You up for some more magic, Micah?" he asked, trying to dispel some of the deeply weird vibes permeating the room.

Micah nodded.

It seemed much longer than two days since the last time Dominic had set up a spell. The circle in the living room had mostly burned out, thanks to the hex bag from— Gods, was it only the day before?

Unfortunately, the spell he was trying to do now was a little more complicated than a general purification ritual, which was why he ended up calling Amanda.

"Let me guess, the angel's decided to kill you and you're calling me for help from under your bed," she quipped, picking up after two rings.

"Ges is fine, other than being consistently surly and condescending. I think I might have figured out something about his collar though."

"Awesome. Do tell."

"Do you still have the photos you took at the crime scene?"

"I'm looking at them right now, actually. Anything specific?"

"There's a jagged diamond shape that repeats on both sides, it's on all five bangles, see it? It's an ouroboros."

"Are you sure? It's kind of a leap."

"It's gotta be. You can see the fangs and the eye on the snake if you look close."

There was a pause on the other end. "I'll be damned. You're right."

"The binding is feeding off something else, and I gotta figure out what. I've got a tracking spell, but it involves dropping the linked item into a fire, and that's not really going to work in this scenario."

"Do you know anyone with Sight? They might be able to look for you."

Dominic closed his eyes, running through the list of people who owed him a favor. Not a psychic, seer, or medium in the bunch. He supposed he could reach out to Amelie, but their last job had gone badly, and he wasn't sure he wanted to reopen that particular can of worms.

"Not at the moment."

"Capricious bunch, aren't they," Amanda remarked dryly.

"Don't I know it."

"You could try summoning an elemental."

Dominic frowned, considering. He tried to remember if there was any bread in the house—maybe half a loaf of store brand white stuff. It would probably do, in a pinch.

"Think they'd be able to track down the link long-distance?"

"Dunno, but it's worth a shot. I'd go for the air types; they tend to have the most range." Amanda paused. "Are you sure you want to do this?"

"Not really. I mean, elementals are annoying in ideal circumstances—"

"No, I mean, with the angel. He got you hexed and then he killed people in your freakin' yard. He's not your responsibility. You can turn him back over to Ian, you know."

"How did you know about— Never mind. Anyway, none of that was Ges's fault."

"It wasn't your fault, either. Just . . . be careful, okay?"

Dominic checked back into the living room, where Micah and Gestalt were working through the photographs. "Yeah. I will."

They said their goodbyes, and then Dominic went looking for baked goods.

It turned out they had less than a quarter of a loaf of sandwich bread, and it was a particularly shitty store brand. Dominic gave it a miss, digging out the flour bucket and mixing bowls instead.

Elementals were useful, but temperamental. They had to be called with a certain amount of deference, and even then, they had a habit of wandering off if you didn't keep them engaged. Some witches kept them as familiars, but it was a tricky process and tended to backfire if their personalities didn't match up.

"Can I help?" Micah asked, but Dominic waved him off. Ian had sent another text message asking about the photos, so he guessed it was important that they finish their identification. And to be completely honest, Dominic wanted them to get that over with while he was otherwise occupied. The snippets of conversation reaching him were dark enough to turn his stomach. Gestalt kept sending glances his way, which meant he was pushing his weirdness through the bond, which meant he was probably upsetting Micah too, not that the freakin' robot would ever complain—

He spilled the salt and cursed, trying to scoop the majority of it back out of the bowl. He failed miserably and decided to press on anyway. It wasn't like it was going to get eaten; it was just a symbol. Gestalt looked over, curious, but Dominic glowered at him.

He stirred the excess salt into the dough, kneading it twice with flour-coated hands before tossing it onto a tray.

"That's gonna take an hour to bake," he announced, "and we should try to do the summoning as fast as possible after that. The fresher it is, the more cooperative the elemental will be."

The house filled with the smell of baking bread while Dominic set up the spell. In this case, the circle surrounded a four-pointed star, arranged to coincide with the cardinal directions. There were candles at each point, three white and one red positioned toward the west to indicate the preference for an air elemental. Four small mirrors were set up around the red candle, facing inward and reflecting each other, indicating a request for information.

Around the outside of the circle, Dominic etched a containment spell in chalk. The spell was weak; its primary goal was to assist the elemental in maintaining a corporeal form, rather than to actually capture and hold the spirit. All but the weakest elementals would be able to break free from the circle easily.

And, just because it had worked well for him in the past, Dominic put a line of peppermint oil up the side of each white candle.

Elementals tended to be very sensory creatures, and the strong scent would attract them and make them more comfortable in the space.

All the while, Micah and Gestalt were clicking through the photographs that Ian had sent. Each time Gestalt said no, Dominic's breath came a little easier, but when he said yes, the stories that followed made Dominic's blood run cold. Micah listened impassively, asking questions to clarify and typing out Ges's words. His typing was getting fast.

Dominic forced himself to stay, and listen, and shut up, though Gestalt's repeated glances told him all he needed to know about how stoic he was managing to be.

But gods damn it, he was gonna do this. He was gonna sit right here and set up his summoning and not lose his shit.

He could do that much.

He *could.*

Micah closed the last photo after forty minutes, and a distinctly uncomfortable silence fell over the three of them. Dominic had finished marking out the containment circle, and now he was just sitting there, trying to process.

After a while, he realized there was a light, cool pressure in his chest, just below his breastbone. When he thought about it, he realized it was Ges, pushing *calm* into the bond.

"Am I that obvious?"

Gestalt nodded, meeting his eyes.

Dominic sighed. "Sorry. I know I'm probably making it worse for you both."

He reached out, trying to find Micah, but came back with nothing.

The oven *ding*ed and Dominic was friggin' saved by the bell because he had no idea how to even *begin* to fix this.

"Okay," he said, clapping his hands. A kind of manic energy was taking over where coffee and rationality had both failed him. "Let's call us an elemental."

Dominic knew how to do that. He'd done that before. He was very confident in his elemental-summoning abilities, and he was going to hold on to that confidence if it killed him. It was his rope across a bottomless pit of horror and outrage and other, darker emotions he didn't even have words for.

He explained his process, retrieving the bread and tracing the last ikons into the circle.

"When you call these guys, there's usually about an eighty percent chance of getting the kind you asked for. It really depends on who's around and what kind of state they're in."

Micah was watching closely; Gestalt was settling cross-legged onto the couch.

"Earth elementals are the hardest to summon," Dom went on, because he definitely couldn't handle silence right now, "because they're lethargic and move at a slower pace than the rest of the world. It makes them great witnesses if you need to know the history of an area, but also pretty terrible about communicating quickly. Fire elementals, on the other hand, almost always show up when called. They're also the most likely to show up when *not* called. You get fire elementals at summonings not for an elemental at all, if they're in the area and in the mood."

That said, Dominic lit the candle, setting the spell in motion.

"And now we wait," Dominic said, collapsing onto the couch. "Shouldn't be too long."

He hoped.

The uncomfortable quiet fell over the room again. The candle flame burned perfectly evenly, without even a hint of a draft.

Without intending to, Dominic poked at the bond, the place where he felt like Micah *should* be.

"He's closed us both off; I'm not sure why," Gestalt said, and Micah looked up sharply. Dominic kept his head down, remembering the night before. When Micah had thrown the bond wide open and he'd responded by panicking and running.

"Yeah, about that—"

"You don't have to explain," Micah interrupted. "I know what I feel like to you. Why neither of you can stand the inside of my head."

Dominic blinked. "Micah, that's not—"

"No, it is." Micah's voice was low. "You pretend like you're fine, but you hate it. All this stuff, it disgusts both of you, and that's probably good. But I liked it. I was *good* at it. Ges lived through it; I *excelled* at it. Whatever they asked, I gave; I was obedient and dignified and I knew my place. More than I know it now, because ever since I've come here, all I've done is *fuck up*." He gestured to Dominic. "I fucked it up for you, and I fucked it up for Ges, and the more I fuck up, the more I think I belong with them more than I belong with you."

Micah glanced up at him then, calm hazel eyes meeting Dominic's horrified gaze. "I think maybe they realized something you haven't yet, and that's why you can't stand to see inside my head."

Dominic opened his mouth to protest, but he couldn't find the words. *No, Micah, you're perfect, I'm just terrified by the ideal you're so in love with, you know how it is?*

"You can't think I'd blame you," he said instead. "For what you did to survive."

Micah let out a dark laugh, dropping his eyes and going straight back into his training. He slid onto his knees and leaned forward, his hands flat on the floor and his head down.

"You don't get it. I tried making this work and I failed. I can't *be* a person like you are, but I can still be something good." Micah risked a glance up at Dominic, his face pleading. "This morning, that was good, right? That's what I can do right; it's what I'm good for, so just *let* me. I could make you happy if you'd stop being so angry about the way things *are*."

"But that's *not* how things are!" Dom insisted. "It's how they *were*, and they shouldn't have been that way!"

Micah just shook his head, staring down at his hands. His shoulders were tense.

"I'll stop talking about it," he said evenly. "Now that Ian has what he needs. I didn't realize what it was doing to you, and I should have. I won't say anything else about it, and we can forget it. *Please*, Dominic. I can be so much better than I have been, if you'd *let me*."

"What do you think we see?" Gestalt asked before Dominic could formulate a response.

"I don't think I want to know," Micah whispered. "Something broken."

Gestalt frowned, and Micah flinched away from him like he'd been struck. "What are you— *Ah*!" Micah clutched at his head, fingers buried in his hair.

"What are you doing? Stop it!" Dominic reached for the daiyura, but Gestalt evaded him easily. The collar sparked, but Micah had already relaxed, his hands returning to the floor and his breath coming heavy.

"Ges, what the fuck did you just do," Dominic deadpanned. Gestalt wasn't paying attention to him. Instead he was peering at Micah, head tilted slightly to one side.

"I was looking for something," Ges answered, distracted.

"What?" Dominic asked, at the same time Micah said, "I hate it when you do that."

"Whatever it is that Micah seems to think is inside him. The broken thing." Gestalt frowned. "I don't see it."

"You saw it before," Micah said. "It's why you couldn't hold the bond unless I was handcuffed. Because there was something inside me that scared you. And Dominic—" Micah's voice caught. "Dominic saw it too. I don't know what it is, and I'm sorry and I'll learn to keep it closed, I swear, I'm trying, I just—"

His breath caught again and he stopped, drawing a slow inhale. "I *forced* you to include me in the bond; it was a mistake and you're the ones paying for it. And I'm gonna keep doing it, keep making mistakes—"

"That's *life*," Dominic interrupted, and Micah looked up at him, eyes widening. "You make mistakes. People get hurt. You scared Gestalt? Big deal. You think *I'm* perfect?"

He should stop, he knew it, but he couldn't stop seeing himself the way he'd been in Micah's mind, confident and capable and strong, ready and able to take on the world.

Micah deserved the truth.

"You think I should be in charge of *anyone*? I let my dad put off doctors' appointments for eighteen months because I didn't want to have an argument over it." Dom's throat got tight. "He'd still be alive if I had more backbone. You make mistakes, but at least you *try*. I was just a coward."

He fixed Micah with a level stare. "Know what I saw in you? I saw what you think of *me,* and it freaked me out because I'm *not* what you see. I can't live up to that, Micah."

Micah had nothing to say to that, just continued waiting on his knees, not meeting Dominic's eyes. Gestalt was watching the two of them with an expression Dominic couldn't even begin to decipher.

"All this from one bond. It's no wonder humans never learned to communicate properly."

"Okay, you know what—" Dominic started, but Gestalt was shaking his head with a sardonic smile.

"I do know. The moment I saw him, I said you were his master."

"I'm *not*," Dominic snapped.

"I think you are," Micah said, still addressing the floor. "I don't think I can help it."

Dominic looked back and forth between them, realizing for the first time how utterly in over his head he was. "Okay. We can work on this. Micah, please, just get off the floor. Please?"

Micah complied immediately, rising languidly to his feet.

For a long moment, they stood there, not sure how to proceed.

Something crunched.

In unison, the three of them turned, silently, to stare in the direction the sound had come from.

There was a little creature sitting in the middle of the summoning circle, munching on the tribute bread.

"So, did you guys *need* something, or . . .?" he took a bite of the loaf and grimaced. "Think you got enough salt there, buddy?" He took another bite. "Word to the wise? Sugar. Tastes way better, gets you a much higher quality— *Hel-lo*, what are *you*, then?" The elemental jumped to his feet, looking Gestalt over with a suggestive grin befitting a man far taller than eighteen inches. He waggled his eyebrows.

Gestalt just stood and stared, forehead furrowed.

The little guy strode out of the circle, headed for Ges. He didn't lose any corporeal clarity—truth be told, he didn't even seem to notice. He rounded Gestalt once, taking in the wings and dirty jeans, finally stopping in front of him with his hands on his hips. He was wearing some kind of tiny toga.

"Aren't *you* a tall drink of water?" the creature asked, and Dominic laughed. He couldn't help it. Whoever he was, this diminutive non-elemental was the weird cherry on top of his weird-ass sundae of a day, and fuck it, he was laughing.

"Watch it, pal," the not-elemental said, sending a glare Dominic's way. "It's not the size, it's how you use it."

Something cracked in Dominic's brain, the rope over the pit of madness snapping its final thread, and he laughed so hard his stomach cramped, and Micah started to look concerned.

"I'm told you can help me with this," Gestalt said, addressing the tiny man. He tugged at the collar, and the little creature didn't bother craning his neck. He took a running leap onto Gestalt's leg and proceeded to shimmy up the denim until he reached hip-height and ran out of cloth.

"Gonna need a boost, here, Gulliver," he said, when Gestalt made no motion to lift him higher.

"My name is Gestalt," the daiyura said, reaching for the creature.

"Nice to meetcha, I'm Lilin," the creature replied, launching himself onto Gestalt's hand and using both hands to shake one finger.

Dominic couldn't breathe. Micah was shifting his weight back like he thought he might have to fight someone but he wasn't sure who.

Lilin climbed up onto Gestalt's shoulder, holding a fistful of dark hair to keep his balance. He gave the collar a quick once-over.

"Nope. Stronger magic than mine, I'm afraid. And *way* stronger than the elemental you were *trying* to summon." Lilin glanced over to where Dominic was catching his breath, then turned back to Ges and stage-whispered, "Your witch might not know what he's doing."

"I know you can't break it," Dominic said. "I was hoping you could tell us what it's tethered to."

"Hmmm." Lilin plopped down onto Gestalt's shoulder and twisted the silver band in his hands. "You got some weird shit here, that's for damn sure," he said cheerily. "What did you say you were?"

"I'm a daiyura."

Lilin let out a low whistle. "Angel, huh? Weeell that explains a lot. Means I finally get the chance to ask . . ." He leaned in and whispered something in Ges's ear. Ges looked confused.

"I did not fall, I was pulled here from my own realm. And manifesting in a physical body was excruciating beyond words. Why do you ask?"

Lilin blinked like that wasn't the answer he'd been expecting.

Dominic grinned. "Did you ask him if it hurt when he fell from heaven?"

"Once in a lifetime opportunity!" Lilin protested.

Gestalt huffed. "This is pointless."

"Hey, hold your horses, there. Just having a little fun. As a matter of fact," the little man said, "I *do* know what the collar is bound to. And I will tell you, for a very reasonable payment."

"I thought that's what the bread was for," Ges grumbled.

"Nope! That's just the appearance fee. Information is extra."

"What do you want?" Dominic asked quickly, before the others could speak. Elementals weren't the bargaining sort, and he hadn't gone over fae rules with the other two yet.

Lilin raised his eyebrows at Dominic. "You agree to do me a favor. And then I'll give you three questions."

"I'll deal," Micah said quietly, because of course he would.

Dominic groaned.

"The benefit is mine," Gestalt protested. Micah shrugged.

"Hold up," Dominic said. "Nobody's dealing. You haven't even told us what you *are*."

"I'd think *that* was obvious," Lilin said, dropping down to sit easily on Gestalt's bare shoulder. "I'm an incubus."

Dominic blinked. "Aren't you guys supposed to be . . . bigger?"

"It's how you *use it*, pal," the tiny demon repeated. "Do you want to know what's got hot wings all tied up, or not?"

"Yes," Micah said deliberately, and Lilin grinned and said "Done" before Dominic could protest.

"Though I do wish it had been you," Lilin said wistfully, draping himself dramatically across Gestalt's shoulder. The daiyura's wing twitched outward, and Dominic was reminded of a horse flicking off a fly.

"How do I remove the binding spell?" Dominic asked, mentally counting off one of his questions.

The incubus patted Gestalt's shoulder. "You came here through a gateway, right? Somebody poked a hole from our realm into yours and yoinked you right through."

"We already knew that," Gestalt said icily.

"Yeah, but do you know where it is?"

"N . . . no," Gestalt admitted.

"Well, that's where you wanna start. Somebody's got a nice little spot of magic holding it steady, and *that's* what the spell's tied to. If you wanna lose the bling, the portal's gotta get gone."

Gestalt shook his head. "The portal's closed. I closed it myself as I was being pulled through."

"The fuck you call me here for if you're just gonna argue with me? The Door's open, babe. Bound up in blood runes." The incubus gave the collar a yank. "It's all written out right there if you know how to read it."

"So we need to find it," Dominic said. "That shouldn't be too hard. You can figure out how to destroy it, then, right, Ges?"

"No, apparently I can't," Gestalt snapped, picking the demon off his shoulder and dropping him onto the couch. "I've likely prevented passage between realms, but without knowing more about the magic currently sustaining it, I don't even know how to find it, let alone close it."

The incubus made a go-on gesture with his hand.

"Do *you* know how to destroy it?" Gestalt asked.

"Ah, rookie mistake," Lilin crowed, looking to where Dominic was rolling his eyes. "Your witch knows better than he lets on. To answer your second question: Yes. I *do* know how to destroy it. Think carefully about your last question."

Gestalt narrowed his eyes at the little demon.

"Coffey," Micah said. "And the rest of his people." He gestured to the laptop, indicating the photos he and Ges had been going through. "If they're the ones who trapped Ges, then it stands to reason that they're the ones who summoned him here. They'll know *where* it is."

"Handsome *and* smart," Lilin quipped, looking like he was considering a change of location.

"So we wait for Piper to pull one of those dickheads in, and grill them for info. Which means—"

"How do I destroy the gateway?" Gestalt asked. Lilin actually looked a bit disappointed. He reached out, placing one tiny hand on Gestalt's temple. A spark rolled down his arm, disappearing into the daiyura's skin.

"Got all that?"

Gestalt nodded. He opened his mouth and said something that Dom didn't hear with his ears. Lilin answered in kind. Gestalt nodded again.

"And that's three," the incubus said. He pointed at Micah. "I'll be getting back to *you*."

And with that, he vanished. Gestalt dropped to his knees, seizing a piece of chalk and beginning to draw a complicated set of diagrams on the floorboards.

"Oh, is *that* all?" Dom said, watching the shapes form without a hint of comprehension. "Well, this is going to be easy."

It wasn't easy, and what's more, it was getting considerably more difficult with each passing development.

The first thing Dominic did was call Ian, to tell him what they'd learned. Only it turned out that Ian had been yanked off the case completely. The way Ian heard it, the feds were now pulling together cases from around half the country, pinning them to an organization Dominic was dubbing the Hellfire Club. Ian had sent everything he had over to Piper and gotten exactly nothing in return. Apparently, the federal government wasn't in a sharing mood.

If the Hellfires had one clubhouse, or two, Dom might have suggested heading over with a dowsing rod to see if they could seek the portal out that way. By the sounds of it, though, there were dozens, not to mention people's private homes and businesses and holdings and who knew what else.

Dominic rubbed his temples.

Okay. So it was big. But not impossible, and he had allies. Plus an angel, not for nothing.

They, he amended. *They* had allies, because this was about Micah more than him.

That train of thought brought him back to the uncomfortable topic of What to Do About Micah.

Because Micah was regressing, and Dominic didn't need a shrink to tell him that. Dominic thought they'd been making progress. Then all of a sudden, it was like a switch had flipped and Micah had slipped back into his please-fuck-me deferential slave mode. It was problematic for several reasons, and Dominic couldn't shake the feeling that it was his fault.

Dominic called Piper, trying to focus on what he *could* do, but the call went to voicemail. He left his number, asking for a callback, and when he hung up he realized Micah was standing in the doorway. For a moment it looked like he was glowing, and Dominic realized he'd been reaching out through the bond.

"Do you need anything?" Micah asked quietly.

"Nah," Dominic said, waving him off. And then, for the first time, he saw the quick tense-relax of Micah's shoulders when he heard the answer. "That's not the question you were asking, was it?"

Micah looked uneasy.

"They—your owners—they used different words, didn't they," Dominic said. It wasn't a question. "They say something, they mean something else."

"Sometimes."

Dominic tried to remember all the times in the last weeks that Micah had offered help and been waved off.

"What are you actually asking me?"

"Where you want me to be." Micah paused. "Normally I'd wait by your side, but you don't like it when I'm on the floor."

Dominic sat on the edge of the bed. "Where do you want to be?"

"Do you want the truth?"

Dominic swallowed, throat suddenly tight. "Of course."

"I don't know. I don't know where I'm supposed to be or what you want me to do or what you expect from me." The words were coming out in a rush now, Micah's eyes fixed on the floor as he spoke. "Sometimes I get lost in a task, or I wake up and I panic because I haven't done my duties and even when I don't know what they are, I know they're *something* and I know I haven't done them. I know you want me here for a reason and if I knew what the reason *was* I could do it better, but you won't tell me. I was supposed to help you on jobs but now you're leaving me behind."

Micah paused, and Dominic could see him fighting the urge to drop again.

"Sometimes," he said quietly, "I wish you'd just punish me, so I could learn to do better. Or so I could know what to expect."

He winced as he said the last part, like he thought this would be the thing that finally sent Dominic over the edge.

Dominic closed his eyes. "If you . . . if you were saying this to your owner, you wouldn't be standing."

Micah shook his head.

"What . . . Can you show me how you would do it?"

Micah took a step toward the bed, then folded easily to his knees. He laid his hands in front of him, leaning forward until his forehead rested on his fingers. Dominic remembered this from the night Micah had told him about Slate.

"I'm sorry," Micah whispered.

Dominic took a breath. "And if I—if your owner—if they wanted to give you what you're asking me for. What do you do then?"

Micah's body stilled, even his breath stopping as he processed Dominic's words. But then he looked up at Dominic, his face only a few inches from Dominic's knee.

"Then I would give thanks. In whatever way seemed appropriate."

Micah's eyes dropped meaningfully to Dominic's waist, and Dominic closed his eyes again. Micah was asking him to be *punished* and promising him a blowjob if he agreed to do it, and gods, that was ten kinds of fucked-up.

"Why does it frighten you that I won't punish you?" he asked instead.

Micah's voice was distressingly level as he answered. "Because I don't know what you'll do."

"What do you *think* I'd do?"

Micah's eyes widened slightly before he got himself under control. "I don't know. You haven't done anything at all for weeks. I'm afraid that when I finally push you over the edge, you'll be driven to something extreme. Not that I can't handle it," he added quickly. "But I don't know what will trigger a punishment, and I don't know when it will come."

"This whole time," Dominic said hollowly, "you've been expecting me to hurt you?"

Micah hesitated. "Not the whole time. At first. And then for a while I thought I could be what you wanted, and I forgot my training and I slipped. I've been getting worse and worse, and I know I'm running on borrowed time."

Micah looked up at him, a brief flash of hazel before he forced his gaze back down to the floor. "Please, just tell me what it will be, when it comes."

Unbidden, Dominic's mind flicked through Gestalt's stories, trying to imagine what Micah could possibly be expecting him to say.

"I told you when I bought your contract: I'm not going to hurt you." How could Micah not *know* that?

Micah shook his head. "I've never had an owner that didn't find it necessary to punish me. I haven't gotten better just because I've been sold again."

"I'm not your—" Dominic paused. He'd been echoing this sentiment since Ian had first told Micah he was free. And as many times as he repeated it, it didn't seem to get any truer. He remembered that day, all those weeks ago in the hotel room, when Micah had fallen asleep next to him and he'd suddenly realized the enormity of what he'd bought. And maybe once bought, it couldn't be given back. Micah and Gestalt seemed to think so.

"What do *you* think the punishment should be?"

Micah almost glanced back up but caught himself. "I hurt Ges," he said slowly. "I marked him and I forced him to open a bond."

"To save his life," Dominic reminded him.

"He didn't want me to, and you were angry with me. But he's a creature, so . . ." Micah's brow furrowed. "I don't know the rules for creatures. But if slaves hurt each other, usually they'd starve us. Just for a few days. They said it took the fight out of us."

Dominic swallowed. "Okay."

"I thought about doing it myself, but I'm afraid, without permission." Dominic opened his mouth to protest, but Micah wasn't done. "I'm not good at being a free man. I've been argumentative and difficult to handle and I can't even fuck you the way you want."

Well, that's *not true*, Dominic thought but didn't say. "I've told you, it's not about what I want."

Micah looked up at him, exhausted. "You want me to want it like you do, and I don't know how."

"What about yesterday?" Dominic asked slowly.

"Someone hexed your house because of me," Micah said miserably. "I don't know how to *start* devising a punishment for that, but you didn't do anything. It's one more thing on top of the *mountain* of things I owe you for, and I don't have anything else to give."

Dominic froze, ice in his veins. "Did . . . did you have sex with me to *punish* yourself?"

"No!" Micah said quickly. "No, I did it for *you*, because I've felt what it feels like for you, and I want you to have that! I want to be the one who *gives* you that. Can't *that* be the thing I want? For me?"

"Micah—"

"Don't," Micah whispered, leaning forward and letting his forehead rest against Dominic's thigh. "Please, don't tell me not to. I don't have anything else to give you. I don't have another way to apologize. Anywhere else, the broken window alone would have earned me a whipping. But you won't do *anything*, and I keep ending up more and more and more in your debt."

"Coffey broke the window, and he's dead. If anything, he was here for Ges, not you, and Ges fixed the window, so it's all fine. Nobody owes a debt." Dominic put his hand out, stroking Micah's hair back and trying not to feel like he was petting a dog. Micah didn't say anything, and Dominic realized his jaw was trembling. "Micah?"

"Please, can I ask for something?"

"Of course. Micah, you can ask me for *anything*."

"When it comes. When I push you over the edge finally. Because I will." Micah took a deep breath. "Please don't hold me under water. I won't fight if you do, but please. Please don't do that."

"I promise," Dominic said hollowly, and Micah nodded.

"Thank you. You don't seem like the type, but it helps to know."

"What type do I seem like?" He wasn't sure he wanted to know the answer.

"You'd use your hands, probably. Before you even thought about it. And you'd probably apologize afterward." Micah paused. "Some owners liked the ritual of it, thought it helped the lesson sink in if we were aware it was coming. Like the owner who held my head under water." Micah licked his lips. "We'd watch the tub fill. But you don't seem like the type to plan it that way."

"No," Dominic agreed weakly, and that seemed to satisfy Micah.

"Thank you," he said, laying his cheek against Dominic's thigh.

"I can tell you something else?" Dominic cleared his throat. He hadn't meant it to come out as a question. "I'm not gonna hit you. But if I did. You'd see it coming. I'm not gonna crack you in the kidneys when your back's turned."

"Thank you," Micah said again, and now his hand was wrapped gently around Dominic's calf, and he was looking up at him with those bright hazel eyes—

A ring of copper blazed around his irises, and for a moment, Dominic could see him, really *see* him.

Micah's jaw tensed, and it was like a door slammed shut. The light was gone. "It was an accident," he said tensely. "May I go?"

"You don't need to ask," Dominic answered, but Micah just shook his head with a wry smile.

Dominic watched him go, and then collapsed back on the bed.

"Don't tell me not to."

What an utter clusterfuck.

CHAPTER TEN

Over the weeks that followed, Micah began to realize that keeping the bond closed was a full-time task. It was like trying to keep a bubble from breaching the surface of the water. He could catch it, force it down, but it was always searching out cracks, seeping through any weakness, moving inexorably upward.

It was the worst when he was asleep.

During the day, he was learning new ways of keeping his mind controlled. It would have been easier if he'd been expected to keep his body poised and still, but most of those requirements were gone now. In any case, it tended to upset Dominic when he came into the living room and found Micah conversing with Gestalt from a position on the floor.

Gestalt, to his credit, was utterly indifferent to Micah's choice of seating, even seemed to prefer it when the larger man took a subservient stance. Gestalt still tended to flinch at sudden movements, keeping his distance from the two of them. Micah found that if he could keep still and stay back, Ges proved an excellent conversational partner.

Without the constant attention to physical details, though, Micah's mind and his focus drifted, and that was when the bond tended to slip open. Gestalt would usually let him know, reaching out through the link to settle gently against Micah's side. He wasn't angry or reproachful, just there, and Micah appreciated that.

Sometimes, though, Micah slipped so far that even Dominic started to notice. And it was easy to tell when Dominic noticed. Gestalt moved through the link like a dancer, sure-footed and quiet, but Dominic was a bull in a china shop. He blundered through the bond and slammed into Micah's side with energy that might have been enthusiasm or plain old velocity.

When that happened, it mostly ended in sex. Dominic was still careful with him, always afraid Micah was offering for the wrong reasons, but . . . well, Micah was usually able to convince him. It was fine.

But every so often, Micah remembered what it had been like to feel himself through Dominic's eyes, and he wondered if maybe it wouldn't be too bad if, just a little, he . . .

These moments left Micah scared, because he couldn't afford to be that careless. Not with the bond, not with anything.

With that in mind, he began modifying his training.

He started using his poses again, holding himself to the standard even if no one else did. He worked his way through Dom's books as thoroughly as he could, taking notes in a journal he'd bought while out grocery shopping. He started really *trying* to have preferences during sex, and was mildly surprised to find that some things *did* feel better—when it was Dom that was doing them.

And he resolved to learn to cook. Or, at least, cook better than Dominic could.

It wasn't a high bar.

Gestalt kept him company in the kitchen, watching his progress with interest. He didn't eat, and he showed no inclination to start, but he did have a weird fascination with the process. Micah had almost no experience making food, but the laptop provided helpful instructions, and he managed not to ruin too many meals.

As Gestalt frequently reiterated, the rules were both arbitrary and baffling. Some ingredients were boiled, some were fried, some were baked. Some were eaten hot, some cold, some lukewarm. Some were eaten raw, some were heated and then cooled. Some were wet, some were dry, some had sauce, some were plain, some were seasoned. Gestalt believed that the seasonings were a form of witchcraft, and Micah's attempt to explain the difference between sweet and sour and spicy and salty did nothing to persuade him otherwise.

The more Micah tried to explain it, the more questions Gestalt had, until Micah finally gave up and suggested that he start eating his own food if he was so curious. Gestalt wrinkled his nose and managed to go nearly two hours without asking any more questions.

He was easier to placate than Dominic, who was growing ever more frustrated with the lack of communication from Piper. Ian and Amanda still hadn't gotten much from her either, just requests for clarification made through official channels. She was adamantly refusing to take Dominic's calls, and attempts to contact her office just routed him back to the same voicemail boxes as her direct numbers.

It had the unfortunate effect of stalling their investigation into the Hellfire Club and the possible location of their portal. Micah noted that this seemed to be upsetting Dominic a lot more than it was upsetting Gestalt. The angel seemed sure that his capture would have alerted his people to the gateway's danger; they were more than capable of protecting themselves. His interest in the case seemed to revolve primarily around his own freedom. When Dominic had asked why he was dawdling around with spice racks, Gestalt had fixed him with a level stare and replied that he was very old and very, very patient.

Micah liked to think that if he got as old as Gestalt, he would be like a redwood. Calm, still, and wise. In Gestalt, age manifested as a restless sort of curiosity, a disinclination to focus on any one thing and a marked inability to separate the important from the mundane.

Every day or so, Dominic and Gestalt would settle onto the living room floor and set up a transfer. Micah stayed on the sidelines for this, watching as the two of them went still, their eyes locked, their breathing slowly synchronizing. Afterward he'd make sure that Dominic made it to the bedroom to sleep off the aftereffects. Micah wasn't any use for the transfers, not with his mind poisoned the way it was, but he could get Dominic through the aftermath, if nothing else.

Gestalt was quiet during these times, his feathers ruffling gently, shivers running down the length of his body as he adjusted to the influx of power. He would sit quietly and watch Micah watching Dominic, his forehead furrowed like he was trying to figure something out but he wasn't sure exactly what it was.

There wasn't *much* that Micah couldn't explain to Gestalt, given time and appropriate metaphors. The angel was both interested in and baffled by a system of government in which authority figures were trusted to mete out justice on another's behalf. Idioms proved no small source of amusement, as did the revelation that over his million years of observation, Gestalt had somehow missed the existence of *seasons*. When Micah had pressed, Gestalt simply shrugged and said that he wasn't completely oblivious; he'd noticed the ice ages.

Micah tried to ask him about historical events, things he'd seen mankind do or develop, a subject on which Gestalt was disappointingly unversed. He'd checked in on humans a few dozen times, but he couldn't provide specifics on where or when. When Micah insisted he must remember *something*, Gestalt fixed him with a level stare and asked if Micah was familiar with the intricacies of the rather advanced anthill that was being constructed on the north side of the driveway.

"Ants have wars, you know," he said dryly, and Micah had been forced to concede the point.

For all his sarcasm and casual superiority, Gestalt was terrible at poker. Dominic could usually beat both of them, but when it came to Micah and Gestalt, Micah never lost. Something about the value system of near-identical cards was lost on the angel, no matter how Micah tried to explain it. Gestalt played him anyway, losing again and again.

Sometimes, Gestalt would ask him about sex. Usually this happened right after Micah and Dominic had some interlude, though on occasion, it happened while Dominic was in the shower, leading Micah to the conclusion that Gestalt was getting his information (such as it was) straight from Dominic's mind.

Micah didn't have a good explanation for why humans would engage in nonprocreative sex, so he shrugged and explained that it felt nice. Gestalt was dubious, but Micah insisted that it really was great. After all, people bought him just to fuck him, so there had to be *something* to it.

In retrospect, with that explanation as the only thing to go on, it shouldn't have come as such a surprise when Gestalt kissed him.

It was right after an energy transfer and Dominic was dead to the world, leaving Micah and Gestalt with a good twenty minutes of solitude. They normally spent the time talking about one thing or another, Gestalt with his wings spread out across the back of the couch and Micah perched on his knees on the floor because Dominic wasn't there to get upset by it. This time, Gestalt had been unusually quiet, watching with a silent regard Micah didn't quite know what to do with.

And then he'd leaned down, catching Micah's jaw in his hand, drawing him in.

Micah opened for him without hesitation, inviting. Gestalt didn't take it, just pressed his lips to Micah's mouth.

Then he withdrew, looking at Micah with a frown.

"I think I'm missing it," he said, and Micah's stomach turned to ice because whatever Gestalt was feeling, it wasn't what he'd expected. And he'd expected something good.

"I can do better." The words came out in a rush. He *could* be better.

Gestalt shook his head, and Micah's heart sank. He leaned up, pressing his mouth to the angel's, nipping at his lower lip and bringing one hand up to card through his hair. Gestalt froze, his hands on Micah's shoulders, ready to push him away. Micah pressed again, delving between Ges's parted lips, remembering everything Arabelle had ever taught him. He could do this. He had this.

"Let me," he murmured against Gestalt's mouth, and Gestalt relaxed slightly. Amethyst light flickered against the edge of the bond, warm and hopeful, and Micah slammed it shut, cursing himself for letting his concentration drop.

Gestalt pushed him away.

Micah's eyes dropped, and he folded back into his position on the floor, kicking himself. "I'm sorry—" he started, but Gestalt waved him off.

"It's not what I thought," he said absently, and heat prickled behind Micah's eyes. He grit his teeth, keeping his gaze on the floor. Slaves didn't have pride, he reminded himself. He was wanted or he wasn't; all he needed to do was respond. If Gestalt didn't want him, then he needed to *sit down* and *be quiet* and *keep the bond closed*—

"This bothers you," Gestalt said. There was a question in it.

"I'm fine."

Gestalt leaned down again, catching his chin and forcing his face up. Dark eyes regarded him questioningly. "You want this," Gestalt observed, and suddenly Micah understood what Dominic had been trying to tell him all these weeks.

I want you *to want this.*

"I'm good at it," Micah answered. "I *need* to be good at it."

Gestalt's eyes searched his face, looking for more, finding nothing. Micah didn't *have* anything else; he had to show Gestalt he could do this, this *one* thing—

Gestalt kissed him again, open and warm, and Micah let him. His lips were soft, pressed easily against his, and Micah knew how to do this, this was what he *did*—

"There!" Gestalt said, pulling back slightly, his eyes widening, and then he was crashing back down onto Micah, hard and insistent. Micah's hands rose, tangling in Ges's hair, nails scraping over the nape of his neck.

Something tickled at the base of Micah's back, and he realized that the angel's wings had encircled him. Gestalt was desperate, hungry, and Micah wondered, distantly, what had changed.

CHAPTER ELEVEN

The physical sensation was one thing.

Micah's body was hot and yielding, opening up and offering, and Gestalt had to admit that it was appealing in a way he hadn't anticipated.

But that wasn't his objective.

Gestalt had been watching the two humans interact for weeks. Micah kept himself locked in and silent, but Dominic was making efforts to be boisterous enough for both of them. Visceral pleasures inspired a colorful sort of poetry in Dominic; everything from showers to sandwiches compelled the man's mind to song.

But it was different—*always* different—when he did this.

There was no purpose Gestalt could see. To the best of his knowledge, nothing actually passed between the men when they touched. Nothing substantial, in any case. They didn't do it often, and they didn't do it predictably, but when they did, there was nothing like it.

For some reason, Micah—doing this to Micah, getting this from Micah—made Dominic *happy* in a way Gestalt hadn't seen from anything else.

He wanted it.

The first time he kissed the human, he felt nothing, just the warm touch of skin on his own. It wasn't unpleasant, but it wasn't anything close to what Dominic felt. There was a little flicker, and he reached out against Micah's defenses, skirting along the edges, but the man only responded by shutting down harder.

Gestalt gave up, settling back onto the couch and resigning the matter, somewhat disappointedly, to another unfathomable human quirk.

He'd expected Micah to tolerate him, to humor his curiosity the way the man did with the other customs Ges had wanted explained.

He hadn't expected Micah to look so . . . broken.

And he *was* broken, Gestalt realized, looking at the kneeling figure before him. Disappointed. Almost ashamed. Micah, for whatever reason, wanted this from him.

So Ges kissed him again, and there it was. That feeling, inside himself. Not as strong as Dominic's, not as vibrant, but there nonetheless. One tiny little spark of light.

He drew Micah closer, hands tangling in his shirt and holding him close. Belatedly, he realized that his wings had encircled them, and he shouldn't do that, it wasn't safe, he needed to pull back.

He didn't pull back.

His primaries pressed a line up the center of Micah's back, holding him flush, and Micah was making little noises, *happy* noises, though the bond was still locked down.

These . . . The things Gestalt was doing made Micah happy, and when Gestalt realized that, the spark of light bloomed stronger.

And it was . . . good. He didn't have another word for it. Pointless, but the avatar liked it, and it was nice to find *something* the avatar liked. Mostly it was just, as Dominic put it, a "pain in the ass."

Surprise bloomed through the bond, surprise bordering on shock and then a flicker of sadness and for a moment Ges thought that Micah had opened the bond after all.

But no.

"Hello, Dominic," he said quietly, regarding the figure in the darkened hallway. Dominic was frozen, like he'd been caught somewhere he shouldn't be, which was ridiculous—it was his house. But the surprise was giving way to a slow-burning discomfort, a general unease obvious enough that even Micah picked it up.

"Can I get you something?"

Dominic shook his head. "Nah, I'm just— I was, uh . . . I'm gonna get some food. You guys want . . .?"

Micah blinked at him, his expression neutral. Gestalt noticed his weight shifting back, his hands creeping toward his knees. Whatever they'd been doing, the moment had passed.

"Do you need help?" Micah asked.

"I'm good," Dominic said. He was smiling now, his big smile, the one he used when he was trying to tell someone else that everything was fine. He crossed to the kitchen and began collecting sandwich ingredients. His movements were quick, deliberate. "So, you guys, huh? Good for you."

Gestalt frowned. Dominic was being vague again. He glanced at Micah, but the human was equally confused.

He reached out gently through the bond, trying to feel out a meaning.

Dominic jumped at the contact, flinching back. The knife he'd been holding clattered to the floor, and he swore. His mind was filled with an image, the image of Micah and Gestalt as they'd been a moment ago. The reaction surrounding it was chaotic to say the least. Genuine happiness mixed with genuine sadness, regret, relief, half a dozen other things that Gestalt couldn't identify. He shook his head, pulling back from Dominic's mind.

Humans.

So needlessly complicated.

"I think I've got a job," Dominic said suddenly, retrieving his knife and tossing it into the sink. "Couple of spriggans Garrett's been nagging me to check out. It's all the way over in Illinois, usually out of my territory, but Frank's probably off on another one of his benders and the pay's good, so I'm heading that way. Be gone a few days probably. Might be more, depends on the infestation. So you guys can . . ." He gestured at them aimlessly. "You know. Whatever."

"I'll come with you," Micah said, rising to his feet and turning his attention toward the bedroom.

The burst of shock that came from Dominic was unmistakable, but his features didn't even twitch. "You want to come with me?"

"It's why you bought me, isn't it?"

Frustration. Sadness. "You don't have to come if you don't want, Micah. You can stay here."

"I know," Micah said with an easy nod, then turned and disappeared into the bedroom to pack.

Dominic turned back to his food, seemingly noticing for the first time that he'd spread mustard on both sides of his sandwich bread.

"Loose clothes!" he shouted suddenly. "You've gotta wear 'em inside out!"

Micah didn't respond, and the house fell into silence. Gestalt drew his legs up under him, resting easily on the upholstery, his wings tucked neatly behind him.

He was keeping an eye on Dominic.

Metaphorically.

Literally, he was looking out the window, past the car in the driveway, trying to read the letters carved into the tree across the gravel drive.

In his mind, he was waiting for Dominic to speak, because Dominic was going to. He had something very important he needed to say, and he didn't know the words for it. They bubbled through his head like a roiling stew, and for the thousandth time, Gestalt missed the company of beings that could communicate like civilized people.

"He still wants you," Gestalt said finally, still studying the tree.

The human sputtered, half-denying and seeking clarification.

Gestalt spared him a glance. "You're trying to decide how to ask me about Micah. I wanted his assistance with a custom that piqued my interest."

"Kissing," Dominic replied, his voice flat.

Gestalt made a noncommittal noise. "Physical contact in general. You seem to enjoy touching him a great deal; I want to know why."

Dominic's mouth opened for a retort, but he closed it again before the words could escape. Gestalt didn't mind—he'd seen the shape of them in Dominic's head. "Yes, that," he answered. "I want that. What is it?"

"I don't know," Dominic said, and his voice was tired. He sat down at the table, sandwich abandoned on the counter. Finally, he said, "Be careful with him."

Gestalt raised an eyebrow. "The two of you are so fragile it's becoming a constant battle not to crush you with an idle gesture," he replied. "I'm always careful."

"That's not what I mean. Micah's . . . He's had it rough. He doesn't always understand . . ." Dominic trailed off, then focused on Gestalt. "Forget it, look who I'm talking to. Just make sure he knows what you're getting into, okay?"

Gestalt nodded. "You want to make sure I don't hurt him like you do."

Dominic flinched. "Jeez, man, I don't—" He paused. "It's not on purpose, okay? It's not my fault I didn't know what I was buying. I just needed help with work. I didn't mean to pick up a trained sex slave; it was a mistake."

"Ready when you are," Micah intoned from the doorway, and Dominic glanced over.

"Micah, I didn't mean—"

Micah nodded gently. "I'm not what you expected. I know that. But you've been patient with me and I appreciate that."

Gestalt watched Dominic as the man struggled for words. Dominic was feeling it again, that same thing he felt when he and Micah touched, but now it was making him unhappy instead of giddy. Gestalt frowned. Maybe the feeling was only beneficial if it was accompanied by physical contact? Or maybe Dominic was getting sick. Or maybe it wasn't related to Micah at all. Who knew.

"Can I go load the car?" Micah asked when it became obvious that Dominic didn't have any kind of meaningful response. "Or do you need me."

"Yeah, go, it's fine, you don't need to ask." Dominic waved him off, and Micah nodded, hefting his bag onto his shoulder and heading out. Gestalt watched him through the window as he opened the back door of the car and threw the stitched bag inside.

"You gonna be okay here on your own? We'll be gone a few days."

"I expect I can keep myself occupied," Gestalt answered. Truthfully, he had some plans of his own, but they were nothing he felt he needed to share with Dominic. He inclined his head toward the window. "Micah's waiting for you."

"I didn't mean I was going *this second*," Dominic huffed. "At the very least I'm gonna finish my damn sandwich."

Gestalt sent a thought Micah's way, sharp, directed, strong enough to push through his defenses. Outside, Micah turned back toward the house, his eyes searching the windows. He met Gestalt's eyes, and Ges sent another thought, beckoning.

"Will it cause problems with you if Micah and I continue?" Gestalt asked, still looking out the window.

"It's not my business. I don't give him orders."

"That's not what I asked."

Gestalt watched the war going on inside Dominic's head, two halves of the same emotion biting and snapping like a pair of dragons, drawing blood and finally resolving.

"No," Dominic answered at last. "I'll make sure it doesn't."

"Good."

CHAPTER TWELVE

Micah looked back up at the house, searching for Gestalt's face amongst the reflected branches. The angel was calling him through the bond. Not with words, there weren't words, but Gestalt was calling him all the same.

Micah checked the bond, searching for holes in his armor, but as far as he could tell, there were none. Satisfied, he set off back into the house.

"I didn't mean we were going, like, literally right this minute," Dominic said when he stepped through the door. Micah nodded, kicking off his shoes. Gestalt was sitting cross-legged on the couch, and since Dominic was up and moving around, Micah took a seat next to him instead of on the floor.

"I've gotta tell Garrett I'll take the gig, and then I've gotta talk to the contact at the site itself. And it's late. Probably won't be leaving until morning. It's about ten hours to Eddansville; we can split it up into two days."

Micah nodded. Two days was fine. Dominic would likely let him drive part of the day, and they'd reach their destination early on the second day. He didn't know much about spriggans, but Dominic could spend the drive filling him in.

He liked listening to Dominic talk, the way his voice changed when he got onto a topic he thought was really interesting. Back when Micah had been silent, Dominic had picked up the slack easily, moving from topic to topic in between bursts of singing along with the radio. Micah liked to think he contributed now.

"I'll leave the bag in the car and be ready when you are."

He didn't know what time Dominic wanted to leave, but he knew he rarely woke up before seven. Micah would get up before that, finish his workout, and shower so he'd be ready as soon as Dominic was.

Dominic gave him a measured glance, like he wanted to add something, but he shook his head and looked away before he found the words. "So yeah. I'm going to email Garrett. You guys . . . you do whatever."

Dominic retreated back into the bedroom without looking at either of them. Micah watched him go, wanting to follow and knowing that Dominic didn't want him to. Ultimately, that was what he needed to focus on. Keep the bond closed, don't be a nuisance, help where he could.

Micah turned back to Gestalt. The angel was watching the doorway where Dominic had vanished, his head tilted slightly to the side.

"Did he say something to you?" Micah asked.

Gestalt's gaze turned back to Micah. "He told me to be careful with you."

Micah dropped his eyes. "You don't need to. If you don't want to. I've had owners that were rough with me before; I can handle it. If that's what you want."

"It isn't," Gestalt said simply, and Micah felt him brushing up against the edge of the barrier again. He held it steady, not letting Gestalt feel the rush of relief. The angel could hurt him badly, and he didn't enjoy the thought of that, even if Gestalt *could* heal him afterward.

Micah wasn't going to inform Gestalt about his worry. It wasn't his place to have opinions on other peoples' tastes. He could take what he was given, even if it hurt. He used to have the scars to prove it, but Gestalt had taken care of that.

"What *do* you want, then?" Micah wanted the answer at the same time he dreaded it, hoping it was something he could give and fearing deep down that it would be just another thing he couldn't.

Gestalt's wings fluffed slightly, and he looked Micah up and down. Micah held still, letting him. Then Gestalt reached forward, the tips of his fingers resting against Micah's cheek.

"Let the barrier down. I want to show you."

Micah panicked for a second, but he got it under control. "Are you sure? You want—"

"Yes."

Micah exhaled deeply, then focused on the bond. He knew how to keep the barriers *up*, that wasn't complicated. He had to think about it nearly constantly, but it wasn't complicated. Letting them down, though . . .

He didn't want to drop them completely. For one thing, he didn't want Dominic subjected to whatever broken thing lived in his mind. He'd have to relax them only a little bit, and that took concentration and a mental dexterity and experience he wasn't sure he possessed yet.

He closed his eyes, mentally surveying the walls he'd put up in his mind. They weren't strong, but they were solid. Slowly he focused on thinning them, letting them grow wispy and transparent, until holes began to form in the fabric of the barrier.

"Is that enough?"

And then Gestalt was in his head, black-bright and solid, and Micah let out a breath. He'd missed this, from the scant days before he'd learned to build the barrier. Gestalt's violet and Dominic's blue had been comforting in their simple *presence*, like the warmth of bodies pressed against him. But he couldn't be part of that because of the damage he'd acquired. He accepted that.

It didn't stop him from leaning into the contact, though, surrounding the hot light of Gestalt's presence inside him.

"This," Gestalt told him, and then Micah saw a memory.

He was momentarily disoriented because it wasn't his memory, or Gestalt's, for that matter. It was Dominic's, though Micah would be hard-pressed to explain how he knew.

The memory was dark—Dominic's eyes were closed. Micah could feel a physical sensation, the pressure of his own body against Dominic's skin, but that wasn't the essence of the memory.

The memory focused on how Dominic *felt*, and there weren't words for that. It wasn't just that he was at ease, relishing the feel of Micah's body on his. It was the way his heart, his *mind* were totally centered as well, as though Dominic had nothing in the world more important than the ex-slave currently making love to him.

Heat built in Dominic's belly and Micah *moved* and Dominic came, hard and fast, his breath coming in ragged gasps.

The memory snapped and Micah blinked, back in the real world with Gestalt's unwavering gaze fixed on him from across the couch.

"That," the angel said. "Can you do that again?"

Micah scrambled to put together what he'd been doing in the memory. "Anything you want."

"Good. Do it."

"I need a minute," Micah said. Then, when Gestalt frowned at him: "Human things."

Ges rolled his eyes but didn't protest.

Micah rose off the couch and went down the hall to the bathroom. Their bedroom door was open a crack, and he could hear Dominic talking to someone, probably about the trip tomorrow. Micah smiled, looking forward to the time on the road. He liked learning about the paranormal, and Dominic's enthusiasm made it easy to ask questions.

He brushed his teeth and used the toilet, trying to remember if he knew anything about spriggans. They couldn't see you if you wore your clothes inside out, which made them easy to kill individually. But they tended to *infest* places, like termites, so killing them individually wasn't usually the trick.

He pushed his hair back out of his face, giving himself a cursory once-over in the mirror. He'd showered this morning, so that wouldn't be a problem. Ever since he'd started sleeping with Dominic regularly, he'd done his best to make sure he was presentable on a moment's notice. It was paying off here.

He pulled his shirt over his head and checked over his body.

Dominic hadn't said anything else about wanting him to cut his hair, or raised any concerns about the dark hair that now grew on his chest and belly. Micah frowned, hoping Gestalt didn't have differing preferences but knowing it was too late to do anything about it now.

He pulled his shirt back over his head and raided the drawer under the sink where they kept the condoms and lubricant. There were a number of small tubes, mostly because they kept losing them but partly because on an ill-fated whim Dominic had bought a variety pack. Amongst the deceptively labeled flavor options was an innocuous tube simply marked "warming," which had culminated in cold showers for both of them and a resolution to never speak of it again. The tube remained in the drawer, a cinnamon-orange warning against the hubris of man.

Micah wasn't sure which type they'd been using in Dominic's memory, so he selected a plain version and hoped for the best.

When he passed their door a second time, the phone conversation was still going on. He paused a moment in the hall, considering knocking, but in the end he decided not to. Dominic rarely needed anything from him and got frustrated if Micah offered too frequently. They were having sex every couple of days, and they'd done that yesterday, so the likelihood that Dominic would want him again tonight was minimal. In any case, it sounded like he was deep in conversation, and Micah didn't want to interrupt.

Gestalt was on the couch, where Micah had left him. His legs were pulled up onto the seat, feet tucked under his knees, and his wings had fallen back into a position that Micah recognized as relaxed. They tended to pull high and back when Micah got too close, and when the angel's eyes settled on him, that was exactly what they did.

"We should go in the guest room," Micah told him. "The couch isn't big enough to do this comfortably."

Gestalt glanced at the door, then rose silently to his feet.

His meager belongings were set up in the room, two pairs of jeans folded next to his as-of-yet-unworn shirts. Beside them on the dresser was a small collection of odds and ends: some stones, a book, a lug nut, a glass bowl half full of river water, the bottle cap off of a milk jug. Micah studied the items, then turned back to Gestalt, his face questioning.

"They interest me," Ges said, a defensive edge to his voice.

Micah smiled at that; for someone who claimed total disinterest in the human race, Gestalt had a good deal of curiosity regarding its customs and creations.

Gestalt relaxed, and Micah leaned toward him, tipping the angel's jaw up and kissing him again. "I like that about you," he murmured, lips ghosting over Gestalt's skin. "The things you find amusing."

"Hmm," Gestalt answered. He stepped away, keeping his back to the closed door. "Take your clothes off."

Micah complied, doing it the way Arabelle had shown him. His body undulated as he pulled his shirt over his head, his arms crossed, skin uncovered inch by inch. He dropped the shirt to the floor and undid the buckle of his jeans. They were snug on him, tighter than Dominic wore his, but Micah liked the way they accentuated the lines of his body. It also meant they wouldn't just fall; they had to be guided down, his fingertips sliding easily over his thighs.

Gestalt watched all of this, unmoving, his wings pulled up and back.

"You'll have to lie down," Micah said after a moment, but Gestalt shook his head.

"Not yet. Get on your knees."

Micah dropped fluidly, folding into the pose for waiting: sitting back on his heels, hands on his thighs. This time, however, he didn't drop his eyes. He knew he was supposed to, but with Gestalt it was different. Ges didn't own him—didn't want to. This, Micah was doing to please a friend. For this, he didn't need to drop his gaze.

Gestalt circled him, wings flaring gently, the feathers over his shoulder fluffing out. The black feathers had an oil-slick shine to them, and not for the first time, Micah caught himself staring.

"There's no magic in them," Gestalt said.

"There doesn't need to be. They're beautiful."

Gestalt smirked, like he thought that was funny.

"Can I touch them?" Micah asked, and Gestalt pulled back, his eyes widening. Then he frowned.

"Put your hands behind your back," he murmured, and Micah obeyed, crossing his wrists behind the small of his back.

Slowly, cautiously, Gestalt's left wing unfolded, feathers splaying like a paper fan. There was a pattern, spots and mottled sections of light and dark. Micah couldn't name it, because he was looking at the colors, and in Gestalt's wing he saw *all* of them.

Gestalt hesitated again, then let the limb rest against Micah's shoulder. The feathers were soft but surprisingly stiff. Micah leaned gently against it, so the feathers slid over his skin, but he kept his hands where they were, letting Gestalt get used to him.

"They're the closest to what I am," Gestalt said quietly. "In my home world, they— *I* don't look like this. The colors . . . They're fearsome and brilliant."

"They're brilliant here," Micah murmured.

"They were never meant to be part of an avatar. *I* wasn't. I'm bound to a physical form by the magic that summoned me, and now that I have one, I don't know what to do with it." He held out his hands, looking down at them like he'd forgotten they were there. "It does things without consulting me. It wants things. It's easily damaged, it fails to respond to commands . . ." He looked up at Micah. "I don't know how you stand it."

"It's all we know," Micah answered, shrugging against the pressure of Gestalt's wing.

"You like yours. You're proud of it."

"I'm proud of what I can do with it."

"And what it can withstand."

Micah frowned. "I like being able to give people what they want."

"Even if they want to hurt you."

"Especially then."

Gestalt was silent, considering the man in front of him. "Do you want me to hurt you?"

Micah shook his head.

Gestalt's expression didn't change. "But you'd let me. If I wanted to."

"Yes."

"I don't think I want to."

"I appreciate that," Micah said, a light smile on his lips. He shifted his weight, letting his knees slide farther apart.

Gestalt didn't react, just stood, watching, considering. Then, abruptly, he drew his wing back behind him. "Get on the bed."

"In the memory—"

"We're improvising." Gestalt retrieved Micah's belt from his puddled jeans, then turned to where Micah was sitting on the edge of the bed.

"Cross your wrists," he ordered, and Micah obeyed, holding them out. Gestalt wrapped the belt deftly around his hands before buckling it. "Test it."

Micah did, twisting and pulling against the leather without managing to loosen it.

Gestalt nodded. "Lie back."

Micah did, stretching out onto the mattress, his bound hands above his head. Gestalt watched him, and when Micah stopped moving, he stepped forward. He reached out, laying one hand against Micah's bare abdomen. His palm was warm, and Micah shivered, goose bumps rising along his body. Micah was distantly aware of his cock hardening, but he ignored it, focusing on the way Gestalt's eyes raked over him.

"Is it yours?" Gestalt asked abruptly. "The avatar. Is it you?"

"It's mine," Micah said. It felt wrong, but he didn't know who else's it would be.

"But you let people damage it. The scars I healed . . . they would have marked you forever."

Micah looked away, letting his vision blur as he stared at the ceiling. "Some people want to mark someone forever. It's something I can give them." It was a lie—new owners would always pay to have his skin wiped clean. Bearing them was just another part of his performance. He could feel Gestalt's eyes on him, and for the first time since being a teenager, he was ashamed. "I don't have anything else to offer."

Gestalt's hand vanished from his belly and Micah waited, letting his body relax, watching the ceiling. He heard the rustle of Gestalt's jeans hitting the floor, felt the mattress shift as he climbed on. And then his view was obstructed by dark eyes and messy hair.

"I'm glad I removed them," Gestalt told him, and Micah glanced guiltily at the white line crossing Gestalt's chest, the silver bangle around his throat.

"I'm sorry—" he started, but Gestalt silenced him, leaning down and pressing his lips to the corner of Micah's mouth. Ges was straddling his hips, and Micah arched upward, experimentally, and was surprised at how *light* he was.

"I like you more, like this," Gestalt said, straightening up and running his hands over Micah's chest. "The people who gave you those marks . . . they had no right. Not to you."

Micah opened his mouth to respond, but nothing came out. He wanted to say Gestalt was wrong, of *course* they had a right, but the words wouldn't come. Not with the conviction they'd held before.

Ges touched him reverently, almost a caress. His hands delved between them, fingers closing around Micah's cock. Micah groaned, rolling his hips upward into the touch.

"Is this what you want?" Gestalt whispered to him.

"*Yes*," Micah moaned. That was the right answer, the answer Gestalt was looking for. One of the angel's knees pressed between his thighs, and he spread them, making room. He could feel Gestalt's hard-on against the crease of his hip, and he arched up against it. "Please, Ges."

Gestalt kissed him, and the world went dark. The angel's wings were surrounding them, blocking out the world. Gestalt's hands cupped his face, and Micah felt him pressing against the edge of the bond.

"Let me in, Micah," he murmured, his lips ghosting over Micah's mouth.

Micah closed his eyes, turning away. "I can't."

"Yes, you can. Or I can make you, if you'd rather."

He could feel Gestalt there, insistent, pressing against his barriers, and he could feel them failing.

"Ges—" His voice cracked and Gestalt shushed him, kissing him deeply.

"Don't hide this from me. Not now."

"You'll hate me."

"No, I won't."

Micah let out a sob, and the barrier fell.

Gestalt surged through his mind, filling it with a dark heat, burning away the last of the wall. Micah's eyes flew open and he saw the sky, reflected in Gestalt's wings, stars upon stars glowing and growing and dying, a million years in a moment, and it was too much, too bright, too dark, too hot, and he was *burning*—

Gestalt's hands were cool on his skin, thumbs wiping the tears from his cheeks, and the angel spoke to him—not with words, there were no words—and he remembered Gestalt's voice: *"We contain each other."*

"Everything I am, living inside you," he murmured, or maybe that was Gestalt, speaking all those weeks ago and only now being understood. It didn't matter, not with Ges flooding through his mind in a wave of stygian violet, filling in all the cracks he'd never known were there.

Micah felt his hands clench hard around the slats of the headboard, and he felt his hands tracing the edge of Gestalt's jaw, the stubble on his skin. His own body was beneath him, arching with want. Gestalt's hands moved to his hips, bracing him down, and he heard the angel groan as he buried himself deep inside Micah's body. He felt himself filled, felt Gestalt's arms, strong as iron, lifting him up and pulling him close.

"Ges—" he said again, and this time Gestalt didn't answer, his face buried in the hollow of Micah's shoulder, rocking into him slowly, filling him in slow, easy thrusts.

Micah opened his eyes and looked out at the stars, bursting like fireworks, burning hot and fast, sparks raining down over the two of them.

"I can see," Gestalt murmured suddenly, "why someone would want to mark you." He thrust down into Micah, filling him totally and still pressing. "Why someone would want to claim you."

His teeth nipped at Micah's shoulder, leaving a mark Micah knew would be there in the morning. Micah stared upward, into the stars close enough to touch, the distance making him dizzy, making the room spin, because it was so *far*.

He gasped, sucking in air because his lungs were on fire, his body was on fire, and Gestalt's hands were like ice, roaming over his skin, dousing the flames.

Through Gestalt's eyes Micah looked down at himself, felt the tension pooling in Gestalt's belly, felt the tight heat of his own body, his legs wrapped around Gestalt's hips, and then he arched back and felt Gestalt's wings flaring wide, and that was it.

He couldn't keep the shout in, couldn't grit his teeth as he came. Liquid fire burned in Gestalt's eyes as he buried himself deep, and the stars went black.

Micah came back to himself slowly, drifting into his own body in a process not unlike waking up from a very vivid dream.

Gestalt was still above him, but he'd pulled his wings tight, tucking them behind his back. He was staring down at Micah with what might have been confusion or possibly awe. On his face, it was hard to tell sometimes.

With a start, Micah realized the bond was still open, and he scrabbled at it, trying to rebuild his barriers.

"Don't. Please."

He paused, looking up at Ges in the half light. "Why?"

"Because I want to feel you. Just a little longer."

Micah canted his hips, emphasizing the way their bodies were still linked. "There's better ways I can make you feel." His voice was smooth, like melting chocolate, betraying none of the panic he felt at still having the link open.

Gestalt's eyes narrowed, and Micah realized he'd said the wrong thing. The angel pulled back, leaving Micah's skin cold in the evening air. "You tell very peculiar lies," Gestalt mused. "They aren't self-serving."

"Why should they be."

It wasn't a question. Gestalt studied his face, and Micah looked away. He could feel the angel through the link, approaching him with what Micah could only describe as a caress.

"So did that help?" he asked, changing the subject. "Did you get what you needed?"

Gestalt sighed, collapsing down onto the mattress beside Micah. "Turn that way."

Micah obeyed, rolling away onto his side, his bound hands coming level with his waist. Gestalt's fingers flicked over his rib cage, and for the first time he noticed the thin fluid streaking his belly. Gestalt's fingertips were like ice, and a chill danced over him, and then it—and the mess—was gone.

"Neat trick."

"Hmm."

Gestalt didn't come closer, but he didn't take his hand away, either. They lay there in silence for a while, and Micah felt himself beginning to drift off. It occurred to him that Gestalt didn't sleep, and he'd probably be leaving soon. He wondered whether he should try to check in on Dominic before falling asleep.

"He's already out," Gestalt told him, and Micah had a brief moment of confusion before remembering—the bond.

"So are you just casually reading my mind right now?"

"Yes."

"I'm sorry."

"Why?"

"For whatever you see in there. I know you don't like it. That you'd prefer to do this with Dom."

Ges's laugh was both incredulous and affectionate. "You perplex me to a degree that borders on frustration. Dominic's motivations are simpler. It does not mean I prefer him."

Micah shifted, trying to keep his arm from going to sleep. Gestalt's hand moved to settle over Micah's belly.

"And you know you cannot become with child," Gestalt said, and Micah had to chuckle.

"No. No, I cannot."

"You do it because of the joy it brings you. And your partner."

"Right. Understand now?"

Gestalt sighed. His arm suddenly seemed very heavy where it draped across Micah's waist. His fingers pressed divots into the skin of Micah's abdomen. "No."

Micah's stomach tightened. "You didn't like it?"

Gestalt shifted, and Micah felt the cool brush of feathers across his shoulder. "On the contrary. You were quite enjoyable. But you and I are linked—when I reached for you, I could feel you there. I was able to know that you enjoyed yourself as well."

Micah hummed, shifting against the blanket. He didn't like the idea that Gestalt would forgo his own enjoyment for Micah's comfort. It seemed antithetical to the purpose of the exercise.

"That's what I don't understand," Gestalt intoned. "I don't understand how humans can interact this intimately without *knowing*. I don't understand how your owners could take pleasure from you, knowing that you would suspend your own desires to please them. I don't understand how the men who bound me could—"

He stopped suddenly, and Micah waited for him to finish. He didn't, and the light touch vanished from Micah's body.

Gestalt sat up, his movements shifting the mattress. "You may put the barrier back up now, if you wish. I think I've seen all I need to."

Micah closed his eyes, mentally reconstructing the wall between himself and the outside world. Gestalt stood, and Micah watched him shuffle back into his jeans. "We need to get you some of your own," he observed. "Mine are too long for you."

"I like them," Gestalt replied evenly. "I'd alter the avatar if I didn't."

Micah blinked, absorbing that information. "You can do that?"

"Given time. I all but built it; I can change it if I wish. Though the basic shape remains immutable."

"Oh."

"Would you like me to unbind you?"

"When you're ready."

Gestalt's gaze was cool, but he didn't comment, just crossed the room and slipped the buckle on Micah's outstretched wrists. Micah nodded a thank-you, rubbing the red marks out of his skin.

"I think next time, I will not need to," Gestalt mused, and Micah tried not to react visibly to the idea of *next time*. Ges hadn't been lying about enjoying himself. Micah pushed down the swell of happiness that brought him.

"That's good. I'm not nearly as vicious as I look," he said instead, flashing a wide smile.

"I'm going out. You may stay here if you wish. Dominic is asleep, but I doubt he would be opposed to your company, in any case."

Gestalt rolled his shoulders, feathers flicking out and then returning to their prone state. Micah was struck with the desire to reach out and run his fingers down the shaft of one primary feather, but he resisted. He and Ges were making progress. He didn't want to ruin it by getting handsy.

The angel paused with a hand on the doorknob, and Micah felt him flicker against the bond.

"He reaches for you. Your defenses aren't strong, but they're enough to keep him out. He reaches anyway."

Micah shook his head. "He doesn't know what he's doing. We connected once already; he didn't like what he saw."

"I think he knows better than you think," Gestalt answered, and then he was gone.

Micah watched the door for a while, then stood and gathered his clothes in the dark. The covers had been rumpled during their activities, and he straightened them, trying to set the room back to the way it had been before he'd come.

Gestalt didn't sleep in here, obviously, but he did occasionally lock himself in for what Micah assumed was some good old-fashioned sulking. Pondering his bottle caps, maybe. Who knew.

The house was dark and quiet, but Micah knew the layout and was used to making his way without light. He carried his clothing in a bundle, not bothering to dress for the simple walk across the hall.

Gestalt had been right: Dominic was asleep. Micah was careful not to disturb him when he slid quietly between the sheets. Dominic shifted slightly, his hand sliding across the distance between them, but he didn't appear to wake.

"He reaches for you."

Micah frowned. Gestalt was wrong. He didn't understand humans. He was mistaking lust for . . . for something else.

It wasn't worth considering.

CHAPTER THIRTEEN

Dominic roused half-awake when the mattress dipped, and for a moment he smiled, reaching out for Micah.

And then he remembered and his hand froze.

Micah and Ges.

Micah couldn't sleep alone. And Gestalt didn't sleep.

His hand stopped on the pillow, pulling it closer. Micah stilled, trying not to disturb him further, and Dominic thought about mumbling a *hello*, a *welcome*, but he found he didn't really want to talk about it.

It would be an understatement to say he was conflicted about the situation, because he was bordering on uncomfortably happy to have Micah back in his bed. And what kind of masochist was happy when his freshly fucked not-boyfriend still slept in his bed?

And . . . yeah. That was gonna be a problem. And it wasn't like he had anyone to blame but himself. He knew Micah had an odd and varied set of motivations defining the relationship between the two of them, and he'd be lying if he said he understood what they were. But Dominic had decided it was fine. Dominic had been the one to forgo the *But what are we?* that might have saved this whole fucked-up situation. Saved it for *him* anyway; Micah and Ges seemed to be doing just fine, and hey, good for them. He should put it aside and not think about it too hard.

That was what he *should* do, but it was approaching the polar opposite of what he *was* doing.

He'd gotten off the phone with Garrett and fallen back onto the bed, ready for a nice long bout of staring at the ceiling and cursing his own cowardice.

Instead, he'd gotten a sudden mental picture of Gestalt on the couch, his wings spread out wide, his head thrown back as Micah licked his way up the length of his cock.

And that? That had not helped the situation, and Dominic had pushed it away. Because fantasizing about people he knew in real life was *bad* and anyway, they hadn't been in the living room. They'd been in the spare bedroom.

Micah had probably been on his belly, his face buried in his arms, his hips high and his thighs spread in invitation. Ges had probably been behind him, strong hands gripping the curve of his ass as he—

Okay, no, that was *not* helping.

But it was giving him what could best be described as an *insistent* erection.

Because Ges was grumpy and weird but he was also *damn* good-looking. His body had changed incredibly quickly, all lean muscle and dark features, stubble that had shown up one day and then *never grew*, and now that the floodgates had opened, Dom couldn't stop imagining this.

It had been simultaneously one of the hottest and most begrudging jerk-off sessions he'd ever had, but once it started it couldn't be stopped. It wasn't like threesomes were a favorite fantasy, but he had broadband; he knew how they worked. And now he couldn't shake the idea of kneeling next to Micah, jerking him off lazily as the two of them took turns sucking Ges's dick. Or the two of them taking Micah at the same time, one on each side, leaning forward to lock mouths as they filled him—

He was getting hard again and that was *also* bad because Micah was actually here next to him now. It was one thing to fantasize about a guy, but another thing to fantasize about him while he was lying literally *right there*.

He needed to go back to sleep. He had a long drive tomorrow.

Dominic closed his eyes, thinking about head colds and math tests and the crunchy skins that cicadas left behind when they molted. It helped a little, and before long, he fell back asleep.

He woke up to an empty bed and cold sheets.

He took a second to feel sorry for himself at the poetic symbolism, but he couldn't keep it up because Micah *always* woke up earlier than he did.

He shuffled out to the living room, following the smell of coffee, because making coffee was another thing that Micah always did in the morning. Micah himself was on the couch with the laptop, his own steaming mug forgotten beside him. Dominic blinked at him, tried to think of something to say, failed, and turned his attention to the coffee machine.

"Hey," he croaked when he'd downed half a mug and felt up to making conversation. "Where's Ges?"

Micah shifted his focus away from the laptop, shrugging. "Haven't seen him since last night. I don't think he's the type for sentimental sendoffs, so he might not be back before we leave." He turned his attention back to the screen.

"Anything from Piper?" Dom asked. "Check the email."

"Already did. Nothing."

"Damn it. What are you reading?"

"Spriggans. I know we've got a long drive, but I thought it'd be helpful if I knew *something* before we left."

Dominic nodded, then downed the second half of the mug fast, before it had the chance to burn him. "I'm gonna grab a shower. I'll be ready to go in forty-five minutes or so."

Micah glanced up at him. "Want company?"

He was smiling that smile, the one with the mischief, the one that made Dominic disregard his better judgment.

Dom hesitated. "I'm fine."

And then he kicked himself all through the shower and then all through getting dressed and packing his tools and checking his gun and looking for his phone. In between kicking himself, he congratulated himself on his willpower and resolved to talk to Micah about this at some point between now and the hotel.

That was going to be fun.

Micah did not want to discuss sex. Or Ges, for that matter. Micah wanted to talk about Cornish fairies and the methods of killing them and whether Dominic thought there might be changelings to contend with during this case.

Dominic drove and listened to Savage Garden and explained about fae infestations and tried to remember if spriggans reacted more strongly to silver or iron. He could google it, but he'd read somewhere that it was good for the brain to try to create interconnecting pathways, and so he tried to remember if there was anything else in the same genus that he knew about for certain.

There wasn't, or if there was, it was getting shuffled to the back because right now, every damn pathway in his brain was pointed unerringly toward the fact that *Ges and Micah were fucking.* He couldn't remember another time in his life that he'd been so unhappy about something that otherwise made such an exceptional sexual fantasy.

He made a conscious effort to keep his eyes on the road, because it was a good practice but also because every time he glanced at Micah, his eyes were drawn to the small bruises marring the side of his throat. It made him think of how Micah tasted, and the sounds he made when Dominic sucked similar marks into his skin. And *then* he'd think about whether Micah had made those noises when Gestalt had marked him, and there was a terrible combination of jealousy and fierce arousal, and quite frankly it was giving him a stomachache and an extremely confused boner.

Micah, for whatever reason, didn't seem particularly interested in discussing it. Every time Dominic mentioned Ges, Micah would steer the conversation somewhere else, like the job or the music or whether there was any bottled water left in the back.

Dominic changed his approach. "I want to talk about plans."

"I'd like to drive some today, if you don't mind."

"No, I mean, in general. Where do you want to be in a year?"

Micah bit his lip. "I'd like to be a controller if I can do it. I've looked into it online. Into getting licensed. There's a lot to it."

Dominic shrugged. "Well, yeah. It's a license to kill; they wanna make sure you know the difference between a nonhuman entity and a plain old weirdo. It's one of the reasons there are so few of us." He frowned. "That's what you want to do? Really?"

"You expected something else?"

Dominic shrugged. "I dunno, you seem like a people sort of person, you know? And you're used to dealing with people who've got money; you can walk the talk up there. Seems like you'd get sick of road trips, monster guts, and solitude."

"It's not solitude if I'm with you," Micah pointed out.

"Yeah, but I'm a dumb jackass with a cabin in the woods. Don't you think about, I dunno, any of that classy shit from before?"

Micah stared out the window. "No. I don't."

Dominic paused. "Not even if you could do it right? Not *everybody's* like the people who held your contract. I mean, you've got money now, and you're smart, you could go to school and really be somebody—"

"I *am* somebody," Micah snapped. "I'm trying my best, but if you don't think I can be any good to you, you can *say* so instead of telling me I need to fuck off to fulfill my *potential*."

"Oh for fuck's sake. I think you'd be a great controller, probably better than me, I just want to make sure you're doing it because you *want* to." He paused, knowing he should stop and barreling on anyway. "It's like the sex, okay? Which has been great. Phenomenal. Really. *Really*. But obviously you and Ges have been getting really close, and it's kinda fucking with me to know you've been sleeping with me out of a sense of obligation when you wanted somebody else."

Aaand there it was. Dominic kept his eyes on the road, completely ignoring the peripheral movement of Micah turning to face him.

"What?"

"Don't get me wrong, I think it's great. He's hot and you guys obviously get along great, and I think that's awesome, but it didn't come out of nowhere. You've liked him for a while, right?"

"I guess so? But—"

"Okay, good, but that whole time we've been sleeping together, and I *knew* that was a bad idea because you're doing it as an apology or a fucking... a punishment for yourself or I don't even know what, and that's not ideal, but I'm only fucking human and I *wanted* it, Micah, I wanted *you*. *Bad*. But if you've wanted Ges this whole time—"

"I want you," Micah interrupted.

"—you have to do what *you* want, not what you think you owe me—" Dominic stopped, rewound. Replayed. Rewound. Replayed. "What do you mean, you want me?"

Micah frowned. "You're usually only interested every third or fourth day. Yesterday was an off day. I didn't see any indication that you were breaking the pattern."

Pause. Rewind. Replay.

Still not making sense.

"So what? If it was my turn, you would turn him down?"

"Or tell him to wait, yes."

"Micah . . . you're not a slave anymore, you don't need to fuck somebody just because they *ask* you to!"

The furrows in Micah's forehead deepened. "I know that. I like Ges. I was happy to go to bed with him." Micah glanced over. "Because I was available."

Dominic sighed. Obviously, something was getting lost in translation here. At least at first, he'd been able to blame Micah's silence for the lack of communication. Now? Now he just plain old wasn't getting it.

Micah was still looking at him, confusion giving way to frustration. "It bothers you," Micah said slowly, "that Ges and I were together."

"No." *Yes.* "It's about what that *means.*" And so much for what he'd told Ges yesterday. He'd promised himself he wouldn't do this—would just let Micah make his choice and accept it, whatever it was. Dominic had *sworn* to himself he'd back out gracefully and let it happen.

To the hells with that.

He'd been trying to *bow out,* damn it; how did the conversation get here?

Micah was talking again. "Why didn't you say something yesterday? Dominic, I would have stopped if you had told me you weren't happy with it!"

"Because that's the problem: if you want to be with Ges, I don't want you to stop because of me."

"I wanted to sleep with Gestalt," Micah said slowly, "and I did. So why are you still upset?"

Dominic opened his mouth, speaking almost before he'd figured out what he was going to say. "Because I thought you wanted to be with me."

Micah stared. "I *do*," he said slowly. "All the time. I was under the impression you were finished with me for the night."

Dominic laughed, incredulous. "So you're picking who to sleep with based on which of us has free time."

Micah nodded. "Exactly."

Dominic blinked.

Opened his mouth. Closed it again.

Listened carefully to the white noise in his brain. Instant replay was officially offline.

"Micah," he started cautiously, "I'm not big on the 'but what are we' talk. I'm really not. But I feel like there are extenuating circumstances here. And I'd like to clarify this."

This was *exactly* what he'd promised himself he wouldn't do. He'd seen inside Micah's head, knew the loyalty that lay there. He was being selfish.

"We didn't meet under great circumstances, and this whole thing has been the weirdest experience of my life. But listen, because I mean this. If we'd met differently—if I'd met you in a bar instead of a van and you owed me *nothing*, I'd still want you to stay. And you're great in bed and you'll never hear me say otherwise, but even if you weren't, even if you weren't into guys at *all*, I'd still be happy to have you as a partner."

He took a breath. And now the hard part, the part he *knew* he was going to screw up.

"If you want to be with Ges—and you really want to, for *you*—then I'm happy for you. I'll help you move your stuff back into the spare room, and you're welcome to stay as long as you want. I can always use the company. But if that's the case, we *need* to stop sleeping together."

"Oh," Micah said quietly. Dominic glanced over and Micah's brow was furrowed. Then, "*Oh*!"

"What?"

Micah looked over at him, his hazel eyes wide. "I didn't realize I needed to choose." He frowned. "You don't want me waiting on you, it makes you uncomfortable—don't deny it, I can tell—so I went to Ges, because he was asking for me and you weren't."

Gears were shifting inside Dominic's head, big gears, important gears, while he tried to formulate an answer to that question.

Why *wouldn't* Micah go to Ges?

Well, because Dominic expected him to act like a free man, that was why. Dominic expected him to choose a partner and be monogamous in exactly the way he'd *never in his life* been able to do.

Dominic stared at the dashed yellow highway markers and realized, through his relief, that he was a goddamn idiot. And just like that, he started laughing. He started laughing and he couldn't stop.

The sedan kicked up clouds of dust as he pulled it onto the shoulder and threw it into park. Micah was looking at him with an utterly baffled expression and that only made him laugh harder because what was he even *doing* with this weird, frustrating ex-slave, other than being completely and deliriously happy that he was going to stay?

"What are you—" Micah started, and that was as far as he got before Dominic pulled him in for a kiss, deep and sweet and filled with all the relief he couldn't put into words.

"Come on," he said when he finally pulled back. Micah's face was flushed, and he was grinning even through his confusion. "It's twenty miles to the third best Reuben in the country."

The roadhouse was big and tacky, and there were blinking electric lights strung around the edges, and Dominic had been there two dozen times and every time he sat in the same booth.

He drove slowly across the parking lot's pitted gravel, wincing at the stones pinging against the car's underbelly. The minute the car was in Park, Micah's hand was on the door handle, but Dominic caught his arm and pulled him back.

"I want to ask you something," he said, almost like a joke, but at the same time, not at all.

"Okay?"

"Go out with me."

Micah frowned. Dominic talked faster. "Go out with me. Like a date. Not like I own you and you're following me because you have to. And not like we're on a job and you're following me because I'm your boss. Because that's what it's been for you, this whole time, hasn't it?"

"Does it matter?"

"Yes!"

Micah hesitated, his hand still on the handle. For a moment, the only sound was the rain on the windshield. "This is about Ges, still, isn't it? I should have asked. I'm sorry. It didn't occur to me that you'd want me to be exclusive for you." Micah's voice was getting louder, an edge of panic creeping into his voice. "I didn't know, I didn't think, and I'm *sorry*."

"Hey, hey now." Dominic reached out, his hand stroking against Micah's temple. "You've got nothing to be sorry for. I didn't . . . Look, half the time I think I scare you and the other half the time you're doing shit I can't even *begin* to understand, and right here just this minute I realized why that is. I've been trying to make you act like me, because I don't understand why you act like you."

Micah shook his head without meeting Dominic's eyes. "You shouldn't have to. It's my responsibility to predict what *you* want, not the other way around. It's what I'm good at. Don't waste your time on me."

"Micah?" He paused, waiting.

Eventually, Micah looked up at him. "What?"

"I want to waste all my time on you."

Gods, that was sappy.

But as Micah looked back at him, surprised and confused, Dominic knew it was also true. "There are things that are important to you," he said carefully, "that you're not getting from me."

Micah paused, then nodded.

"But you get them from Ges."

"I don't need to if it bothers you—"

"It doesn't bother me. That's not the problem, Micah." Not exactly true. It bothered him a little bit, mostly because the idea of it was giving him a persistent half-chub, but that was a different conversation. "The night the house got hexed, I saw something. In your head."

Micah looked away, focusing his gaze solidly on the glove compartment. Dom pressed on, determined to get this out.

"No, listen. I saw how you saw me, and it scared the shit out of me, but I didn't understand. And then before we summoned Lilin, you tried to tell me, you and Ges both, and I *still* didn't get it, but I think I might, now. You kept saying that I owned you, and I thought you were confused or mistaken and if I could convince you that you were free, it would all be fine. But you *know* you're free, don't you?"

Micah nodded, but Dominic wasn't waiting for his reaction.

"But you still belong to me, because that's the only way you know how to love someone. It's just how you are. And you've been telling me this whole time and I wasn't listening."

Micah kept his eyes on the glove compartment. Dominic focused, trying to sort out the blizzard of thoughts running through his head.

"So I guess we have to figure out how to move forward. Because we're in two different relationships here. One of us needs to learn to be what the other actually needs."

Micah glanced over sharply, his eyes going a little wide. "Me, I should be the one—" He paused, frowning, gathering his thoughts. "I'm the one who should learn to change. I'm not a slave, and I need to learn to stop acting like one. I just . . . I don't know if I can. You can't understand how difficult it is to *know*, my whole life, exactly what to do, and then have it suddenly be *gone*."

Dominic thought briefly of his father but said nothing. It wasn't the same. "So ask me."

Micah blinked. "What?"

"Ask me. Ask me when you don't know. And I'll tell you. Trust that it's safe to ask me."

Dominic let go of Micah's arm and gestured to the door. Silently, the two of them stepped out into the rain. Micah fell in step behind Dominic, and Dominic let him.

It wasn't as easy as he'd made it sound. Over the following hour, Dominic began to seriously doubt whether he would ever really understand what was going on in Micah's head.

They went into the diner, and Dominic headed straight for his booth, and Micah followed behind. Dominic slid into his preferred seat, and Micah paused, glancing around. Dominic didn't miss the way his fingertips skated over the tattoo on his forearm.

"What are you thinking?"

"Where do you want me?"

"Across from me."

Micah nodded and slid into the opposite bench. Dominic looked around the building, trying, for the first time in his life, to specifically locate indents. There weren't many, at least not that he could tell. A couple guys had a woman with them. She was sitting next to one of them, his arm slung possessively around her shoulders. The two men were speaking animatedly; she sat in silence, not participating in the conversation. Another man sat at the edge of a table of teenagers; it wasn't clear which one he was with.

No one sat opposite their indents, and aside from the occasional glance or comment, no one spoke to them.

Dominic realized that any number of these people could be tongueless or silenced—would anyone even notice?

He turned back to Micah, shaking his head to get the morbid thoughts out. There was one menu on the table, sticky and laminated, a list of sandwiches beside a list of beers. Dominic tapped it with one fingertip.

"The one we're after is the Big Miner. It's got onion rings and sauerkraut and it's better than sex."

Micah looked dubious. That was all right; he'd see when it showed up.

"Okay, so, talk to me. How do I be an owner?"

Micah smiled a little bit. "It's an attitude more than any particular behavior. It's the idea that you know what's best for somebody better than they do. You can manage their time better and utilize their body better." Micah hesitated, his cheeks heating, then added, "Choices should be left to those who can make good ones."

Well, this was going down like a lead balloon. "I don't think I have that attitude."

Micah looked down with a smile, shaking his head. "No. No, you do not."

"I'm not sure I want to develop that outlook, either."

"You don't have to. But . . . meet me halfway? Tell me what you want. Because you don't. You tell me things that you think I might be okay with you wanting, and I have to calibrate to that, and it's . . ." He paused. "It makes it difficult for me to determine what I should do."

Dominic opened his mouth, the phrase *Do what you want* already on his tongue, but he shut up before he could vocalize it. He didn't understand, but this *was* what Micah wanted. And he needed to accept Micah's words at face value, or this was never going to work.

The waitress caught his eye and he signaled her, nodding when she gave him the *one moment* gesture.

"Right now? I want you to get a Big Miner and eat it with me, even though I know you'd rather have a bowl of carrots, because this thing is a religious experience, honest."

"All right."

The waitress had a barcode on her arm. She was young for it—late twenties, early thirties maybe. She set two glasses of cold water on the table, not meeting their eyes. Micah smiled at her when he ordered. His right hand rested gently on his arm, covering his own marking. It stayed there even after she left.

"Why do you do that? Cover it like that?"

Micah glanced down at his hand. He pulled it back, like he hadn't realized it was there. "You looked around the whole place when you came in; do you see any other indents sitting at the table having a conversation with their holders?" Micah shook his head. "Indents are reminded of their places in a dozen subtle little ways, and there usually isn't anything good that comes from being presumptuous."

"They'd hit you."

Micah tipped his head to the side, considering. "Sometimes? Or they'd keep you inside, or give you worse duties, or sell you. There's a feeling of having disappointed them, that's what really does it for most of us, at least at my level. We're already the dregs of society, given the most basic and menial of tasks to accomplish, and if we can't even do *that* right . . ." He trailed off, shrugging.

Micah had talked before about focus. How his whole world narrowed to one task, one person, one goal at a time. And now, Micah didn't have that goal. Because Dominic wouldn't give him one.

"I think you should be a controller," Dominic said abruptly, mentally adding the *if you want to*. "You've already got my textbooks; they're a little out of date but they should get you through the preliminary exams, at least. And I'll help you study."

"I appreciate that."

"You're not a dreg. You belong right up here at the table with me, having a conversation like an equal because you *are*."

"Thank you."

"So what else haven't I been clear on? As an owner, I mean."

"Rent," Micah said immediately. "You don't own me and I'm not a member of your family, and that means I should owe you money, right? But you've never asked for it so I don't know if I should be doing something else in payment."

His gaze was steady, and Dominic knew exactly what the *something else* was. "My grandpa built the house and it was paid off decades ago. It doesn't cost me anything but taxes, so there's no reason it should cost you either. My turn. Why haven't you ever taken that stud out?" He gestured vaguely to his mouth.

"You said it was kinky. I thought you liked it."

"I do, but you should take it out if you don't like it."

Micah frowned, considering. "I think I do like it. It's . . ." He paused. "It's hard for me to tell, in a person, what I find attractive. My preferences weren't taken into account anyway. These, the jewelry, they give me something about myself that I *know* is good, that I *know* is appealing. So I like them for that."

Dominic nodded. "Fair enough. Your turn."

"Do you want me to stop having sex with other people?"

A woman at the next table glanced over. Dominic ignored her, instead focusing his attention on the table. The condensation on his glass was dripping down onto the lacquer, and he pushed his silverware across the puddle, letting the napkin soak up the water and ignoring the fact that he didn't know the answer. "Why'd you sleep with Ges?"

"He asked me, and I saw no reason not to."

"Did you want to, though? Did you like it?"

Micah sighed, turning his palms up. "I don't know if I'll ever 'like' sex the way you like it, or the way you want. It makes other people happy and it doesn't hurt, so I like it. I'm good at it, so I like it. I know it makes you happy, so I like it. I don't want it for its own sake, or for myself. But I want to please you, and I wanted to please Ges. It feels good with you. And maybe someday there will be other people. So the question is: Do you want me to stop?"

Dominic stared at the table, watching the cheap napkin dissolve under the weight of the water it had absorbed. His knee-jerk reaction was to say yes, because of *course* he wanted Micah to stop, because that was what people *did* when they were in a relationship with somebody they cared about: they stopped fucking other people—that's just what people *did*, right? Because being with one person and fucking somebody else was a pretty shitty move, right?

Only, no matter how he turned it over in his head, Dominic couldn't see it as cheating. Not only due to the distinctly rosy glow around the idea of Micah and Ges together. It just seemed like he and Micah had never really clarified what they were doing. He'd sort of assumed they'd both known the kind of relationship they were in.

Then again, those relationships were supposed to start by getting to know each other over coffee or something, not by buying a drugged stranger in a parking lot and then getting an angel to staple your psyches together, so maybe that was a bad assumption, in retrospect.

Then there was Micah. Micah, who didn't want sex but wanted to make him happy. And Micah wanted to make *Ges* happy, which Dominic wasn't so sure about, because wasn't there supposed to be *some* kind of exclusivity when you loved somebody? Sexual, or emotional, or something?

Micah didn't seem to think so, and Dominic didn't think that sort of conviction was something that could be learned. Or faked. Somewhere along the line, Micah had become convinced that affection was about being available, not about being exclusive.

So it was important to Micah that people want him. Need him. Have use for him. And Dominic didn't, not all the time. He couldn't. It was impossible. So maybe Micah needed more than one partner and that was just . . . Micah.

"I don't need you to stop."

There would need to be a longer conversation about this, but for now, Micah's shoulders relaxed, and Dominic realized how much the answer had been weighing on him. He smiled, just a little, and then the conversation was derailed temporarily because the waitress was back with their food.

It was the kind of sandwich that had to be mashed flat unless you could unhinge your jaw when you ate. Micah eyed his with skepticism, while Dominic demonstrated the sandwich-flattening technique.

Dominic finished his. Micah didn't, probably because he kept stealing Dominic's onion rings, beer-battered things that Micah insisted were better than the sandwich. Dominic accused him of blasphemy. When the waitress asked them about dessert, they both shook their heads and groaned.

Micah got his chance to drive after dinner. Dominic handed over the keys with mock-solemnity, making Micah promise to tread gingerly until they were out of the gravel lot. The sun was going down ahead of them as they headed west, and Dominic leaned his head against the window, watching the telephone poles go by. There was a Conversation coming, he could feel it. He considered just hiding behind his phone, playing Words with Friends with Garrett and Amanda until they stopped for the night.

"I want to get one bed," he said at last.

Micah glanced over. "At the hotel?"

"Yeah. I don't think there's any point pretending we're not gonna share. Might as well call it what it is, right?"

"Sure." Micah was grinning, some private joke inside his own head.

"What?"

"The day you found me. I offered to blow you, and you said that wasn't why you bought me." Micah elbowed him gently. "Called it."

Dominic groaned, looking back out the window. "So I gotta ask," he said after a while. "I'm not sure I even want to know, but I can't get it out of my head; it's driving me crazy."

"What?"

Dominic hesitated, making sure this was a topic he *really* wanted to broach. "Ges. I mean, Gestalt. The angel."

"I'm familiar."

"What was *that* like? I mean, he's so—" Dominic gestured, trying to come up with the word. "—*Ges*," he concluded.

Micah snorted, keeping his eyes on the road. "What, like, did he scowl at me the entire time?"

"Yeah! Exactly! I can't . . . I just can't see it, you know? I mean, I can *see* it, I just can't imagine him wanting to get our germs all over him." Dominic was laughing at the image of Gestalt, the daiyura, suddenly finding himself sticky and defiled.

"He saw something in one of your memories; he asked me to recreate it for him."

Dominic paused at that, sobering. "Really?"

"Yeah. It was some feeling you had while we were having sex. He wanted the feeling, I guess."

"What feeling? Was it the one where you suck and do that thing with your finger—"

"No, no, like an actual emotion."

Dominic stared at Micah. "He had sex with you because he wanted to feel an *emotion*? Which one?"

Micah shrugged. "You tell me, it was your memory. All I could tell was that you were paying really close attention to me."

"Well, *yeah*."

"No, not your *dick*," Micah insisted, then hesitated, like he'd said something he hadn't meant to. "Me. You were paying really close attention . . . to *me*."

He said it like he was realizing it as the words were coming out of his mouth.

"Well, I mean . . . I care about you, you know?"

"Then I guess that's what he wanted to feel," Micah said, shrugging again.

"What, he didn't describe it to you?"

"No, he just sort of played the memory for me. In my head."

"He can *do* that?"

"I guess so."

"Were you gonna mention that at some point?"

Micah frowned. "I guess it didn't seem odd to me. Back when he was teaching me to use to bond, we exchanged a lot of thoughts and memories. Hasn't he been doing that with you?"

"Not really. Mostly it's just light. And colors. And sometimes I could feel what *you* were feeling, back before you learned to close it off."

Micah was still frowning. "You mean he hasn't been telling you things or showing you things while you've been doing the transfers?"

"That's what I'm saying, yeah. Why, has he been playing psychic story time with you?"

"He used to, before you took over the transfers. And he—" Micah paused again.

"What?"

"He wanted me to open the bond before we had sex. The whole time, it was like we could see each other, you know? I think he was afraid he was going to hurt me; he wouldn't do it unless he could see into my head."

"Kinky."

"Yeah."

"S . . . so did you do it?"

"Do what?"

"Let him into your head."

"He insisted."

Dominic paused, mulling that idea over. Micah, who hadn't protected a damn thing since he'd been bought, protected his side of the bond. *Obsessively.* But if he'd opened the bond just because Ges *asked—*

"Would you do it for me?"

Micah glanced over, his eyes widening. "Open the bond?"

"Yeah. So I can see."

"You don't want to see, Dominic, remember? We tried that once already."

"I was surprised, that's all. I didn't expect it. Let me try again. It'll be better this time."

Micah's shoulders slumped. "Please don't make me do this, Dominic. We've got something good here; we can keep going like this. Don't overthink it."

"We *can't* keep going like this, and you know it. You were making progress, and then you started backsliding, and I don't know how to help you."

"I don't need help. Like I keep telling you—it's not your job to worry about me."

"I worry anyway, Micah, that's the problem." He took a breath. "You said being an owner was an attitude, right? Feeling like you know what's best for someone?"

Micah eyed him warily. "You said you didn't want to pick up that attitude."

"And you said to meet you halfway. So. My side's open. Meet *me*."

"Not while I'm driving."

"Fair enough." He was stalling. Dom knew he was stalling, and Micah knew he knew. Dominic let him, switching his attention over to building a playlist on his phone.

Meeting halfway, and all.

They got into Eddansville at quarter after eleven. Micah drove the last seven hours straight through, even after Dominic told him to start looking for a motel and nodded off with his head against the passenger window.

Dominic woke up when the engine shut off, Micah announcing, "We're here" in a voice that sounded more resigned than tired.

True to his word, Dominic got a room with a king bed. He'd never done that before. Not intentionally. With his dad, it had always been two queens. Even when he'd been working by himself, he'd stayed in the habit. Two queens, always.

Micah hesitated inside the door, looking around like he wasn't sure where he should be standing—which was probably exactly the case, Dominic realized after a moment.

Dominic ditched his bag in the corner, rolled the kinks out of his shoulders, and kicked out of his jeans with all his customary grace.

"So'd you drive all this way because you're trying to put me off?" he asked when a minute had gone by and Micah hadn't moved.

"Partly."

"Partly?"

Micah shifted. "Mostly."

"What if I swear to you that I won't leave? That I want to see."

"You can't swear that. Not when you don't know what you'll find."

"Can you open, like, just your side? Look into my head and see that I mean it?"

Micah shook his head. "I know you *think* you mean it."

Dominic climbed onto the bed, sitting cross-legged like he did when working with Ges. He gestured for Micah to join him, and after a second of hesitation, Micah did. He sat across from Dominic, still fully clothed, keeping his distance.

"So I wanna tell you something and I'm not sure how to say it. Because this whole thing is a lot . . . I dunno. Deeper than it would normally be."

Micah regarded him impassively. Dominic picked at the hem of his T-shirt.

"I want to try. I want this to work. And I spent most of today thinking I'd blown it, so sorry if this seems rushed, but I think you should know." Dominic looked at Micah carefully. "I think I love you."

Micah's expression didn't change. Dominic waited for something, but it didn't come. "Well?"

"That's why we shouldn't do this."

Dominic blinked. "What?"

Micah paused, considering. "I am working very hard," he said slowly, "to be someone you can love. Someone who is good for you. But you know you're not the first one I've needed to be good for. And the things I've *done*, in that regard, disgust you. Ever since you bought me, everything you've learned about my past has made you sick."

"You *had* to," Dominic protested, and Micah groaned in frustration, rubbing his palms against his face.

"And I so *want* to let you think that. You think you love me because you assume these were things that were *done* to me, but you're wrong. Ges saw it, why do you think he hated me straight from the start? Because I *let* all those things happen. I participated, I helped, sometimes I even *wanted* it. And now I want you, but . . ." He took a deep breath, bracing. "You can't love me, because there's nothing real here, Dominic."

Dominic opened his mouth to protest, but Micah didn't stop, and Dominic realized he'd probably been practicing this for the last seven hours of highway.

"There's nothing to love—I'm a blank slate that happens to have your name written on it. I'll be everything you need me to be, but when you get tired of me, I'll go be someone else, *for* someone else. So if we do this—" he gestured between them "—I don't think you're going to see what you want to see."

He dropped his eyes, and Dominic could see him fighting to stay still, to stay where he'd been told to be. Dom's heart ached for him. He'd predicted that Micah would say something like this, but it didn't make it any easier to hear.

"That's why we *should* do this," Dominic said quietly.

Micah looked up. "What?"

Dominic leaned forward, stretching the edges of his balance, and barely got close enough for his lips to brush Micah's. He closed his eyes, feeling the soft, warm skin against his, the hair tickling his jaw, the way Micah opened for him without protest or hesitation. He stayed there, thinking, trying to figure out how to explain.

"I don't love you," he said at last, "because of what you *do*. The shit you've been through—it terrifies me. You're right. It frustrates me and it makes me sick. But it didn't break you. I don't care what you did—you walked through hell and you still came out the other side *strong*." He punctuated the statement with a kiss. "And *brave.*" Another kiss. "And determined, and loyal, and fair, and honest, and kind, and that's all shit you can't *fake*, Micah. *That's* who you are, way down under that blank slate. And that's what I love about you. Everything else is just . . . incredibly attractive set dressing."

Micah was shaking his head; Dominic could taste salt on his cheeks. "You're wrong. You're wrong, you're wrong, you're *wrong*."

"I'm not," Dominic murmured, "and when you're ready, I want to prove it to you."

Micah passed out in his clothes, king bed or no.

The stuff Dominic had said scared him, and Dominic didn't need any psychic shit to see that. The first time he'd seen into Micah's head, he'd been terrified of the pedestal he'd been placed on. It was kind of weirdly ironic to realize he'd turned around and done the same thing.

He didn't make Micah open the bond. He could have. Micah would do *anything* for him if he insisted. But he didn't.

He just held him close, let him get all his protests out. And eventually they both drifted off.

CHAPTER FOURTEEN

Dominic awoke to sunlight shining through the open curtains, and was not at all surprised to see that Micah was already up. He'd been out and come back with breakfast, and Dominic opened his mouth to say, *You didn't have to*, and then realized that Micah already *knew* that, and so he said, "Thank you," instead.

Micah just nodded, but Dominic imagined he saw a glint of copper before he looked away.

Micah sat across from him again, and Dominic could tell that he wasn't quite sure about it. Dominic caught his eye, giving him a little nod.

He checked in with Garrett, letting him know they'd made it to Eddansville. Garrett said Frank was still being a hedgy bastard about the whole situation, which tracked. But Garrett was *also* able to forward the client's emails to Dominic straight from Frank's inbox, which . . . also tracked.

They made a supply run, *finally* getting Micah his own phone—a slim thing with a huge screen that Dominic was immediately jealous of. It was slightly less slim with the case, a big thick rubber beast whose packaging claimed could survive being run over by a car. Dominic inspected it thoroughly and then pronounced it fit for use on a job.

The next stop after that was a gas station, where Dominic picked up a collection of heavily salted crunchy things and, more importantly, a map of the local area.

This ended up tacked to the wall of the motel room ("Won't they care about the holes in the drywall?" "No, they will not, Micah. I pick these places on purpose.") with a collection of colored stickers mapping out the infestation.

Fortunately, it was limited to one neighborhood, a subdivision on the northwest side of the city called Willow Hill. Dominic had a theory, which Micah confirmed by checking home prices in the area: The subdivision was new construction, where the area's wealthy could gather together to put a buffer between themselves and the people who rode public transportation. One main road in and out, trees and fields on the other three sides. It tracked; spriggans were tricksters and thieves, so it made sense they'd shack up in the good part of town.

They spent the next day and a half setting out an iron perimeter. Like most of the fae folk, spriggans didn't do well against iron, which meant a ring of iron pins around the hem of each pant leg. Dominic had forgotten to pin them *once*, a long time ago. His father had found him wandering, lost, after stepping on a stray sod a piskie had left in a *parking lot* of all places. So now he put the damn pins in his damn jeans, every single time.

The second part of the perimeter was horseshoes (also iron, of course), though fortunately symbolic rather than functional. It had been a glorious day at creature control when someone out west had discovered that an inch-wide representation worked as well as the real thing, and it had stopped being necessary to carry a hundred and fifty pounds of iron horseshoes out into the field.

The miniatures were roped together using reels of kite string, but they had to be set out at odd angles to ley lines. This meant a long day of walking through the fields surrounding Willow Hill with a tape measure, a load of stakes, and a tuning crystal on a string.

Micah thought the whole thing was incredibly interesting and had about a hundred questions, and Dominic spent a lot of time thinking about learning from his dad.

Ley line plotting was pretty simple stuff; he'd learned it back when his granddad had still been alive. They'd gone camping sometimes, plopping down some tents right in the middle of the job and working until it was too dark to go on.

This time, he was happy to have a motel room.

He and Micah got in late, bone-tired but with the perimeter complete. Dominic took the first shower and was not at all surprised when Micah joined him. He didn't make a comment, just kissed Dominic deeply.

Micah went over Dominic's entire body, washing the mud and grime from his skin, working his way down until he was on his knees. The water was hot, hot enough that Micah's tongue seemed cool when he took Dominic into his mouth. Dominic leaned back against the tiles, his eyes closed, lost in the feeling of Micah's mouth and hands on him.

When it was over, Micah stayed kneeling, sucking gently at Dominic's sensitized skin. The water sluiced through his hair and over his bare back, and all Dominic could think was *I don't deserve you.*

"Today was good," Micah said when they finally got done with the shower. The white hotel towel looked laughably small in his hands. "I think I could do this. Really."

Dominic stared at him, watching the way he dried off without an ounce of self-consciousness, his motions fluid, almost practiced, and . . . yeah.

"I think I could do this too." He cleared his throat. "So is there anything . . . I mean . . . can I do anything . . . back?"

"Let me sleep with you," Micah answered with a little grin, and Dominic smiled.

Micah awoke to a sound he couldn't identify. The blankets were too heavy, making it hard to breathe.

"Wha—"

"Hush," a familiar voice said. "It's just me."

A snap, and then a greenish light illuminated the speaker. Lilin was sitting on Micah's chest, his fingers cradling a puff of witchlight. The incubus looked significantly worse for the wear.

"What happened to you?" Micah asked. He reached for Dominic, shaking his shoulder, but the controller didn't respond.

"Nothing happened. And don't bother, he won't wake up unless I let him," Lilin said. "We need to talk. Some new information has come to light, and I'm calling in that favor."

CHAPTER FIFTEEN

Gestalt frowned at the sheet of paper in front of him. It was a drawing—a good representation from a blurry and distorted original—of a wrought iron gate. The gate connected two brick walls, waist high, ornamental, backed by blurry and indeterminate shrubs.

He didn't like it. The connection wasn't good. His Feeling of the area was nebulous at best, and the distance was several hundred miles. But his window of opportunity was now, and he fully intended to take advantage of it.

When Dominic had incredulously announced that the man Gestalt recognized was a *senator*, Ges hadn't known what a senator was. But he'd looked the term up on the computer that Micah had taught him to use. And, apparently, there were exactly one hundred of them at any given time. Furthermore, they were public figures; the first link had led Gestalt to a full list of all one hundred.

Complete with photographs.

That was how he found himself staring at the smarmy face of a bastard he knew *very* well, this time paired with a political affiliation, a state, and a name.

Jeremiah Locke.

The name got him an address. The address got him a street photo.

The photo got him a Feel.

He pushed the living room rug out of the way, revealing Dominic's crudely painted summoning circle. It was primitive, but it would work.

He went around it several times, making small alterations with a felt-tipped marker he'd appropriated from the kitchen. The lights in the living room buzzed as the power in the room fluctuated, making space for Gestalt's magic.

The angel finished marking his sigils and went, for the second time, to sit in the center of the circle. Last time, Dominic's candles and oils had chafed against Gestalt's magic. This time, the spell was all his.

He sat cross-legged, breathing deeply, wings wrapped around himself, letting his consciousness expand. It took a small amount of concentration to hold his avatar together, but most of his mind was free to wander.

Very distantly, he was aware of Dominic and Micah, but he'd closed them off before he started. There was almost no way they'd be able to stop him, but nonetheless, he didn't want to have to worry about any more variables than he needed to.

He closed his eyes, crumpling the drawing between his fingers, letting himself Feel the place he needed to be.

The living room began to melt away. He was floating, balancing, ever so delicately on the edge of a precipice. He could hear insects and wind, smell pine and wood smoke, feel the damp chilled air of the Pacific Northwest whispering against his back.

He exhaled deeply, leaning backward into the other place, letting himself fall—

And then he caught.

His eyes flew open, but there was nothing to see. Nothing but darkness, the darkness between places, the utter and absolute *nothing* that existed between the everything.

He struggled against it, bitter cold seeping into his skin, making his fingers numb and stupid.

There was warmth where he had come from, and where he was going, but he couldn't go either way. He was drowning in ice and darkness. The silver cuffs were dragging him down, drawing him to this not-place, fighting against the surety of the places he existed between.

Of course. They were portal magic. Of course they'd be drawn to the places between. This was their home.

He gathered his magic to himself, holding it like a bauble, letting it warm him, and then he *shoved*, forcing himself through the nothingness and back into the world.

He hit the ground hard, making somewhat more noise than he'd originally hoped. Rolling twice, he ended up in the shrubs he'd seen behind the brick wall.

Someone was coming, but that was all right, that was expected.

The man who came into view was dressed entirely in black, his vest emblazoned with the logo of a private security company. As expected, he had a rifle cradled in his arms.

Here, Gestalt gambled that he was faster than the man with the gun. A gunshot wound wouldn't kill him, but it *would* give away the element of surprise.

He launched out of the darkness, tackling the man to the manicured lawn, snuffing out his mana before he could even shout an alarm.

Gestalt landed on top of the body and froze, listening carefully for anyone else approaching. Nothing: no shouts, no running, no alarms. The lawn did not erupt with sun-bright security lights. All was quiet.

He grabbed the body and hauled it back into the shadows, finding a space for it in the corner between two hedges.

He raised his wings and regarded them carefully in the dark. As much as he regretted it, he was forced to admit that this next part would be easier without them.

He closed his eyes, focusing, pushing at the avatar to mold it into what he needed it to be. His nails dug crescent grooves into his palm as the feathers and bones contracted, growing small and dark and withered. They sank into the flesh of his shoulders with a smoldering hiss. He turned his head, regarding the dark outlines marking his arms and shoulders. They stung slightly, but he didn't think they'd interfere with his plan.

His hands moved over the dead man, pulling at buckles and straps, divesting him of his equipment one piece at a time.

Underneath the black windbreaker, Gestalt found an armored vest, which he quickly appropriated. The jacket he took as well, covering the vulnerable skin of his arms. It would disguise the fact that the bulk of his scars were missing, and might give him an edge against Locke, when he found him.

He looked carefully at the gun for several minutes, avoiding the trigger but not finding any obvious method of locking or securing it.

He slung it onto his shoulder, carrying it the way he'd seen the guard doing.

His bare feet were silent on the grass, and he kept to the edges of the lawn, close to the hedge. When he reached the first corner of the house, he stopped and listened. There was one man on the next side. Slowly he edged closer, keeping an eye on the figure that came into view.

The guard didn't see him, not until it was too late. Gestalt watched carefully as he raised his weapon, pulling one part to the side with a characteristic sound that Gestalt recognized. The man's finger slipped behind the trigger guard, and Gestalt raised his own weapon, jamming it forward into the man's chest. He followed it with a brief touch to the throat that stole his breath away for good.

Gestalt caught him before he hit the ground, keeping his gun from clattering against the cobblestone path. He stuffed the body into a shadowy corner beneath a stairway, and waited.

There were two more. One had been stationed on each of the four sides of the house, patrolling, and the one on the far side had noticed his teammate's absence. He would be signaling to the others over the radio, and the two remaining guards wouldn't take long to figure out that they were alone.

Gestalt crouched, patient, beside the body of the man he had killed, gun slung over his shoulder. His back felt exposed without the weight of his wings, and he twitched phantom feathers in anticipation of the upcoming struggle.

They were coming opposite ways, guns raised, ready for him this time. He could hear the crackle of their radios as they approached. Gestalt glanced up at the front of the building. The windows were deeply recessed, and it didn't take much to get himself up into a casement on the second floor. The room inside was dark, unoccupied. He tucked himself up against the glass, listening to the men below him.

They met fortuitously, under his window and slightly to the left. He risked a glance, determining their exact location, and then he was on them, striking them simultaneously on the back of the neck, below the helmet. They were dead before they even knew he was there.

The front door was unlocked.

Gestalt pushed it open and strode into the darkened front room, looking around, listening. The first floor was empty, but there were muffled sounds coming from the basement. Gestalt wrinkled his nose. The whole building smelled of humans in enclosed spaces, sweat and pain and fear.

The basement likely housed the slave quarters. There were none of his own kind down there; whatever other monsters Locke kept for his amusement were none of Gestalt's concern.

The main hall had several wide French doors. Gestalt picked one at random and went through, looking for a staircase. It took him a minute to find it, a big curving thing with a banister carved from a single huge log. Gestalt hated it.

He went up the stairs, light on his feet, following the sound and smell of humans. There were two of them, a man and a woman. The man, at least, Gestalt recognized. They murmured softly, unaware of the danger. The scent of intercourse was leaking past the closed door, cloying and sweet, and Gestalt thought suddenly of Micah, and how Micah had felt beneath him when they'd coupled—

He shook his head. This wasn't the time.

The element of surprise was key here; he couldn't give Locke the time he needed to evaluate the situation, put two and two together.

The door didn't so much splinter as *explode* inward, and before the pieces had finished falling, Gestalt was following them. He raised the rifle he'd taken from the dead guard.

"Jeremiah Locke," he said, "we have things to discuss."

Locke blinked stupidly at him from the bed, temporarily at a loss for words. Surprisingly, it was the woman, a brunette in her middle forties, who gathered her wits first.

"This doesn't have to end badly," she said evenly. "My name is Piper Hayden. I'm an investigator for the FBI, and I—"

"Why won't you call Dominic back?" Gestalt studied her carefully in the half-light of the room. "You're distressing him greatly."

Piper blinked. Then her eyes narrowed. "What do you know about it?"

"Don't *engage* him," Locke snapped. He looked back to Gestalt. "What are you here for, money? It's in the vault on the first floor. There's nothing up here. No reason to shoot us."

"I want to know where the portal is."

"The what?"

"The portal. To my own realm. You were there when I was pulled through. Where is it?"

Piper's hand was creeping beneath the pillow, and Gestalt cocked the gun, the way he'd seen the guard do outside. With his thumb, he pressed the lever he assumed was the safety.

Locke's eyes widened. "Oh. Oh, you're the—the thing. I remember now. Didn't recognize you without your wings. So if I remember correctly . . ." He grinned. "Drop the gun."

Gestalt did, unwilling to give up the charade quite yet. It clattered to the floor near his feet, and he hooked his toe underneath it. He could have it in his hands in a second, if he needed.

"One more time. Where is the portal to my own world?"

Piper relaxed, the tension visibly leaving the set of her shoulders. "I heard about your little adventure back in Milgram Lake. The local authorities released you back into Dominic Blackburn's custody." She shook her head. "This does not bode well for his career, Gestalt. Assuming, of course, that we turn you in to the proper authorities." She looked sideways at Locke. "Are we going to do that?"

Locke shook his head, a smile on his lips. "No, we are not."

Piper kissed his temple. "You're twisted."

Locke reached out, flicking on the bedside light, and Piper stood. She was a beautiful woman, utterly unconcerned with her own nudity, and within a moment she was close enough to reach out and rest her fingertips on Gestalt's chest.

"So, all I have to do is mark you," she mused.

"I won't ask again," Gestalt said quietly.

Piper nodded. "The cheek, I think," she said to herself, looking up into Gestalt's eyes, scrutinizing his face. "Just under your left eye."

Gestalt sighed and reached out his hand.

CHAPTER SIXTEEN

It took six days to clear up the entire infestation, moving block by block and wiping out the little creatures holed up in basements by the dozens. One of the spells didn't work like it should have, leading to a re-infestation of an area they'd thought was cleared. It extended the job by another day, but in the end, Dominic had made a mock sign of the cross and declared in a high falsetto that this neighborhood was *clean*.

By that time, they'd made decent progress establishing an equilibrium. Micah found a place at Dominic's side, a half-step back, not immediately obvious to anyone who didn't look closely. He sat across from Dominic in diner booths without asking, only rarely casting sideways glances at other indents waiting beside tables. He woke up before Dominic and laid out the day's clothes and tools and fetched breakfast and then woke Dom up, more often than not, by kissing his way up a thigh.

And Dom *let* him. His fingers stroked through Micah's hair, his voice low as he murmured encouragements and praise. And afterward, Dom pulled Micah into his arms, their legs tangled together, Dom's face nuzzling against his chest.

Dom said *thank you* and *I love you* and didn't ask him what he wanted in return. It was enough to be held, to be touched the way Dominic touched him. Dom wasn't trying to turn him on, or pawing at him for his own gratification. He touched him like a lover, soft and gentle, satisfied with the warmth of Micah's skin on his own.

Micah gave up worrying about whether it would last. Maybe Dominic *would* get bored with him, send him away like the others had. He didn't know what he'd do then, and he didn't care. It was worth it just to have him, here and now.

They finished the job and gathered up their supplies, spending a warm afternoon walking silently through fields, winding up their horseshoe rope. Micah texted Garrett to verify that the payment had cleared (it had), and they headed back home.

The first thing they noticed was the smell of smoke.

Mostly it smelled like wood smoke, burning oak or cedar, but underneath was the definite tang of magic.

It was, Micah figured, better than the smell of burning plastic, which would indicate a house fire. But at the same time, it smelled like *magic*. In some respects, that was definitely worse.

"Ges?" Dominic called into the empty living room. "*Gestalt*! You in here?"

"*What*?" came Ges's reply from his bedroom, and a minute later he was standing in the doorway. The doorway . . . well, the doorway answered the question of what had burned. Micah crossed the living room to inspect it more closely.

The wooden frame was covered in ikons, hastily drawn, some of them in runes, some of them unrecognizable. The symbols had been burned deeply into the frame, and the surrounding areas were smoky and charred.

"What the hell did you do?"

"I needed a Doorway," the angel grumbled. "My normal method was proving difficult for me."

Micah looked him over carefully. Gestalt was wearing the same worn jeans that Micah had given him, but his normally bare chest was now covered with a windbreaker, and under that—

"Ges, are you wearing a bulletproof vest?"

Gestalt glanced down at it.

"Is that what it's for? I thought it was armor."

Micah asked, "Why are you wearing armor?" at the same time Dominic asked, "Where did you get *armor*?" Then both of those questions were ignored in favor of Micah's sudden exclamation of

"Oh my god, Ges, your *wings*!" This was cut off by Ges's decision to lean forward, catch Micah by the collar of his shirt, and draw him down into a deep kiss.

There was silence for a few seconds as Ges explored Micah's mouth and Micah let him, and Dominic watched in stunned, wide-eyed silence.

"Dominic has been thinking about you—*imaginatively*—for the past three hours," Ges said when he pulled back, his forehead resting against Micah's. "It has been incredibly distracting."

"Okay, let's go back to the wings," Dominic said. His cheeks were getting a touch of red. "And the armor."

"I did some research while you were gone," Ges explained. His hands dropped to wrap around Micah's hips. "It was necessary to 'go undercover,' as I believe you'd say."

He leaned forward again, rising up onto his toes in order to reach Micah's mouth. His body pressed flush against Micah's.

"You okay, Ges?" Dominic asked, a touch uneasily. "You're acting a bit . . . odd."

Ges spared him a glance. "You were gone a long time. The isolation was . . . more difficult than I would have anticipated. Considering."

Dominic rolled his eyes. "Okay, yeah, we missed you too. So where'd you go undercover? Find anything out?"

"I went to talk to Jeremiah Locke."

Dominic blinked. "The senator?"

Gestalt nodded. He stayed beside Micah, their bodies pressed comfortably together. "He was there when the portal opened. I correctly assumed that he would remember the location."

"He told you where it was?" Micah asked. "How'd you get him to blab?"

"I broke into his house and killed his lover in front of him," Gestalt answered, leaning forward against Micah again.

Micah recoiled.

"You *what*?" Dominic dropped into a defensive position, drawing his gun. "Down, Ges. Get on your knees. Hands behind your head."

Gestalt eyed him coolly but did as he was told.

"You were not quite so horrified when I killed the men sent to hex you."

"That's different from killing an innocent person in their own bed!"

Gestalt blinked. "I'm disappointed you think so little of me. Piper was neither innocent nor in bed."

"*Piper*?" Dominic asked incredulously.

"Why don't you start at the beginning," Micah said, taking another step away from Gestalt.

Ges held his hands out, a weirdly human gesture. "I went to Locke's home with the intention of getting the location of the portal from him. His security team provided me with both the armor and a large weapon, which I used to threaten Locke and Piper. Locke was under the impression that I was still bound to him, which I used to lull the two of them into a false sense of security. Piper took the opportunity to monologue about how she planned to use me now that I'd been recaptured. In doing so, she came close enough that I was able to simply reach out and pull the life from her body." Ges looked evenly at Dominic's gun. "After which Locke became significantly more cooperative."

"I asked you not to kill anyone else," Micah said.

Gestalt shrugged. "You also placed your faith in an investigative body that has been quite literally in bed with the enemy." He looked back to Dominic's weapon. "You can put that away; the chances of harming me with it are absolutely negligible."

"It makes me *feel* better," Dominic snapped. "Ges, you have to understand the position this puts me in. You went into someone's house and *killed* them. I'm a controller; you're basically a job now."

Gestalt frowned, narrowing his eyes. "I went to get information from a man who *bound* and *tortured* me. He's dead now because he—and Piper, as well—expressed both a willingness and a desire to enslave me again." He lifted his chin. "Piper's very presence indicated without a shadow of a doubt that *your* methods have irretrievably failed. Now it is my turn."

He was silent then, looking defiantly up at Dominic. His eyes flickered a dim violet, and Micah could almost see Dominic's recoil as Gestalt reached out through the bond. Dominic frowned, like he was listening or considering. There was silence for a long time.

"I'm having a hard time believing a creature who's admitting to killing people in cold blood," he said at last.

Micah moved toward him, standing close. "He's admitting to killing monsters," Micah said quietly.

Dominic glanced over. "You just take his word on it?"

Micah nodded. He could open the bond, of course, look into Ges's head and see whatever Dominic had seen. But he didn't need to. "You know what they did to him. Would you have responded differently?"

Dominic sighed and reholstered the gun. "You can get up."

Gestalt rose to his feet, light and graceful even without his wings. He kept his eyes on Dominic. "You believe me."

Dominic paused before letting out a resigned "Yeah. Not sure what that says about me, but yeah." He shook his head. "I keep going over it in my head. Like, I should report Piper to someone, but who? If she was crooked, who else can we go to? I mean, I'm pretty sure Ian's good, and Amanda, but any higher—"

Ges was shaking his head. "No. I'm done dealing with your people. I know where the portal is, and I know how it was opened. I intend to close it, for good." He glanced to Micah, then dropped his eyes.

Dominic frowned. "There's something else. Something you're not mentioning."

Ges nodded once, looking him dead in the eye. "I will tell you this because you've been fair to me. But understand that I am not seeking your permission. Or your approval."

Micah shifted slightly, preparing to get between Ges and Dom if needed. He wasn't sure which of them he'd be protecting.

"The magic they used to tear it open was strong, beyond what humans should be trusted to wield. It would have taken quite a few of them. And this . . ." He tugged at the silver collar. "We know they use blood magic. It's possible, even likely, that they opened the passage—and are holding it open—using their own mana as a counterpoint. The spell lives, and dies, with them."

"How many people?" Dominic asked quietly. Micah tried to think back, to remember how many of Slate's friends might have been interested in magic.

Gestalt shrugged. "A few dozen, perhaps. Possibly more. Possibly less."

"Okay, but you're immortal, right?" Dominic asked. "Can you just kick around another forty years or so? They'll die of old age and this whole thing will go away on its own. We could even use the connection as evidence if we can prove it—"

"I'm not making myself clear," Gestalt replied. "This is bonded magic. It is utterly symmetrical. When I say that the bond lives and dies with them, I mean the inverse is true, as well. It will keep them alive, even as it eats at them. They will not die, not so long as the gateway remains open."

"But what about Coffey and Locke? They're dead, right?"

"It's possible they weren't involved in the spell proper. It's also possible that I'm wrong about the source of their power, and there's something else holding the bond open."

"So if we close the portal, we run the risk of killing a few dozen people. Or maybe no one," Dom summarized. "Good, okay, that's an easy ethical decision."

Gestalt's eyes narrowed. "It's not a decision I'm asking you to make. I am telling you what I intend to do. If the gateway was opened using mana, it was done willingly and given freely; it *cannot* be any other way. What happened that day was an attack on my home and my people. I will not allow it to stand, and I will not allow it to happen again, to my world or any other. I intend to close the portal *regardless* of the cost."

Dominic slumped a little. He turned and went into the kitchen. He set his gun on the table with a quiet *thunk*, and retrieved three glass tumblers from the shelf beside the fridge.

Micah could see him struggling. All Dom needed to say was *Don't*. One word, and the cuffs would flash, and he'd save gods only knew how many people. And Ges would stay here, trapped and hating him. Forever.

"I know you don't eat," Dominic said, pulling a bottle of amber liquid from a cabinet, "but do you drink?"

CHAPTER SEVENTEEN

Ges looked at Micah. Micah looked at Dominic. Dominic looked at his drink.

He'd poured a couple fingers into each of the glasses, contemplated them for a couple of seconds, then topped it off with coke from the fridge. Two in the afternoon was a little early for straight whiskey, even if you were drinking to deal with a major mental paradigm shift.

Dominic picked up the glass and downed half of it in one swallow. He stared at the second half like he thought it might have an explanation for his sudden desire to side with a creature over his own species.

The whiskey was unforthcoming.

"You're sure that it was Piper?"

Ges nodded. He took the seat to Dominic's right, across from Micah. Neither of them made a move toward their drinks, which suited Dominic just fine. He was in a use-it-or-lose-it type mood.

Weirdly, Dominic was glad his dad wasn't around for this. Benjamin Blackburn had been a real stickler for rules. The only reason Dominic had ever passed his exams was because of all the time his father had spent drilling him. Going over the laws and regulations, again and again and again. Get it right. Screw it up, and innocent people got killed. There were procedures for a reason.

Dominic looked to Ges, then to Micah.

The laws had failed both of them.

Were failing both of them.

Were going to *keep* failing them.

He downed the rest of his glass.

Micah reached for his, hesitantly, like he sensed that it was in danger. Ges mimicked him, and when Micah raised the tumbler to his lips, Ges did the same.

"This is horrid," the daiyura said a second later, wrinkling his nose at the offending beverage.

"I'll get rid of it for you," Dominic said, taking the glass neatly out of Ges's hand. His own sat empty on the table in front of him. "You said Locke told you about opening the portal. That means you know where to go to close it, right?"

Ges nodded. "I'll need time to work the spell. Ten minutes, maybe less."

"And it's where?"

"New York. A small town outside Troy. Locke was good enough to provide me with coordinates."

"Little town, probably not well-guarded, then," Micah said, ignoring him. "Maybe we'll get lucky and it'll be an easy in and out."

Ges shook his head. "I was there for months after my summoning. I remember it being a sizeable facility—an estate, like the one I was in when you met me."

"Awesome." Dominic looked sideways at the whiskey bottle again, but thought better of it. "This is outside my range of expertise. I'm used to dealing with supernatural creatures, not humans. Humans are a whole different ballgame."

"Humans might be our in," Micah said. "If we can get inside. Trained slaves would probably die before betraying their masters, but if we released some of the creatures, maybe a vampire? The others would flee. That would give us a distraction for Ges to do what he needs to."

"I'd only need about ten minutes," Ges said before Dominic could ask how Micah knew what creatures would be there. "If they were released from their bindings, they would certainly more than cover it."

"That's not a good idea," Dominic said. "Once they're loose, what's to stop them from attacking the slaves? Or the town, for that matter?"

"Can we set up a containment spell?" Micah asked. "Like the horseshoes?"

Dominic grimaced. "Maybe? Iron will contain a lot of stuff but not everything. If you're talking vampires, though . . . I can't see anything good coming from releasing any number of starving vampires. Best-case scenario they attack their captors. Worst-case, they attack the other creatures, or the indents, or us."

"We could start a fire," Gestalt suggested. "A small one."

"All right, so we don't release any creatures," Micah said, ignoring the suggestion. "Just the people. Easy enough, at least physically. If this estate operates like Slate's, the slaves are left to manage each other. Security is little more than a precaution, since the punishment for running is exceedingly worse than the experience of staying." He glanced at Dominic. "For the most part."

"So they need motivation," Dominic said. "The last raid, the Hellfires had advance warning, and they used it to slaughter the evidence: the creatures and some of the worse-off indents. Would the indents run if they knew their masters were planning to kill them?"

"From what I've seen?" Micah shrugged. "Safe money's on yes. For most of them. The trouble will be convincing them."

"This is all predicated on someone already being inside," Ges pointed out. "That's its own problem."

"Can't you get me in?" Micah asked, surprised. "Like you got to Locke?"

Ges shook his head, grimacing.

"I already tried. The compound is warded against that kind of magic—most likely against magic creatures in general. It's a standard precaution for keeping things in as well as out. Not to mention these—" he yanked at the collar "—make it very difficult to move as I normally do. That's why I needed to create the Doorway in order to return here."

"Yeah, thanks for that, by the way," Dominic grumbled.

Ges carried on as though he hadn't spoken. "Creating a Doorway is not subtle, and it's very difficult to do if I don't already have a Feel for the place I'm going. Opening a Door into an unknown and warded building would be . . . inadvisable. I can do it if there's no other choice, but the chances of coming out *right* . . ." He made a face.

Micah frowned, considering. "I could always go through the front door."

Dominic scoffed. "Yeah, like they wouldn't notice one of us waltzing in."

"They absolutely would," Micah replied. "But I'm willing to bet that Slate wants to kill me more than he wants me dead. Especially now."

"I'm failing to see how this ends well for us."

"Because if Slate isn't there," Micah continued, "they'll call him and put me in holding until he gets there. That gives me a couple hours, minimum, to get to the other slaves. Maybe days. It should be plenty of time to sabotage the warding and convince the slaves they need to get out."

"Yeah, you can get a lot done in the 'couple hours' before he shows up and *tortures* you to death," Dominic said.

"If the plan works, we'll all be long gone before he shows up."

"That's too big an 'if.'"

Micah dragged his thumb against his lower lip. "Who could we get as backup?"

Dominic rubbed his eyes. The local police wouldn't be much help in this situation. They'd need a warrant, and the process of getting one was almost certain to tip off the Hellfires that they were coming. Everyone inside would need to be evacuated by then. He mulled it over.

"I'm positive Ian will believe us about Piper. He might be willing to help us with a covert operation if we asked. And I'm positive Amanda's clean too. I can get Garrett to sound a red alert when we're ready. That gives us a witch, a controller, a cop, an angel, and possibly an AI."

"It's not nothing," Micah said, shrugging.

"You're overlooking another large advantage," Ges interjected. He looked back and forth from Micah to Dominic. "The bond. We'll be able to adapt to changing circumstances much faster if we communicate that way."

Micah paled.

Ges reached out, laying his fingertips on Micah's temple. "You'll have to keep the wall down, Micah."

Micah shook his head violently, pulling away from Ges's touch. "We've been over this, I can't. I'll find a way to signal you when it's safe; you don't need to see all of it."

"We *have* a way to signal, Micah—"

"No!" Micah stood up suddenly, his hands planted on the table. He stared at the empty glasses in front of him, avoiding eye contact. "You probably haven't considered," Micah said in a low voice, "what's likely going to *happen* to me before they decide to lock me up. If they catch me, I can play that I'm repentant, that I want to come back. And I can make them believe it."

Dominic's stomach sank, but Micah wasn't done.

"You keep talking about how you want to see into my head because you *love* me. But could you watch me do that? For them? For *all* of them?" He turned to Dominic, hazel eyes flashing. "Because I could do it. I wouldn't even hesitate. Do you understand that? The fact that it bothers me so little that I wasn't even going to *mention* it? That's what I *am*, and that's what you want to see?"

Dominic opened his mouth, the protests building in his head. This plan was awful, they couldn't let him do that, they'd find another way—

He couldn't say it. He couldn't tell Micah that he knew better. Not honestly.

So he said the only true thing he could think of. "Yes."

Micah stared at him, and Dominic swallowed, trying to find words. "If that's what you are, then that's what I want. And if you're determined to do this, and watching that happen is the way to keep you safe, then . . ." He hesitated. "Then that's what we'll do."

"You don't mean that." Micah's voice was barely a whisper.

"He does," Ges said. He was looking at Dominic as well. Dominic felt suddenly self-conscious, with the two of them staring at him like that.

Micah's face broke, and his gaze dropped to the table. His voice was thick when he spoke. "I can't bring that to you. Please . . . I can't."

Dominic stood, pulling Micah close to him, ignoring the protesting noises he made. "Yeah, you can."

The muscles of Micah's back were strung tight under Dominic's fingertips. Ges's chair scraped against the floor, and when Dominic looked over, the daiyura was shrugging out of his jacket. The backs of his arms were smeared dark with something that seemed to go deeper than his skin. When he discarded the vest, Dominic saw that the black markings covered his shoulders as well.

Ges shivered, and as he did, the blackness deepened and expanded, rippling outward like a shadow. It spread from his body across the kitchen, deepening into darkness, solidifying into the familiar shape of wings.

Dominic held Micah a little tighter, the two of them gaping wordlessly.

"I can help you turn the bond into something we can use," Ges said earnestly, as though he hadn't just performed a minor miracle in front of them. "We can do it slowly, but we should start now."

Micah swallowed hard and then nodded.

Ges sat on the living room rug, his legs crossed, his wings splayed out to the sides. Dominic sat across from him, close enough that his knees almost brushed against Ges's when he moved. Micah sat behind him, his chest pressed to the length of Dominic's back, his hands resting easily on Dominic's thighs.

Dominic would have thought that Micah would be in the center, with one of them supporting him, holding him, having his back. Instead, just like the first time they'd slept together, Micah had slipped in behind him. Something in Micah's head made him feel safer holding, rather than being held.

Dominic let him do what he needed, leaning back into the warmth of his body, letting Micah mantle him. Micah's back was against the couch, and Dominic once again remembered the early days, when Micah had spent much of his time on the floor, in corners.

He let out a breath. It would be fine. This was fine.

Ges leaned forward, and Dominic could feel him, not just physically. He could *always* feel Ges there, in some corner of his mind, with some sense he'd never known he had. Like waking up and knowing, somehow, that someone was in the bed beside you. Ges was just *there* and as he leaned toward Dominic, Dominic felt the bond thrumming with energy.

Ges's hands rested on Dominic's knees, palms down over Micah's, but it was Dominic he was looking at.

"I'm going to come through you," the daiyura told him. Violet sparks circled the darkness of his irises. Dominic swallowed.

"Okay."

"Close your eyes and focus your breathing. I can force this to happen, but it will be much easier for everyone if you can allow me to do what I need to."

"I'm not gonna lie, I have no idea how to do that."

"It comes to you," Micah said quietly.

Dominic took a deep breath, letting his eyes slide shut. He could still feel the two of them, Micah's solid heat and Gestalt's static energy. He focused on breathing. In and out. Slow and easy.

Ges's presence brightened slightly, and Dom felt the pressure, behind his pubic bone, that he'd come to associate with the bond. Micah's breath was hot on the side of his throat, and he tried to slow his own breathing to match.

The pressure increased, and Dominic realized he could sense *himself*, as well. With his eyes closed, Gestalt saw Dominic as a form of bright, roiling cobalt, light and dark places flickering and mixing and curling like smoke. It was nothing like Ges's pure, luminous amethyst, but the daiyura didn't seem to hold it against him.

Micah shuddered and then, suddenly, there was another form there—a dull, lustrous copper, more dark than light, but brightening by the second. Micah tried to pull back, to tear his hands away, but Ges held them firm, pushing them down into the tops of Dominic's thighs.

"It's all right, Micah," Dom murmured, and then his hands were on Micah's as well, steadying him. Micah's face was buried against his shoulder, and Dominic could feel hot tears against his skin. "I love you."

The bronze light flared, the dam bursting wide, and for the second time, Dominic *saw*.

Micah was his. Micah loved him, would give anything for him, *belonged* to him in a way he never could have predicted in that parking lot, not in a thousand years.

And it scared him, it terrified him to be given something that precious, but he didn't close the bond. He didn't look away.

Micah wanted to belong to him, and he could understand that now, because he wanted to belong to Micah too.

He felt the realization happening, and what was more, he could feel *Micah* feeling it. He could feel Micah distrust it, feel him turning it over, inspecting it like a jeweler seeking flaws.

He found none.

Micah burned brighter as the fear and shame dissolved into a cautious kind of hope. The disbelief and caution weren't *gone*—Dominic wasn't sure they ever fully would be—but it was a start.

Ges dropped the last of the barriers between them.

The light changed immediately but almost imperceptibly, the gold spreading over the lapis like honey, brightening the dark places in him until he shone. Dom remembered to breathe, gasping for air that had vanished from the room, because Micah's light was flooding through him and he *remembered*.

He remembered dirty hotel rooms and hunger and fear. He remembered lavish parties and gold body paint and confidence and pleasure. He remembered bright lights and desperation and pain.

And then Ges was there, guiding them apart, keeping them from sinking too deeply into each other, and Dominic settled into him. Gestalt was freezing, an icy counterpoint to Micah's torrid heat. When Dominic looked closer, he could see cracks through the black-white of Gestalt's light, broken places that had only just begun to heal.

The house seemed suddenly filled with ghosts, laughter and memories that Dominic could hear over the sounds of singing. A choir, a memory of an infinite chorus, sang through his blood until he ached from missing it.

He was alone, one of a million million, a single voice in the dark, and Dominic shivered, feeling the cold sink into his bones. He realized distantly that it was Ges he felt, not himself, and he reached out, pressing his hands to Gestalt's frigid skin.

He could feel a part of himself spreading into Ges, and part of him into Micah now too. He wondered if he was going to pass out again. Heat surged through his hands, sinking into Gestalt, and cobalt flowed through the cracks, filling the empty places, even as he was engulfed in a blanket of auburn fire. Ges shifted to his knees, making space between Dom's thighs, his fingers digging into the couch on either side of Micah. His lips found Dominic's and light poured through the connection.

And then, somehow, it began to balance. Dominic was no longer trapped between ice and fire, light and darkness. The colors he saw roiling inside himself moved a little slower, the lights and darks a little less distinguished.

Ges's mouth was warm skin rather than hard ice, and Dominic kissed him slow and easy. The daiyura's wings engulfed them, and Micah's arms tightened around him. His eyes flew open.

Ges looked down at him with concern, and Dominic wasn't surprised to see there were now three colors circling his irises.

"There were so many," Dominic breathed, and Ges smiled, pressing another kiss to his mouth.

"Yes. And I will see them again soon, as you will see the ones you have loved. But that's not for us here, or now."

"Do you want him?" Micah asked, and Dominic didn't know how to answer.

Ges did, uttering a simple yes before leaning in to kiss Dominic again. Dominic was vaguely aware of Micah's hands on him, slipping beneath his shirt to skim along his belly. He let his own hands run up Gestalt's back, feeling him tense slightly when they reached the soft, downy feathers at the base of his wings. His body froze, but Dominic could see the shape in Ges's mind. He sent out a reassurance even as he let his fingers press deep into the muscle beneath the tertial feathers. Ges shivered and relaxed, letting the appendages rest against Dominic's palms. His fingers carded through the feathers, and Ges shivered again, letting out a little moan.

"Being physical has its upsides," Micah murmured, and Dominic laughed a little. The feel of Ges's wings beneath his hands was incredible—setting aside the rest of the daiyura's physique, he felt like he could do this all day.

The rest of Gestalt was not so easily set aside, he realized as Ges shifted against him. Micah's hands were the only thing between them; Micah had been busy working open the buttons of Dom's shirt.

Sneaky bastard, he thought to himself, and Micah chuckled in response.

Just following orders, he answered.

Before Dom could respond to that, Micah and Ges ganged up on him, taking his shirts in four hands and pulling them off him.

"No fair," he sputtered when his face was free of the cotton undershirt. "It's two against one here."

"We're just talking, Dominic," Ges said, his hands exploring Dominic's now-bare chest. "You could hear us, if you listened."

Dominic closed his eyes, trying to focus his breathing, trying to tune in to the connection between the three of them. He didn't hear words, not exactly, but he could . . . sense something. He focused, trying to turn the gentle buzzing into a language he could recognize.

"Not like that," Micah whispered in his ear, and the bond echoed with his words, not with sound, but in some other form that solidified as Dominic focused.

And then he could feel it, could see it. It wasn't a buzzing so much as a stream of words and images and sensations and . . . and . . .

"Oh," Dominic said quietly. "Yeah, okay."

Micah took hold of his wrists, lifting them and putting them where Ges wanted them, on the joint of his wings. Dominic stroked along the feathers, feeling the oily softness of them, and Ges let out a breath like a pant, raising the limbs, splaying the feathers for him.

Micah's hands delved beneath the waistband of Dominic's jeans, thumb popping the button on the way down. He palmed Dominic's hardening cock through the thin cotton of his boxers. Ges hissed in response and pulled at the rough denim, hiking it down Dominic's thighs, and Micah held Dom steady while he wriggled out of them.

He could feel them, he realized as Ges pressed their mouths together again. He could feel himself, held flush to Micah's broad chest, Micah's cock jutting against the small of his back. He could feel Ges against him, could feel his legs wrapped around the daiyura's hips. He could feel his own hands on Gestalt's wings. He dug his fingers in and his vision whited out. He heard Micah's answering hiss of pleasure.

"Gods, Ges," Dominic groaned, and he couldn't get further because Micah's hands were on his cock, stroking hard and firm. His fingers were clenched in Ges's wings, and Ges's hands were on his hips, pressing between his spread thighs—

He could see himself, he realized. He could see himself through Ges's eyes, through Micah's, a sheen of sweat rising on his skin as Ges pushed against him. It was too much—

Everything I am, living inside of you, Dominic thought, or Micah thought, or Ges thought—one of them thought and it didn't matter because Dominic wasn't trying to distinguish anymore. He was too lost in the feel of hands and mouths and the taut, hot feel of his body—

He wasn't sure when he came, not exactly, but he knew when every nerve in his body turned to lightning. His back arched and one of them cried out and Ges came down on top of him, the three of them in a splayed tangle of limbs.

"Being physical *does* have some upsides," Ges said, when they'd caught their breath a little bit. Dominic was busy watching the auras that the things in his living room had suddenly obtained. They were fading as he came down off his afterglow. "I'm glad I got to do this again."

Micah laughed. "Always happy to oblige you in your investigations, Ges."

"I'm being sincere," Ges said. He shifted onto his knees, pulling his wings close to his back. He regarded the two humans in front of him. "I think I may miss you when the portal has closed."

Micah tensed, and Dominic got a flicker of something through the bond. "What do you mean, you'll miss us?"

Gestalt was rolling his shoulders, almost too nonchalantly. "When the portal closes, I'll be on the other side. With my brothers and sisters."

Dominic was paying attention, and he didn't miss the pang of apprehension. "That *is* where you'll end up though, yeah?"

"Where else would I go?" Ges asked, and Dominic didn't know how to answer.

Dominic looked to Micah, saw Micah's confusion as well. The question broached the distance between them, and Ges scowled.

"It's not important. You don't know about my people, and I am not going to tell you." And then, somewhat unexpectedly, he leaned forward again, pressing a gentle kiss to Dominic's mouth. "Don't worry yourself."

Dominic didn't miss the note of sadness.

Ges retreated, tucking himself into the couch opposite the one Micah was backed against. He settled his wings behind him and regarded the humans as though he were waiting for them to do a trick.

Dominic realized that he was still totally naked, in counterpoint to Ges's jeans and the fact that Micah was still dressed. He couldn't seem to bring himself to care. Micah's legs were bracketing his, the other man's long arms encircling him. When Dominic leaned his head back, it rested against Micah's shoulder like they were made for each other.

Micah smiled, and though Dominic couldn't see it, he could feel pleasure resonating through the bond. "Could you hear me thinking that?"

"Yeah."

"Made for each other," Ges supplied.

Dominic scowled. "So I'm a poet in my own head, sue me."

He didn't stop leaning against Micah's shoulder. Micah's thumb was making idle circles around his arm, and for the first time, Dominic realized that Micah was doing it on purpose. It wasn't an idle motion; Micah was very carefully—

The thought retreated and Dominic chased it, coming back with a whole set of very detailed actions and circumstances under which to use them.

Micah froze. Dominic could feel him scrambling, trying to recover, trying to find an explanation.

"You're fine," Dominic murmured, shifting against Micah to remind him he was there. "It feels nice."

Things went through Micah's head very quickly: Satisfaction at his success, happiness at Dominic's happiness. Pride in his training, and then a stifling, an attempt to shove it down. Sadness that these actions did not come to him naturally, that he could not enjoy what Dominic wanted him to.

Dominic laced his fingers through Micah's, listening to all these things happen in a second.

"I'm sorry," Micah mumbled. "I didn't want—" And then he paused, listening. Dominic squeezed his hand, letting him.

"I told you," Ges said, and the pressure against the bond increased as Micah raced through Dominic's mind, searching for a condemnation that wasn't there.

"You *love* me," Micah said. His voice was almost a whisper. And then, "You— How *can* you?"

Dominic's eyes flicked to Ges, but the daiyura was unchanged, regarding them silently. Nobody spoke. The answers to Micah's question were easily seen.

Micah leaned forward, resting his forehead on Dominic's shoulder. There was no point trying to hide his face; the disbelief and awe thrummed through the bond as clearly as though he were speaking out loud.

"Thank you," he whispered, finally. His long arms tightened around Dominic's body, holding him close, and Dominic wondered if Micah had ever believed—really *believed*—that he could be loved.

Micah laughed a little, wiping his face against Dom's shoulder. "I'm not *that* hopeless, am I?" he asked, but the truth was searing through his mind, ice-cold in its severity. Dominic and Gestalt reached for him at the same time, treading lightly through the bond to soothe and encircle him.

For a while, they stayed there, listening, feeling the reassuring presence of each other.

At some point, Dominic began to get cold, and Ges felt it and passed him a blanket.

"We can't stage an offensive like this," the daiyura said finally. "We need more time."

Dominic didn't ask him what he meant. It was plain that neither human understood, and in any case, he was too comfortable to talk.

Gestalt let out a breath. *You two are like children*, he said through the bond, and Dominic understood the full meaning of the words. Gestalt could send thoughts, ideas, plans, all clearly defined and articulated. That was the sort of communication they'd need, and it was communication that Micah and Dominic were not yet capable of.

They shared in broad strokes, emotions and images. They'd need to be more specific if they planned to orchestrate a battle this way.

"A time," Gestalt said out loud. "Send a time."

Dominic felt Micah at the edge of the bond sending him the sky, orange and red, the sun kissing the horizon.

"Sunset?" Dominic guessed.

Micah frowned. "Eight PM."

Dominic picked noon, sending the time to Micah as clearly as he could.

"Lunch," Micah guessed.

Gestalt laughed. *You see what I mean*, he said, and Dominic had a sudden glimpse of *home*. Young daiyura reaching out in joy and excitement, proudly letting their first thoughts cross the spaces between themselves and their families, uncertain voices joining the choir that never stopped—

The homesickness hit him like a physical force, and Micah's arms gripped him tight as the other man felt it as well. Gestalt's face remained stoic, showing no sign that he knew what he'd shown them.

"Was that— Were they yours?" Dominic asked.

Gestalt frowned, searching for the meaning of the question. His eyes widened, and he shook his head. "No. I don't . . . My people . . . I don't think another daiyura would . . ."

He stopped, frowning, then rose to his feet and crossed to the door of his room. He considered the Doorway for a moment, chewing absently on his lower lip. Then he reached out, laying his palms against the ruined wood, and the burned runes glowed momentarily blue.

"A daiyura is a mixing of spirits. It requires two complementary beings, gifted with traits that enhance and beautify the other. It is pointless to create, otherwise. The resultant child is . . . off-balance."

The runes faded, leaving unblemished wood behind. Gestalt surveyed his handiwork with satisfaction. He flexed his fingers absently.

"Out of all my people, there is a reason it was me who was closest to this plane."

"You're off-balance," Micah said quietly.

Ges nodded. He kept his eyes on the doorway. "I don't add to the harmony," he agreed. "It's why I was alone, watching the physical plane when the gateway opened. I was the closest to . . . to you."

"Because we're off-balance too," Dominic said quietly.

Ges only smiled. Then he shook his head, dismissing the topic. "It doesn't matter. Nothing can be done about it. I can't understand you, and you can't fix me. It was an experiment that failed. That's all."

"You don't need fixing," Dominic protested, but Ges waved him off, turning back to where the two humans were sitting.

"We need to work on your communication. We'll start with places."

CHAPTER EIGHTEEN

By the time the humans got hungry enough to break for dinner, Micah and Dominic were both capable of sending static images. Micah had come up with the idea, sending Dominic an image of red clock numbers, glowing in the dark. Gestalt had scoffed at it, calling it a simplification bordering on cheating, but their accuracy had improved almost immediately.

The way they learned wasn't like young daiyura. Human minds did not organize things the way daiyura minds did. They developed in isolation and, as such, lacked the universal syntax that formed in the minds of a collective.

They spoke to each other in broken, simplistic phrases. Gestalt would have abandoned the entire experiment in despair if it weren't for the genuine *mirth* the humans shared when they realized they'd successfully communicated a thought. Periodically, they stumbled on something that made them collapse into laughter. Gestalt didn't understand the references, but he felt the joy that came from them, and he laughed as well.

It wasn't a harmony. Their triad did not make a choir. But as Gestalt listened to the two of them babbling to each other, he found he missed the song a little less.

It was getting dark by the time they stopped to eat. Gestalt watched silently as Dominic dressed and Micah moved to the kitchen to reheat something frozen.

Dominic saw him watching and turned with a grin. "See something you like?"

"Yes," Gestalt answered simply. He could tell that Dominic was making a joke, but he couldn't understand the meaning, so he answered honestly. "I've come to have a grudging admiration. I suspect it has something to do with the avatar's reaction to intercourse."

Dominic rolled his eyes, which Gestalt didn't think was called for.

Dinner was frozen pizza, which Dominic insisted he try. Gestalt pretended to hate it, mostly in the hopes of not being pestered to try more things.

The two humans finished it off themselves, all the while making broken eye contact across the table and sending each other simplistic phrases and half-formed mental images.

Dominic tended to send jokes and sexual innuendos, refusing to take any of it too seriously. There was still a part of him that couldn't accept the idea of sitting at his kitchen table and communicating telepathically with an *angel* he'd taken as a lover a few hours before. Gestalt suspected he'd come to terms with the idea eventually.

Micah stuck to facts. He tried to convey times, places, and faces. Concepts that would aid them in the coming fight. His mind was a practical counterweight to Dominic's playfulness. Even still, Micah's thoughts occasionally overflowed the boundaries of his own mind. An affection or appreciation so profound that the bond resonated with the praises he sang.

He caught it quickly when it happened, trying to stifle it. He retreated back behind his wall, hiding from the repercussions. His eyes would drop, and he would briefly fill with fear: That he was presumptuous, that his advances were unwanted. He worried his affection was inappropriate or unseemly, that he would displease the others.

When this happened, they would wait, sometimes reaching for his hands, sometimes letting the bond speak for them. They would wait until he let his barriers back down. It took time, but when they fell, he was always pleasantly surprised to find that he was, still, loved.

It wasn't a harmony. Combined, their minds were chaotic and boisterous, nothing like the serene melodies of the daiyura.

Gestalt thought that maybe he understood it now. Why humans reached out when they received no response. How they lived and interacted in such silent isolation and still managed to care for each other. They were not expecting a complementing melody. Their affection was self-contained, existing entirely within themselves. They reached for each other in order to feel the light that bloomed within themselves.

Being loved in return inspired new joy, but it was not a requirement. Love existed with or without reciprocation.

Gestalt thought of the time he'd spent at home, alone and as quietly as possible, listening to the others and watching the earth. And he understood.

He missed the harmony, but he didn't add to it.

He thought maybe he added to this.

After dinner, Dominic got the computer and found a map of Troy. Gestalt gave him Locke's coordinates, and they ended up with a small red X in the middle of an otherwise featureless patch of woods.

"You're sure that's the place? There's no way in or out."

"That's where Locke said it was," Gestalt answered.

Micah took over the computer, switching it into satellite view. "It's a private road," he said, zooming in and pointing. "Look, it branches south off Route 12 near Arlington. It's not named, but you can see where the path was cut through the trees."

Ges looked at the image on the screen. Sure enough, a single lane traversed the woods, culminating in a parking lot.

"Does it look familiar?" Dominic asked.

Gestalt shook his head. "I don't know. I had a hood on when they moved me outside. I only ever saw the inside of the complex. But it looks like it's about the right size."

"All right. For now, let's assume this is our target." Dominic glanced to Micah. "You're our advance. If it's the wrong place, you'll let us know. If it's the right place . . ."

"Then I get to the slave barracks," Micah interjected, glossing easily over Dominic's pause. "I tell them to head north. That'll take them straight up to the main road."

"Right. Once everything's moving, we'll put a call in to local authorities. Here and here." Dominic gestured to the map, pointing to the two towns closest to the compound. "Plus Troy. The Hellfires have almost definitely got a couple cops in their pockets, but if we call into three different departments with news of a medium-scale rebellion? News will spread too fast to cover up."

"Dominic and I will use the pandemonium to get inside, find you, and close the gate."

"With Amanda and Ian covering us, if we can convince them to help," Dominic concluded. "Speaking of which, I should call them. Should probably give Garrett a heads-up too. If this place is like the others, cleanup is gonna be a big pull on controllers. He might be able to consolidate some people for us."

Dominic flipped his phone open, dialing as he stepped outside onto the darkened porch. Gestalt could hear the rumble of his voice as he greeted his friend.

Gestalt turned back to Micah. "You're not nearly as confident as you're pretending to be."

Micah squared his shoulders. "I can do this."

"I have every faith in you. But you're frightened nonetheless."

Micah let out a laugh. "Well, yeah. The whole plan is based on the hope that Slate will want the chance to torture me before he kills me. And waiting for him . . ." Micah's face went momentarily blank. "I don't have illusions that I'll be treated kindly."

Gestalt could see it in his mind, the grim determination and the fear. Micah was confident he could withstand whatever they planned to do to him. Gestalt could see the memories running through his head, the pain he had endured, the scars he'd been left with.

"You could walk away," Gestalt said quietly. Micah glanced up, meeting his eyes. Gestalt kept going. "You stand to gain nothing from this. At its heart, this is my battle. Not yours."

"I said I'd help," Micah said, then hesitated, dropping his eyes again. His fingers twisted together, then released. He watched them, choosing his words. "Do you know why Slate got rid of me?" he asked after a while.

"No."

"Because I was willful. I defied him and challenged his authority."

Gestalt frowned. "You did everything you could to please your masters. I've seen memories of abuse that go on for years—"

"There was someone else," Micah interrupted. "Another slave. They were hurting her and . . . and I told him to stop. I would have taken her place. Slate was furious. He took it out on both of us, and when he was done with my punishment, he sent me away."

"Why didn't he kill you?"

Micah smiled, letting out a breath. "I think he wanted me to die slow. A slave's death. Run ragged at one of his work camps until I got sick or hurt or just . . . wore out. But I got lucky. Another slave sold me instead of taking me there. It was a long shot for her—not many people would gamble on a disgraced hospitality slave. But Dominic did." He cast a fond look out the window, to where Dominic's silhouette was visible against the darkening sky. "He believes there's more to me than the things I fake to make my masters happy. Maybe he's wrong. Maybe I'm doing this because you *need* me. But maybe he's right and I'm doing it because out there, they're hurting *somebody*, and I'm still willing to trade places."

Gestalt opened his mouth to respond, but before he could say anything, Dominic came back through the door, a wide grin on his face. "They need two days, but they're in."

Gestalt nodded. "Two days will give us time to work on communication."

"Right. The other question is when to leave. The earlier we go, the more recon we get, but it also increases the risk of being noticed."

"We wait," Micah said instantly. "They hexed the house, which means they know our faces. The longer we stay there, the greater chance we have of being recognized. They might even be watching us."

"So we wait," Dominic agreed. "We can get the layout from Micah once he's inside."

Gestalt looked between the two humans. Both of them were ready to do this to help him, though it might get them killed, and they knew it. He was suddenly filled with gratitude, and they must have felt it through the bond. Micah looked down, while Dominic gave him a rakish smile.

"Who wants to get old, anyway?" he joked, and Gestalt saw a flash of two men, their hair streaked with gray, sitting beside a crackling campfire—

Dominic pulled back, looking away.

That night, Micah had a nightmare.

Gestalt saw it as it started, from his customary place by the stream. He watched the two humans and their nonsensical hallucinations, smiling to himself as they moved through their imaginary worlds.

And then Micah's went dark, invaded by men with blank faces, men who held him down, hands around his throat—

Gestalt was on his feet, bolting for the house.

Micah whimpered in pain and fear, and Ges forced his way into the dream. He tried to take Micah away, to separate him from the faceless men, but it was like fighting smoke. Micah's mind controlled this place; he couldn't be saved from his own fear.

The door to the bedroom stood open, and Gestalt was inside in a second, gathering the human against him and shaking him awake. His wings encircled the trembling man, blocking out the world. The noise roused Dominic from sleep, but he only needed a moment's connection to Micah to understand what had happened.

Micah quieted, letting Gestalt hold him inside the dark shell of the angel's wings. Ges sent reassurances through the bond, telling them both that they were safe.

The humans eventually fell back asleep, but Gestalt didn't leave. He stayed, watching over them, and there were no more dreams.

CHAPTER NINETEEN

The drive north was tense, to say the least.

Amanda and Ian went up in their own cars, taking slightly different routes to try to assuage some of their shared paranoia. Gestalt, Micah, and Dominic headed up in Dominic's car, and Micah could tell it was taking every ounce of Dominic's self-control not to turn around.

"We're not ready," he said for the tenth time.

"We're as ready as we're going to be," Micah answered back, for the tenth time. "Every day we delay, they're building up resources too. And they can do it faster than we can. We can't sit around waiting for them to hex the house again."

Dominic looked to Micah, pain in his eyes. "I just wish it didn't have to be you."

"I know." Micah straightened his shoulders, trying to look confident. "Anyway, Amanda says she's pretty sure she has a spell that can cloak me. I've got a good thirty minutes before they can even *see* me. I'm pretty sure I can find the slave barracks in that time. If it's anything like the last place, we'll be dealing with about a hundred club members and a little under two hundred slaves. Not counting creatures. Two hundred slaves making a break for freedom is a hell of a diversion. More likely than not, they'll never even see me."

The optimism was a total lie. Micah knew it, and he knew the other two sensed the deception.

Outside the window, the landscape got darker. They drove on in silence.

The ragtag group rendezvoused in a park about a quarter of a mile from the club entrance. Amanda and Ian parked end-to-end, blocking Dominic's car from sight. It was probably pointless; it was almost ten at night and far too dark to see anything from the road anyway.

Dominic began laying down a chalk circle for the concealment spell, but had to stop when Amanda pulled him up into a bear hug.

Micah barely had time to laugh at Dominic's confusion before it became clear that he would not be spared a similar treatment.

"I've been so worried for you guys. Ever since I heard what happened with the hex bag, I've been expecting to hear you've been offed!"

"We're fine, Amanda," Dominic grumbled, but he was touched by the concern.

Micah smiled. "We've had a guardian angel," he added, winking at Gestalt.

Gestalt stared blankly back.

"We'll need a hell of a lot more than that to make this work," Ian griped. "I've got a written explanation for all this laying on my desk back in Selina, in case I don't come back, but still." He tipped his head back, staring up into the darkness. "If the corruption goes as deep as you say it does, I don't know if that'll do any good."

"Well," Dominic mused, returning his flashlight to where he was still drawing the circle. "Before, you were trying to nail them on indent endangerment and the unauthorized slaughter of creatures. A couple dead free men would change the scope of the investigation."

"I sincerely hope it doesn't come to that," Ian said.

"You and me both," Dominic said cheerily. "Micah, you're up."

Micah steeled himself and went to sit in the center of the circle. This was Amanda's spell, not Dominic's, so he wasn't quite sure what to expect.

As it turned out, her spellwork was based on crystals. Amanda had brought along a plastic toolbox filled with a dozen different crystalline minerals. She arranged these around the circle, occasionally pausing to step back and survey her work. She had just enough Sight to see how the crystals reverberated into the air around them.

After she'd gotten them how she wanted them, she went to the toolbox and returned with a small, circular gold cage on a long chain.

This, she hung around Micah's neck, adjusting the length of the chain until the cage rested above his belly button. Micah inspected it in the beam of his flashlight. There was a clear crystal inside, six-sided, pointed on both ends.

"It's a Herkimer diamond," Amanda explained. She'd moved back to the edges of the circle, and she was sliding a large, rough emerald along one inch at a time, pausing and then repositioning it again. "Your energy is centered in your second chakra, so that's the best place to put it for this. Since it's basically your life force that powers the spell."

"Isn't that dangerous?" Ian asked.

"Nah," Amanda answered, abandoning the emerald in favor of rotating a set of small rubies. "Human life force is basically endless. Unless you're trading a huge chunk of it to some deity, most spells use so little it regenerates as you go."

"And we're *not* trading chunks to a deity, right?" Dominic asked.

Amanda shot him a look. "Of course not. Do I look like a crazy bitch to you?" She settled the rubies, then stood back, surveying the whole scene in the darkness. She squinted, taking a few steps to the side. She readjusted the emerald again. "We're repositioning his aura so that he resonates slightly out of sync with the rest of Gaia. It'll effectively make him invisible until the spell wears off. It's just taking me a second . . . Micah, your aura is larger than you seem."

"Thank you?" Micah guessed.

As Amanda moved the crystals around, Ges approached, holding something out. Micah took it, turning it curiously over in his hands.

"It's an auspicious talisman," Ges said, nodding at the bottle cap. "For luck." His face was solemn, but his side of the bond bubbled with mirth. Micah laughed and promised not to lose it.

Amanda made one more adjustment, which seemed to satisfy her. She retrieved a small brass bowl filled with an assortment of herbs and dropped a match into it, muttering under her breath as she did so.

Micah felt a sickening lurch, like he'd just awoken from a dream about falling.

Amanda grinned. "Perfect. Come on, in the car. We've only got half an hour until you're visible again."

Micah cast one last glance back at his friends as he got into Amanda's Volkswagen. They couldn't see him, but they could feel him through the bond. Dominic waved. Ges just stared.

Micah tried to shake the feeling that it was the last time he'd see them.

Amanda parked at the far end of the lodge road. If anyone approached, the plan was to pretend she was lost, but the whole place was still and quiet. She left the engine running as she got out of the car, opening the back door and pretending to search the back seat. Micah slipped out unseen, squeezing Amanda's shoulder in silent thanks as he passed.

Getting over the fence was easy, and then he was in the parking lot. He crossed the blacktop quickly, heading for the main doors. The place was decorated like a hunting lodge, all rough-hewn wood and antlers. Orange light spilled outside through plate glass windows. With any luck, the front doors would be unlocked.

Micah palmed the set of picks in his pocket. Dominic had been showing him how to work them for the last two days. He couldn't get through a modern lock, but he was fairly certain that handcuffs and cell doors were within his abilities.

He also had a pair of knives: one in his pocket and one strapped to the vest that Ges had liberated from Locke's guard.

Micah eyed the surveillance camera as he crept up the rough granite steps leading to the entryway. Cautiously, he tugged the worn wood handle of the door, almost letting out a sigh of relief when it opened. He released it, letting it swing shut. He pulled twice more, only a few inches each time, before finally drawing it open wide enough to slip through. With any luck, it would appear to the cameras as though the motion were due to an errant gust of wind.

The lobby continued the rustic theme, hunting trophies and warm lighting. A fire crackled in the granite fireplace, but the wooden reception counter had only one person working, and she hadn't noticed the door. Above him, Micah could see a darkened balcony, chairs, and tables, probably a restaurant of some kind.

Open hallways led off to either side, and he went left, choosing at random. He walked lightly, trying not to disturb anything. He didn't know the layout, but if he had to guess, he'd say he needed to head down.

It took ten of his thirty minutes to scout the full left wing. Nothing but conference halls and private rooms. Micah moved past them silently, not wanting to disturb the occupants. He was used to navigating in bare feet; his boots made it difficult to move quietly.

A door opened and Micah froze, afraid to risk the motion of pressing against the wall. They went the other way.

When he was certain he'd searched the whole left wing, he went back to the lobby. The receptionist was gone, and he crouched behind the reception desk, quickly unthreading his bootlaces.

Not a good idea, Dominic said. His voice was clear as a bell in Micah's head.

The place is designed for slave occupation, I'll be fine, he answered back, pulling the heavy shoes off and stuffing them into a corner of the desk.

If you need to run for it—

I'll have bigger problems, Micah interrupted, rising silently to his feet.

He crept into the right wing, immediately coming across a kitchen. There were three slaves here, busy preparing trays of hors d'oeuvres. They were dressed in simple tunics, and Micah didn't miss the bruises on their upper arms. One of them had a black eye. Micah grimaced in sympathy.

I guess that means we have the right place, he reported back. The other two didn't respond.

Beyond the kitchen were the rest of the facilities: laundry, housekeeping, and a recreation area for the slaves. It took Micah another five minutes to find the staircase to the lower level. It was behind a door, and Micah paused. He couldn't fake a gust of wind this time.

Taking a deep breath, he pushed it open.

There was no one behind it. No one had seen.

He slipped through and moved quickly down the stairs, bracing himself for what he would find. If the lower level was like the last one, he was about to walk straight into a carnival of misery.

The stairs ended in a set of warded fire doors, and for a moment, Micah feared they would be locked. He reached out, and the handle turned easily.

By the time he'd pushed it open, it was too late to run.

The door was yanked forward, out of his grip. Strong hands pulled at his clothes, jerking him forward into the room. Distantly, he heard the door at the top of the stairs bursting open; others were coming, cutting off his retreat.

He went for his knife then, drawing it from his vest and slashing at the men holding him. He caught one of them across the forearm, drawing blood.

"Son of a *bitch*!" the man shouted, and then Micah tasted blood as a fist came down hard against his cheek.

Someone kicked his knees out from under him, and he went down, dropping the knife. Someone kicked it, sending it skittering across the marble floor.

Micah could feel Dominic and Gestalt in his head, feel them watching as a boot caught him in the ribs, flipping him onto his back. He felt Amanda's diamond being yanked away. Micah wrapped his arms around his head, trying to protect his face from the blows. One of the men was laughing now. Micah breathed deep, sinking away from his body.

They'd do what they'd do. He couldn't fight them all.

I'm so sorry, Micah, Gestalt said, and he tried to reassure the angel that it was fine. He'd counted on this. Whoever these men were, they'd keep him alive until Slate could get there and deal with him—

He heard a click, and then his body turned to fire as electricity flowed through him. He could hear himself making a sound that wasn't a scream.

The blows suddenly stopped. The crowd around him parted, silently making way for someone.

"Welcome back," Slate said, grinning down at him.

Micah stared up with barely concealed terror. Already, he was recalculating, trying to find a way to turn this back to his advantage.

"We were expecting the angel," Slate said. "A little birdie told us he's after revenge."

"Well, you get *me*, you son of a bitch," Micah snapped, pushing himself up onto his elbows.

We tried, Ges said, and Micah could hear the defeat in his voice. *Brace for this. Pulling you out from this side of the warding is going to be . . . rousing.*

No, Micah sent back. *I can do this. I'm not dead yet.*

I'd rather keep you that way, Ges said, and there was an edge in his voice. Something came through the bond that, from anyone else, Micah might have called affection.

Someone kicked him, and he went back down with a groan. There was a low buzzing in his head that he assumed was Dominic.

I've got this, he assured him. *They think I'm here on my own. They won't start the cover-up yet.*

"Search him," Slate ordered. Two slaves stepped forward, grabbing Micah by the shoulders and yanking him up onto his knees. They stripped off the vest and patted the rest of him down, removing the picks and knife, as well as the burner phone he'd brought, just in case.

"I'm free. You can't hold me and you know it," Micah spat, staring defiantly up at Slate. The man laughed, grabbing Micah's wrist and yanking the sleeve of his shirt up to reveal his obscured tattoo.

"Someone gave you your voice back," Slate said, leaning down into Micah's face. "I'll have to fix that." He dropped Micah's wrist and grabbed his shirt collar with both hands, yanking hard. It tore easily, and someone whistled as the two slaves pulled the garment off.

Slate crouched down, running his fingers over Micah's chest.

"I remember putting my mark here, last time I saw you. Apparently I should've used something more permanent."

Micah closed his eyes as the men holding him yanked him to his feet. He wouldn't accomplish anything by fighting, not right now. He had to survive the first round, wait until they got bored. They'd put him away eventually, they always did. He just had to hold out until they got tired of him.

Hold on, Micah, we'll pull you out, Dom told him.

Not yet, Micah sent back. *If I go now, this whole thing falls apart.*

Dominic was protesting, too worked up for clear words. Micah took a deep breath, settling back into his training.

It'll be a while, now, Dominic. Rest. Be ready when I call.

Dominic's frustration echoed back to him, but Gestalt was there, doing his best to calm him. Micah listened to them, focusing on them, letting his captors do what they wanted.

His hands were shackled together and drawn high above his head, forcing him up onto the balls of his feet. His back was against a pillar of some kind, probably built for this purpose. Sharp points protruded from it at regular intervals, forcing Micah to arch his body away from the support. Almost immediately, the muscles of his back began to protest, but he ignored them. He could hold.

He listened to Gestalt's voice, the soothing cadence, telling him it would be fine.

Ever since the nightmares had started, Ges had been watching over him at night. More than once, Micah had awakened to find himself encircled by strong arms and dark wings, Gestalt murmuring to him in a language he didn't understand—

Someone slapped him, and he came back to the present with a start, the warmth of the angel's chest replaced by the ache of overstretched muscles.

Slate was pouring rubbing alcohol over what looked like a scalpel.

"Normally I'd get a doctor to do this," Slate was saying, "but we seem to have a shortage of those lately. As I'm sure you know."

Micah kept his mouth shut and his eyes forward. He remembered this. Slate would want him quiet—he could do that.

His breath caught as the wet blade pierced the skin of his chest, above his right nipple. Slate stared at him, his mouth twisted up in sadistic glee.

Micah focused on keeping his breathing even, not letting even a hiss of pain escape his lips as he was sliced again and again. He didn't need to look. He knew what would be written there.

Damaged goods.

Hot blood dripped down his belly, and he remembered the feel of Dominic's mouth, how the man had taken him to bed and kissed every inch of him. Like he was making a map. Like he was committing Micah's body to memory.

"I can't lose you," he'd whispered into the darkness, and Micah had pulled him close and promised that he wouldn't.

His chest burned like it was on fire, each carefully measured breath pulling at the incisions. Slate was finished, standing back to admire his work. One of the other men stepped forward, lifting the bottle of rubbing alcohol and pouring a liberal splash over the wounds.

Micah's vision turned red and white, every thought driven from his head by the pain of it, clawing through his body and mind. He realized he was hyperventilating and hoped against hope that he hadn't screamed.

"How quickly they forget," one of the other men said, shaking his head in mock disappointment.

"Shouldn't have let Godfrey talk me out of taking his tongue," Slate said.

Ah. So he *had* screamed, then.

Micah silently berated himself as he watched a woman come closer. It was the woman who'd straddled him the night he'd first disobeyed. She was holding a small black case, and with a bolt of panic, Micah recognized it.

Unzipping it quickly, she revealed a set of shining needles in their sterile wrappers.

She looked up at him, her eyes dark. "Free man, hmm?" she said in a high voice. "I think you just need a bit more training."

The first one went through his septum, threaded through with a gold ring that he could feel resting above his upper lip. The woman took pity on him, pushing the needle through skin but not bone. He sent her a silent thanks as he licked a drop of blood off his lip.

If she understood his gratitude, she didn't show it. Instead, she turned her attention to his chest, pinching his nipples until they stood in hard peaks.

Micah let his vision blur, his gaze still set straight forward. He didn't want to look and he didn't dare close his eyes. The leering faces of the people around him dissolved into soft masks. Someone moved to his side, rough hands moving over his skin. He didn't think about that, either.

She did the left first and Micah stopped breathing. He held the air in, not daring to inhale, as she replaced the needle with another gold ring. He could feel his heartbeat, throbbing hot and heavy and painful with each second that passed.

She pushed the needle through his right nipple and he exhaled, hoping it was silent and dreading the alternative. Very carefully he inhaled, letting air back into his lungs, trying to ignore the pain hammering through his body. His side was pounding where he'd been kicked.

The woman searched her case and returned with a gold chain. She held it up for Micah to see, and raised a couple chuckles at his confusion.

The mystery was solved a when she clipped the ends to the gold rings. Micah had only a moment to anticipate her intentions, and then she had hooked a finger through the chain and beckoned him closer.

She pulled with barely the strength of one finger, but the pain was enough to have Micah responding instantly, straining against his bonds to arch toward her. He couldn't hold the position more than a few seconds, and they both knew it. She met him halfway, leaning in to capture his mouth in a kiss, biting him hard and then releasing him.

He slumped back, unable to take his full weight off his toes, the spikes of the column still jutting painfully into his spine.

The woman turned to the crowd, raising her hands, drawing cheers as though she'd performed a magic trick.

"Ready for the fun part?" she asked them, and there was a general roar of approval. Micah guessed there were probably ten people here, maybe twenty.

This is turning into quite a party, he thought dully.

I'm so sorry, Gestalt told him, and he smiled at the sound of the angel's voice. There were hands on him again, pulling his jeans down over his hips. He grabbed the handcuff chains, quickly taking his weight onto his arms, keeping the cuffs from breaking his wrists when they stripped him naked. He'd expected this too. It didn't frighten him. He was accustomed to being seen without clothes.

He thought back to two days ago, when he'd gotten out of the shower and found Gestalt waiting for him. The angel had made love to him against a wall, holding Micah's weight easily, Micah's arms on his shoulders and legs wrapped around his hips. It wasn't until they'd finished that they realized Dominic was in the doorway, a grin on his face.

"Huh," the woman said. She was crouched down in front of Micah, absently fingering the piercing in his cock. "I would have bet money he'd have taken this out by now."

Micah bit back a grin, happy to have ruined it for them, if only this little bit.

The woman looked back to Slate. "What do you want me to do? It's already here. I can put in a wand . . ."

Slate strode forward, grabbing a fistful of Micah's hair and forcing his face up. "You think that's *funny*?" he snapped, and Micah let his face go blank, not wanting to antagonize him further. Slate searched his expression with a sneer. "Still think you're *free*?"

He caught the chain between two fingers, forcing Micah to lean closer. Micah was silent, but he knew Slate could see the pain on his face.

Slate chuckled, pulling harder, until Micah was sure the rings were about to tear free. "Still want to tell me I *can't*?"

Micah shook his head vehemently, knowing that was the reaction Slate wanted.

"You're the same as you've ever been." His voice was too low for the rest of the crowd to hear. "You say you're free and strong because those are the desires of the man who *fucked you last*." Micah stiffened beneath him, feeling his blood run cold. "He takes you to bed and you pretend to love it. Maybe even pretend to love *him*, because that's what he needs from you. I bet sometimes you even believe it. *That's how good you are*." Micah tried to shake his head, but Slate tightened his grip. "How convenient for him, to fall in love with exactly the man who could do this job for him." Slate's voice dropped lower, until Micah could barely hear it over his own heartbeat. "I bet coming here was your idea and everything. No. You're not free. And you never will be. You don't know *how*."

The words rang true, clear as a bell in Micah's head. Slate had seen what Gestalt and Dominic couldn't—

Inside him, the truth of Slate's words were cold and clear as ice. He turned toward the bond, the connection to the men outside, hoping to show them what he understood, but as soon as he did, there was a new truth.

Dom believed in him. Ges, too. Whatever fears Micah had about his own motivations, they were just that. Fears. If he could be free for Dominic, then he could be free for himself.

He could, and he would.

Slate laughed, releasing the chain. "I'm gonna pass you around like a fucking party favor," he growled into Micah's ear. "By the time I kill you, you'll forget you were *ever* free."

Micah's burst of fear was swallowed up in the pain of the needle penetrating him again. He bit his tongue trying not to scream, the familiar taste of blood filling his mouth. He didn't look, didn't want to see the metal bar through his flesh.

Slate turned back to the crowd.

"Who wants first go?"

Last chance to put the wall back up, he thought as his wrists were released and he was shoved to his knees. *There's no unseeing this.*

Dominic's response was instantaneous. *No. I'm not leaving you alone.*

I'm not alone.

Black silk dropped over Micah's eyes, tightening until there wasn't a scrap of light shining through. He told his body to be calm, pliant. Strong hands gripped his jaw, forcing his mouth open.

They used a ring gag on him, which he thought was a little insulting. He knew how to keep from using his teeth.

Someone pulled at his chain and he lurched forward, almost losing his balance. Someone else caught him by the hair, thrusting deep into his mouth as they did. With the ring in place, his participation was limited, so he focused on breathing. Slow and steady, in and out. This was familiar territory.

The man wasn't gentle with him, the head of his cock driving into Micah's throat, and Micah had to focus to keep from gagging on it. There were hands on his hips now, yanking back, pulling him up—

"Bring him over here," someone said, and he was dragged to his feet.

I'm sorry, he sent through the bond.

For what? came Dominic's instant response.

They pushed him down over a table, thankfully letting him lie on his back rather than his front. Someone grabbed his shoulders, tugging until his head hung over the edge. Even without the gag, Micah knew this was when he'd need his mouth open.

I'm sorry you had to see this, Micah answered.

Hands pulled his legs apart, and he forced his body to relax. He wasn't naïve enough to think they were going to prep him for this.

Someone shoved into his mouth, just as big, just as deep. It cut off his air, muffling his cry as someone else buried themselves between his legs.

Micah, no . . .

It wasn't as bad as it could have been. The man was wearing a condom, the lubrication working to lessen the pain. Micah didn't think this rated in the top ten. Not yet, anyway.

At least I don't have to look at them, Micah thought. In his place, Dom would probably have tried to make a joke.

If the others responded, he missed it. Someone had taken hold of the chain, lifting it ever so gently upward. Micah arched helplessly, trying to relieve the pressure. People held his arms down, limiting his motion, and the man between his legs groaned in pleasure as he squirmed. Micah wondered if it was Slate.

I'm going to kill them, Micah. If nothing else gets you through this—

Hush, Dominic. Gestalt's voice broke through Dominic's threat. Micah was grateful. Being angry wouldn't help him now. He was nothing right now. He was a hole, a void. He was pliable, he was formless. He was water, he was stone, he felt nothing.

He couldn't breathe.

His body hurt so much, but he was not his body, he was stronger than that, and he always had been.

His body twisted, trying to breathe.

He remembered home. He remembered holding Dominic in his arms, remembered watching Gestalt's face as the angel kissed him.

They'd take care of each other, Micah knew.

Micah?

They'd be fine.

MICAH!

"What's happening? Dominic, talk to me!"

Amanda wasn't sure whether she should shake him or just get out of his way. Dominic's brow was furrowed and his palms were pressed to his eyes.

"He's gone, I can't feel him at all— Ges! We need a Doorway!"

"He's not gone, he's unconscious," the daiyura said calmly. He was sitting cross-legged on the grass, his wings wrapped around him. "I can still feel him."

"Are you sure?"

Gestalt turned his face to Dominic, raising an eyebrow in a particularly human expression. "I'm sure."

"We need to go get him," Dominic declared. He grabbed the chalk they'd used to make the concealment spell and pressed it into Ges's hand. "We need a Doorway."

"He's waking up," Ges responded. He didn't attempt to take the chalk.

Dominic's eyes widened, and he pressed his palms to his face again, groaning. "We should never have sent him in there; I'm never going to forgive myself."

"What are they doing?" Ian asked hesitantly.

"You don't want to know," Dominic muttered.

Ges shot him a sharp glance. "They're doing exactly what Micah predicted they'd do," he said, still looking at Dominic. "Working through a fairly standard set of sexual sadomasochistic rituals. For all their power, they aren't particularly creative. It'll be over soon. He knows that."

Amanda and Ian exchanged glances. Gestalt closed his eyes again. His hands rested on his knees, and as they watched, his fingers tightened on the denim.

"None of this is new to him, Dominic," Ges said quietly. "Your distress isn't helping."

"No, that's bullshit. We need to get him out of there, and if you won't get me inside, I'll go myself."

"Dominic, wait—" Ian started, but he could have saved his breath. Dominic froze, pressing his hands to his eyes.

"Fuck," Dominic murmured. Gestalt shuddered, the small feathers along his shoulders standing on end.

"This might be more than he's used to," he admitted.

Dominic picked the chalk back up, pressing it into Ges's hand and forcing his fingers closed around it.

"You don't have to activate it," Dominic said hollowly, "but at least have it ready."

Ges looked up, meeting his eyes.

"What did you see?" Amanda asked.

"They're going to brand him," Dominic said, his voice getting higher as he talked.

Ges shifted onto his knees and began to draw.

Don't.

Micah wasn't sure if he was talking to Gestalt or Slate. He couldn't tell how much time had passed. He was still gagged, but he could breathe. His mouth tasted salty and bitter. His chest was bathed in fire, and he felt like someone had punched him in the gut.

Maybe they had.

He wasn't going to think about that.

We're going to get you out of there, Micah, hold tight—

No! He squeezed his eyes shut, trying to block out what Slate had been showing him. *I can hold. Don't come anywhere near this, I don't want you anywhere near this—*

His hands twitched in their bindings, a memory of the first time he'd tapped out of a fight and been told no. No, his job was to see it through, and he would. Everything rested on this, people were depending on him, *Ges* was depending on him, and he wasn't quitting just because it was gonna *hurt* a little.

The stylized *A* was glowing red, and Slate examined it with glee as it began to smoke.

"I got it for the angel, of course. Figured if I was going to have to mark him up again, might as well do it in style." He twisted the brand around in his fingers, watching it turn. He cut his eyes back to Micah. "There's an *S* too."

This is going to knock me out, I think.

"Fucking hell, Ges, *open the Door*!"

"Not until he asks."

"He won't ask, Gestalt, it's *Micah* we're talking about—"

"Then you should know he knows his limits."

Dominic closed his eyes, listening to Micah. He couldn't see everything Micah saw, only what Micah was focused on. The glowing *A* turning slowly in the dark. He could feel Micah's fear and the pain, but distantly. Like a memory.

"He doesn't *have* limits."

"You aren't hearing me." Gestalt stood, leaving the chalk markings. Dominic had begun pacing. "There are decisions you're given to make. This isn't one of them."

"This isn't *sex*, Ges, this is torture, I didn't send him in there to be *tortured*."

"You didn't send him in at all. He went on his own. *He's* the one weighing the risks here."

"But I'm responsible for him, he's mine—"

Ges was in front of him in three steps, taking his shoulders and pushing him back against the car. "Look at me, Dominic. Listen to my words. *Micah walked through that door knowing what would happen to him.*"

Dominic gaped. "But . . . he said sex. He said they'd—"

Ges's eyes were soft as he leaned in, pressing a chaste kiss to Dominic's mouth. "Because he knew if he told you the truth, you'd protect him."

"Two strikes," Slate instructed, handing the brand over.

Of course he wasn't going to do his own dirty work, Micah thought bitterly. He tried shifting minutely, just to reassure himself that he couldn't.

The tabletop felt rough against his torn skin, and the piercings were points of fire where he was forced to rest his weight on them. His hands were bound behind his back now, wrist to elbow. Easier to hold him still, he assumed.

Slate approached him, stepping out of Micah's vision as he trailed a hand down his captive's back. He paused at the curve of Micah's ass, then drew back and slapped him hard, across the top of his right cheek.

"Right there," Slate said smugly. "Right on that red mark."

The man with the brand nodded, disappearing from Micah's vision.

Strong hands held his hips and thighs, immobilizing him. Someone put their hand over his mouth, and Micah was grateful. He didn't think he could be quiet for this.

Last thing, he thought desperately. *Last thing. They always save the worst for last.*

He was beginning to hyperventilate. He could feel the heat of the brand as the man positioned it over his skin.

Last thing—

The brand pressed into his flesh, and he screamed, bucking up against the people who held him. He couldn't help it, couldn't stop the tortured cries escaping his throat.

The man was pressing down hard, and counting. Micah didn't know what to.

Infinity, maybe.

Dominic—

The brand lifted off his skin with a wet hiss, and Micah let out a sob. He wanted to thrash, but he didn't dare move. Moving would make it worse.

"Perfect," he heard Slate say. "Now do the other one."

CHAPTER TWENTY

"He's out," Gestalt said quietly. He'd returned to drawing his chalk Doorway. Amanda was crouched beside him, watching with interest as he formed the sigils. "They'll be moving him to the cells now."

Ian was sitting in his car, thumbing his radio and watching the stars.

Dominic was sitting on the blacktop beside his car. He'd been there since the first brand had touched. His arms were folded over his knees, his forehead resting on his forearms.

Amanda angled her head toward Dom. "Is he okay?"

"He's not used to being helpless. This is new to him."

"I can hear you," Dominic called, not lifting his head.

"And I, you," Ges agreed, nodding. He completed the last of the sigils and dropped the chalk. "It's ready. It's linked to Micah, so once he breaks the warding, we'll be able to get to where he is."

Dominic turned his head toward Ges. "Assuming that he'll get the chance. Assuming he isn't gonna wake back up to more of the same."

Gestalt shook his head. "No. Micah's experiences are the same as mine. They've been at it for more than an hour. By now they're beginning to get bored, and their victim is beginning to weaken. The branding is the grand finale before they move on to something else. He'll have a few hours to recover and be fresh for the next session." Ges paused. "Relatively speaking."

Dominic put his head back on his arms and groaned.

Micah did not want to wake up. It was dark where he was, and cool. Someone was singing to him.

He was being carried. Two people. An arm over each of them.

His feet dragged along the ground. He didn't bother trying to catch his balance. He wasn't sure he could stand, let alone walk.

The person on his left stumbled, pulling him off-balance, and he hissed in pain as the scabs across his chest tore open.

"God, I'm sorry," the person exclaimed. A woman. In a minute, Micah would open his eyes to look at her.

A minute.

"Who'd you piss off, kid?" the other person asked him. This was a guy. Older guy.

"Slay," Micah muttered. A drop of blood ran down his chest. He was having trouble forming words.

"Sounds about right," the guy answered. "Don't die on us, kid. I don't wanna end up in your place."

Micah opened his eyes, content to watch the floor passing by. It was no longer flagstones or marble; this was linoleum, the cheap pebbled stuff that could be cleaned with a hose, which meant—

I made it.

"We gotta go," he muttered, pulling ineffectively at his captors. "We have to go."

"Dunno what you're thinking, but you're not going anywhere," the woman told him. She and the man were both dressed in plain cotton scrubs. No Signatures, which meant they weren't trained. And they had key rings, which meant overseers.

Micah let out a sigh of relief.

They came to a row of cells. Most of them were open or empty. No one looked out at them as they passed.

They stopped in front of an empty cell, and the man reached for his keyring. Micah's hand shot out, catching his wrist.

"There are monsters here, aren't there?" Micah asked. His mind was clearing, and he looked up into the man's dark brown eyes. "I mean real monsters. Creacon stuff."

The woman frowned. "What makes you say that?"

"Seen it before. Somewhere else . . ." He struggled to form the words that would make them understand. "It was raided; they killed *everyone.*"

"The cops?"

"The owners. Can't talk if you're dead."

The woman's grip tightened on his arm. "You're a liar."

"Bet your life on it?" Micah asked. His voice was gravel in his throat. He needed a drink. "I know for a fact there's at least one succubus here."

The two slaves exchanged glances. "Lucky guess. I think it's more likely you're looking for a chance to run," the man said.

Micah shook his head, the blood pounding through his brain as he did. He was so goddamn tired. "Leave me here. But take the others. As many as you can. At midnight, go north. The police will be waiting for you at the road."

The slaves exchanged another look. "Are you sure?" the woman asked quietly. "If we go, and we're caught—"

"Believe me, I know," Micah interrupted. "But if you stay, they'll kill you. All of you."

The woman bit her lip, considering. The man shook his head, turning the key in the lock and dragging Micah inside.

"We're not running. If it doesn't work and they catch us, we'll end up worse than you."

Micah lowered himself gingerly onto the cot. The letters on his right side pounded with each beat of his heart. He could feel the other two watching. Listening.

If he couldn't make these slaves understand, it was all for nothing.

He couldn't think.

In a minute.

"Please," Micah whispered. "Please, can I have some water?"

The man nodded. "You'll need some bandages too. Not that they won't be getting torn off in a few hours."

He and the woman exchanged another glance, and the man left.

"Is there . . ." Micah paused, trying to gather his thoughts. "I came looking for a gate. A Doorway. To a different place. It would be . . . There would be ikons surrounding it, warding . . ."

Her eyes widened, but she said nothing.

Micah pressed on. "Please, it's important. My friend . . . his life depends on me finding this thing. Anything you know. Please."

"How do you know that?" she hissed. "Nobody talks about that."

"My friend came through it. He told me. Please, where is it?"

The man reappeared, holding a cup of water. "The angel," he said. "You saw it?"

"He sent me here," Micah responded, reaching for the cup. It was soft silicone—unbreakable. Micah wondered if it was precautionary or a reaction to something a slave had done. The water was cool and tasteless; he'd half-expected the sour tang of the relaxants Slate had used in the past. "Thank you."

"We don't go near it," the woman said. Her voice had dropped to a low whisper. "They tried to push people through. To see the other side. It was awful. I've never heard screams like that."

Micah eyed her silently. She had the scars and bruises he was beginning to expect on the slaves here. He didn't doubt she'd heard a lot of screams in her life.

"What's your name?" he asked.

"Carol. That's Robert."

"Carol. I'm Micah. I came to warn you. The masters are going to kill you, unless you run. Soon."

"Bullshit," Robert muttered. "Prove it. Prove any of it." He turned to leave, catching Carol by the arm as he did. "Come on. Leave him to his delusions."

Micah closed his eyes, leaning his head back. The sound of the cell door locking echoed loud in his ears. He wanted to lay down, but it hurt to move. Instead, he settled for leaning his shoulders back against the painted cinderblock wall.

Tears gathered in his eyes.

I couldn't do it.

Ges's reply was instantaneous. *We have time yet, Micah.*

Dominic was silent, but Micah could feel the anger there, the frustration. *Dominic—*

You lied to me.

Micah rolled his shoulders back, feeling the scabs pull, letting Dominic's words sink in. *I had to. You couldn't know.*

You know I would never have agreed to this plan if you had been honest with me—

I asked you not to look. The tears spilled from Micah's eyes now, running down his bruised cheeks. Damaged goods. *This is what I'm good for, Dominic. This is my part to play. It always has been. I asked you not to look. I told you that you'd hate what you saw.*

Micah, I—

"Hey, you alive in there?"

Micah's eyes flew open, and he stared toward the door of the cell.

A young man was standing there. He couldn't have been more than nineteen, and Micah's heart broke to see him. The bruises on his bare hips indicated pretty clearly what kind of slave he was.

"Still breathing," Micah rasped. The water cup was empty.

"Were you telling the truth? About the cops waiting for us?"

"Yeah."

The boy bit his lip, refusing to meet Micah's eyes. "There's some messed-up shit that happens here," he said quietly.

"I know."

"A lot of 'em here haven't heard the gossip, but . . ." The boy looked up. "I've only been here a few weeks. I was free, before. And I heard people talking. There actually *have* been raids. In other places."

"They shut down other places like this," Micah said. "You were free. You *have* to know this is illegal."

The boy laughed. "I know that. I just didn't think anyone cared."

Micah struggled up into a sitting position. "People care. And they're coming. Trust me."

The boy eyed him warily. "Can you give me something? Anything I can show the others? They'll be too scared to run, not without some evidence."

Micah groaned, leaning back. "Give me half an hour. You talk to the others. Tell them to get ready. It'll take time to spread the word. Tell them midnight. Not sooner."

The boy nodded and disappeared from the cell door.

Micah let his head rest against the cinderblock.

He could deal with Dominic's rejection later.

We have half an hour. Half an hour to prove there'll be help from the outside. What do we do?

Gestalt sent a wordless assent. From Dominic, there was nothing.

The wall beside the bed was smooth, painted cinderblock. Micah brought his hand to his chest, smearing blood across his fingertips.

Wincing, he began to draw, re-creating the shape that Lilin had shown him in the motel room.

When it was complete, Micah spat on his hand and pressed it to the bloody brick, sparking the ikon with his mana. Somewhere in the manor, a warding icon turned to ash and vanished. Beside him, the bed creaked as Lilin's weight settled on it.

"You can get to her from here?" Micah asked without looking over. His hair fell across his face and he realized he was slumping forward.

"I got it," Lilin said. He paused. "You really do pay your debts, huh."

"Yeah." Micah hummed, too tired to nod. He slumped forward a little further. "I think one of my ribs might be broken."

The incubus stood, heading for the door. Then he paused. Micah heard footsteps as the little demon approached him.

"Full disclosure? I've picked up some extra energy checking in on you these last couple days."

"Sex demon, yeah," Micah said. He tilted his head, looking at the diminutive creature. "Makes sense."

"We're even on the favor," Lilin said, reaching out to touch Micah's knee. "But I figure you're due a little interest. For whatever good it'll do you."

Warmth bloomed in Micah's chest, dulling the pain somewhat. He opened his eyes. Lilin was gone.

Careful to breathe slowly, Micah got to work on the rest of the warding.

Amanda popped the trunk of her car, rummaging around until she found the box of books she was looking for.

"Are those . . . foam swords?" Dominic asked, raising an eyebrow.

"It's called LARPing, and it's cool," Amanda said distractedly, flipping through the book on the top. Whatever she was looking for, she didn't find it. She picked up another book, slapping it against Dominic's chest. "Look through this. We need something obvious and nondestructive."

"Why nondestructive?" Gestalt asked, coming to stand over Dominic's shoulder.

"Because if we blow a wall out, we could hurt somebody," Amanda answered.

"Not to mention, it would give the Hellfire boys a heads-up that we're coming," Ian added. "We'd lose the element of surprise, though not by much."

Gestalt looked unimpressed, but he accepted the book Amanda handed him.

"We could summon up a storm or something," Ian suggested, looking at the sky.

Amanda shook her head. "No, this needs to be obvious. And it needs to be obvious even in the basement."

Dominic frowned. "What about a spirit? An elemental, something ethereal we could send down to deliver a message?"

"They wouldn't be much more persuasive than Micah," Ges said. "This needs to come from the outside."

"Oh," Dominic said suddenly, slamming the book shut. "Oh, I'm an idiot. How much time do we have left?"

"Twenty minutes."

Dominic glanced at his watch.

"That should be plenty. Stay here. I'll be back."

Micah's jaw tightened as fingers brushed over the brand.

"Sorry," Carol murmured. "But if this gets infected, it'll probably kill you."

"If I live that long," Micah said.

Carol didn't respond, just kept applying the antibiotic cream. A bandage was waiting by her side. Micah hadn't been able to bring himself to look at the wound, but the bandage was six inches to a side. He couldn't seem to stop staring at that.

AS.

Adam Slate.

Never mind that, Micah, Gestalt told him. *Hold on a little longer. Fifteen minutes until this all starts. Be ready.*

As ready as possible, Micah thought. He still felt like shit, but at least he was awake now.

People kept wandering past the door to his cell, glancing at him as they passed. Micah didn't know if news was spreading or if they just wanted a look at the Hellfires' newest punching bag.

Carol handed him the cream.

"I assume you can do the piercings?"

"Yeah."

Micah picked up the washcloth she'd brought and tried to dab the worst of the blood off his face. Very gently, he felt the area around the gold hoop, trying not to disturb it. Every touch sent waves of pain shooting through his head.

He abandoned the exploration in favor of a hasty application of the ointment.

He was equally perfunctory about the new barbell through the head of his cock. He brushed the cream on quickly, then pulled on the scrub pants Carol had brought him.

More of the slaves walking past were fully dressed now too. Micah hoped that was a good sign.

"Do you think they'll go?" he asked quietly.

"Can you show them they'll be safe?" Carol was wrapping Micah's chest in a long bandage, and she didn't look at him when she spoke. "This isn't the worst the owners can do to us. Many of them would prefer to stay with the devil they know."

Ges? Dominic? Anything?

Yeah, I've got you covered, Dominic answered. He didn't elaborate. Micah didn't push.

"They'll be safe," Micah promised. "Will you help them? If you run? I saw some were locked in."

"The flight risks," Carol agreed. "I'll do what I can."

The boy from before was back again. He looked to Micah with wide eyes.

"Got anything for us, Stretch?"

Micah blinked.

Dominic?

Working on it.

Dominic moved through the woods as quietly as he could. The lodge was supplied by a single access road, and that was what he was following. The roadside was muddy, the trees crowding in on the narrow lane, but he didn't dare move to the center. He kept his eyes on the sky, when they weren't watching his feet.

It couldn't be far now.

"Everybody back to your damn bunks," Robert growled, coming down the hallway. Some slaves listened; most didn't. They were gathering by Micah's cell, murmuring to each other.

Like a flock of starlings, Micah thought. Waiting for the signal to fly.

"He's a fucking liar," someone hissed.

"He said they're going to kill us."

"Jess, I know for a fact you're supposed to be up in the ballroom," Robert snapped. "Move it, or I'll strap you myself."

"Word is spreading," Carol mumbled. She stood, moving to the door of Micah's cell. She unlocked it without looking at him.

"Head north," Micah said.

"That's it," Robert growled. "One more word outta you, and I'm gonna—"

Micah never found out what Robert would do, because at that second, the lights went out.

CHAPTER TWENTY-ONE

Dominic holstered his gun, staring up at the blown transformer. He'd put a dozen iron rounds through it, and a bullet had apparently lodged inside, because it was beginning to smoke and buzz.

He turned and headed back the way he'd come. His phone hummed against his thigh, and he glanced at the screen.

True to his word, Garrett was calling for all hands on deck.

Please tell me that was you?

Depends, did it just get really dark?

Gestalt listened to the humans babble, excited at their victory, apprehensive about what was to come.

He turned to Ian. "Things are beginning to move now. Can you take this from here?"

"The police will be waiting on the road, like Micah promised," Ian said, keying his radio again. "And some people Mia suggested we contact. Not to mention a few dozen free members of the NYU indentured autonomy movement. And their livestreams, of course. Just to make sure nothing goes awry."

These words meant nothing to Gestalt, but he relayed the information anyway. Whatever it meant, it pleased the two humans.

"Dominic says that if he were here, he would kiss you," he relayed to the detective.

Ian wrinkled his nose. "Tell him to keep his weird psychic ass away from me."

We might also be getting some visits from the electric company, Dominic added.

Hurry back, Ges told him. *The Door is ready when you arrive.*

Got it. Micah, you somewhere inconspicuous?

. . . You could say that.

The blackness had lasted only a few seconds before the emergency generator kicked in with a bang. Emergency lights lit up the hallway, casting a dull gloom over the assembled slaves.

"That's them," Micah said, breaking the silence.

"Good enough for me," the boy muttered, turning and disappearing through the crowd.

"North," Micah said again, looking at Carol. She turned from the dissipating crowd back to Micah.

"The thing you were talking about, the gate," she said finally. "It's here. Down this way. You take a left, the second right, and then right again. There's a metal door covered in wards. You can't miss it."

"I'm sure I can try," Micah answered.

Carol didn't smile. She looked to Robert instead. "You coming?"

"Hell no. I'm going back to my damn bunk before shit *really* starts going south."

"Hide under the mattress," Micah suggested, rising shakily to his feet. Vertigo hit him, and for a second he thought he'd fall, but he didn't. Instead he straightened, taking slow steps toward the door and the two overseers waiting there.

"Left, second right, right," he said.

Carol nodded. "It's locked," she apologized. "I don't have the key."

"I'll manage." He met her eye, giving her a nod. "Go with the others. And thank you."

Jennifer waited at the front desk, watching the glass doors. The main lights hadn't come back, and she didn't have instructions for this situation. She glanced nervously at the other slave, a strong young man on duty as a bellboy. She hadn't done anything, it was stupid to worry she'd done something wrong, but after last time . . .

Her fingers darted to the scar on her shoulder, and she forced her hand back to her lap.

The back door swung open and she flinched, but it wasn't one of the owners. It was a slave.

Two slaves.

"What are you guys doing up here?" the bellboy asked. "You know we aren't supposed to be topside unless we're on duty."

People were streaming upstairs faster now. Some stopped; most didn't.

"We've gotta go," one of them said, hurrying past. "There's going to be a raid."

"I'm supposed to stay," Jennifer said quietly, her eyes darting to the door. "I'm supposed to stay here."

"Suit yourself," the other said, shrugging, and then he was gone.

Jennifer huddled behind the desk, waiting for directions.

A moment later, the alarms started.

"That's not our jurisdiction," the woman on the line explained.

Ian rolled his eyes. "Trust me, this is gonna be *everyone's* jurisdiction today. You got medics? We're looking at probably a hundred and fifty cases of severe slave mistreatment before we're done."

The line was quiet for a moment.

"Sorry, *how* many?"

"One fifty. At least," Ian repeated, and hung up the phone. Immediately, he began dialing again.

He had at least twenty numbers, saved and ready, on top of the dozen people he'd trusted enough to notify in advance. He hadn't told them everything, of course, just that there was a development in the angel case and they'd best not make plans.

Now he was giving out details. Nearly seventy-five synchronous emails had gone out twenty minutes earlier, alerting police departments and emergency services all across the state that something was going down. It was almost midnight, which meant a lot of people would be getting called in unexpectedly, scrambling out of bed to make it here. It would be chaos, which would make a cover-up nearly impossible. There was no way to know how deep the corruption spread—but it couldn't be everyone. It couldn't be *everywhere.*

They just needed to contact the right person, one ray of light to break through the clouds, and this whole thing would explode.

Someone picked up on the other end, and Ian began to talk.

The hallway filled with flashing red lights, and a blaring siren cut into his head. Water poured from the ceiling, cold and stagnant, drenching Micah instantly.

He squeezed his hands over his ears and pressed on, ignoring it.

Someone had pulled a fire alarm, maybe to cover the exodus, maybe just to cause trouble.

The water quickly soaked through his shirt and the bandages beneath, but he ignored that, pressing on.

Left, second right, right.

"Made it!"

Dominic stumbled out of the woods, a little worse for wear. Amanda and Gestalt were bent over the chalk Doorway, reinforcing some of the sigils. Ian was already gone, off to help coordinate the forces that were arriving on the main road.

"He broke most of the warding but not all," Ges said. "I can get in, but we don't yet have a way out."

"I'll keep working on it in the meantime," Amanda said.

Gestalt looked to Dominic. "You ready?"

"As I'll ever be."

Micah, you ready for us?

As I'll ever be.

Gestalt pressed his palms to the blacktop and his magic pulsed through the ikons written there. He resisted the urge to look up at Dominic one last time. It was enough to feel him there, as the pavement blazed and swallowed them both.

They did not pass through the middle ground, the nowhere-place. Instead, one moment they were in the parking lot, and the next moment they were in a darkened basement, getting rained on.

"*Fuck* that's cold!" Dominic shouted, shaking the water out of his eyes. "A little warning next time?"

"Sorry," Micah muttered. He was leaning against the wall, soaked to the bone. He had blood blooming through his cotton shirt, and even from five feet away, Dominic could see Micah's teeth chattering.

"Oh, gods. C'mon. C'mere, put your weight on me."

Dominic helped Micah get an arm over his shoulders, hoisting him up. Micah's skin was cold to the touch, and Dominic began to worry seriously about blood loss.

"Ges, can you fix hi—"

Dominic turned slowly, trying not to jostle Micah too much.

"Ges?"

Gestalt stared at the gate. It was like glimpsing the sun through a pinhole, but even obscured, he could feel the warmth and power echoing through. He spread his wings in the empty room, letting them catch the light like solar panels. Water ran over his feathers, distorting the colors.

He could hear his brothers and sisters, just beyond the veil.

Home.

He closed his eyes, breathing out. Steadying himself. He wasn't making it home, he knew that.

He'd realized it the moment he'd almost been caught in the blackness inside Locke's Doorway.

There was no way to escape the cuffs while the gateway was open, and there was no way to close it from the outside. The containment magic would trap him in the not-space, and there—

Dominic's voice cut through the gathered voices. *Ges?*

I found it. Dominic, get Micah to safety, I need to do this alone.

Ges, he's hurt bad, I'm not sure he's gonna make it out of here.

Gestalt paused, focusing on Micah. He was in bad shape, and something inside Ges tugged. He could go to Micah, heal him, they could leave, come up with another plan, he could—

No. The gateway put power into the hands of people too dangerous to hold it, and he wasn't letting that continue, not matter *what* it cost. Micah hadn't made excuses; he wouldn't either.

He'll live.

How do you know? Where are you?

On the other side of the door. I sent you to Micah, help him.

Ges withdrew a small blade, using it to nick the tips of his middle and ring fingers. He dropped to the floor, drawing hastily on the smooth marble surface.

The floor was wet, the blood diluting into nothing as he wrote, but it didn't matter. Blood magic drew its power from life, and life could not be washed away.

"He's not coming. We've gotta go," Micah muttered, and Dominic was forced to concede the argument.

"Do you know how to get out?"

"Head back this way. There's stairs."

Their progress was slow. Micah was losing energy with each passing step.

They passed rows of empty cells, dozens of them. Roughly one in ten had a slave inside—not locked, not bound, just . . . waiting. The slaves looked at them with trepidation as they passed. Dominic didn't make eye contact. He kept his gaze straight ahead, focused on getting Micah to safety.

"It's still partly warded down here," he told Micah. He wasn't sure if the other man could even hear. "Once we get outside the warding, Amanda can get us the hell out of here. Okay? Just to the stairs. We just have to make it there."

Micah didn't respond. His face was down, hair streaming across his pale cheeks.

You there?

Yeah. I'm good. Keep going.

"*There* you are," a cold voice said.

Gestalt's head snapped up. He'd heard something.

He scanned the edges of the room, all marble pillars and heavy velvet curtains.

The fire alarms were still blaring, making it difficult to locate the sound he'd heard.

Nothing moved.

"Have you found the gateway yet?" Slate asked conversationally. Dominic didn't answer, just continued backing slowly down the hallway. Beside him, Micah was frozen, barely staying on his feet. Slate kept walking toward them.

"I'm guessing not," he continued. "Or you'd have found my little surprise. I pulled it through, just now, *just* for you. You'd be *amazed* at the Doors we can open. The things that come back."

"You've gone *through*," Micah breathed.

Slate's eyes flashed, and his grin had too many teeth.

Gestalt forced himself to be still, focusing on the room around him. The air currents, the water, the sounds beneath the alarm—

There it was.

The ground was cold beneath Carol's feet. She didn't have shoes; none of them did.

When she was a little girl, she'd read a book about rabbits on a journey. She imagined they must have looked like this. Quiet, frightened things, moving forward in fits and bursts.

The woman next to her tripped, and Carol caught her elbow, stopping her fall.

The woman gave her a smile.

Up ahead, red and blue lights began flashing through the trees.

Dominic reached for his gun, but Slate drew first.

"Where's the angel?"

"Go fuck yourself," Dominic answered.

Slate shot him.

The beast launched itself out of the darkness, or maybe it *was* the darkness, Gestalt couldn't tell. It seemed to destroy light, but at the same time, he had the distinct impression of *sharp*.

It barreled toward him with a howl and he dodged, reaching out and striking it as it passed.

The attack landed, Gestalt's power flowing through his hands and burning its skin.

It howled again, ricocheted off a far wall, and pounded back toward him faster than he could have imagined. He spread his wings, but he was too late.

Micah's ears rang with the echo of the gunshot.

In his mind, he could see Gestalt fighting off some monstrosity.

He could see Slate smiling at him, a crazy, broken smile full of too-sharp teeth.

Dominic's support was gone. Micah couldn't lean on him.

He stumbled to catch his balance as Dominic went down, slow as molasses, blood already blooming red across the belly of his shirt.

"You three have been *such* a pain in my ass," Slate said.

Gestalt shoved the beast off him, rolling onto his belly and pawing at the ground, trying to finish the sigils. Two more ikons would complete the spell, he only needed two more—

The thing landed on his back hard, jaws closing on his wing with a sickening crunch.

Gestalt screamed in pain, immediately writing the wing off. Agony jarred through his body as the thing gnawed at him.

Micah's voice exploded through his mind, a picture of Dominic, a crimson stain spreading like a starburst. Ges's heart dropped as he searched for Dominic's mind in the chaos—

"Leave him," Slate ordered, gesturing for Micah to come closer. "The monsters will finish him off soon enough."

An inch of water covered the floor, turning red with Dominic's blood. Micah stared blankly, his thoughts frozen.

Then he dropped to his knees with a splash, pressing his hands against the wound, trying to staunch the flow. Blood flooded over his hands.

"*Ges*! *Help me*!"

Ges rolled hard, his wing tearing as he wrenched it from the monster's grip. He reached out, plunging his hands into the darkness, screaming in pain and anger as he shoved his power through the beast. It writhed and twisted, clawing at him, drawing deep gouges down his face and chest, but it couldn't withstand him forever.

It collapsed on top of him, hot and wet and heavy and stinking like the pits of hell. Gestalt shoved it off, not bothering to check for life. It wasn't dead. The concept didn't apply, not to a thing like this. He only had a few seconds before it was up again.

Somewhere in the distance, Micah was screaming his name.

Dominic was dying.

Ges closed his eyes, trying in vain to block what Micah was seeing. Dominic's blood blurred into the blood on his own hands. There wasn't time to mourn. He couldn't help Dom. He *might* be able to save Micah. The beast stirred as he scribbled the last few lines of the ikon, the blood's power beginning to thrum through his body. Groaning, he hauled himself to his feet, healing just enough to keep the avatar moving.

The gate's hold on this realm was faltering; it stood taut, like a mousetrap, ready to snap shut at any second.

Over the sounds of the alarms, Gestalt heard singing.

Dominic's blood was hot on Micah's hands, and until he felt it, Micah hadn't realized how cold he'd been. He could hear Slate coming toward him, sloshing through the bloody water. His fists tightened on Dominic's clothes.

A roar echoed down the hallway, followed by a scream.

"You let them out," Micah realized, looking to Slate in horror.

"Our little menagerie. I thought they might slow you down." Slate stood at an odd angle. Beneath his cheek, something slithered like a worm. He raised the gun, leveling it with Micah's eyes. Water dripped off the barrel.

Micah didn't blink.

Slate pulled the trigger.

The creature rose to its full height, growling at Gestalt.

Gestalt growled back.

They circled each other, Gestalt edging ever closer to the gate. He could feel Micah's fear, Dominic's ebbing vitality, but they seemed pale and far away.

He couldn't get to them. Not now. Not with the beast on his heels.

His fingers brushed the edge of the gateway, and he turned, staring into the blackness of the nowhere-place between the realms. The band around his wrist shifted, pulled inexorably toward the power of its home.

Once inside, there would be no leaving. That was the spell Lilin had given him. The first time he'd tried to close the portal, the humans' magic had fed it, allowed it to resist him. This time, it would be cut off, the power of their blood trapped inside.

Theirs, and his.

The sounds of home flooded through the gateway like a river. Gestalt closed his eyes and breathed it in, letting his hands rest against the edges of the Door.

Behind him, the beast charged, and Gestalt waited for the impact that would carry them both into oblivion.

The barrel roared as Micah lunged, leaving his left ear ringing as the bullet passed harmlessly over his shoulder. He was younger and experienced, but Slate was fresh. Micah tackled him backward into the water, wrestling the gun away and heaving it down the darkened hallway when the trigger did nothing. They rolled once, Micah coming out on top, straddling his former owner like a sick parody. His hands closed around Slate's throat.

Slate reached down and squeezed, digging his fingers into the fresh brand. Micah screamed, his grip momentarily lost. Slate didn't hesitate, just rolled them over, landing a fist hard into the side of Micah's face. Micah cried out, falling backward.

Slate tutted.

"And to think, you were my favorite once."

Jennifer watched the glass doors.

She'd stayed at her post, even when the alarms had gone off and the water had started to fall.

Now she sat on the chair, her knees pulled to her chest, and watched the men advancing up the front steps. They were dressed in black. Some of them had badges. One of them had a dog, a big mean-looking thing.

They pushed through the doors with guns drawn, fanning in all directions.

She didn't like the look of the dog.

"Welcome to Greater Banks Lodge," she said through chattering teeth. "How can I help you?"

Someone approached her, and she did her best to smile. It was important to always smile for the guests.

"I'd like you to come outside now, ma'am," the man in black said to her.

She nodded. She could go outside.

Micah went down hard, Slate coming down on top of him, his face inches from Micah's. Something dark slithered lazily in the iris of one hateful gray eye.

Micah's vision was getting dark at the edges. He thought he was bleeding again, but that might have been Dominic's blood. His shirt rucked up. Everywhere he wasn't bandaged, bruises were spreading across his belly, dark blotches he didn't like the look of at all.

He brought a knee up into Slate's groin, and the other man screamed. Micah took advantage of the distraction to scramble backward, back toward Dominic. Slate stayed doubled over, retching.

Micah couldn't feel Dominic in his mind anymore. He scrabbled at the bond, but Dominic was gone.

Gestalt! Ges, please!

The angel didn't respond. When Micah reached for him, all he saw was darkness. A cold icier than he'd ever felt. And the sound of singing.

Micah reached Dominic's body and didn't hesitate, just began searching through his pockets. True to form, Dom had a foil med pack in his thigh pocket, and Micah could have cried with relief. He cracked it even as he tore the foil open, pressing it against the hole in Dominic's shirt.

Work, Micah willed it. He lifted Dom's arm, using one limp hand to pin the pack in place. *He's alive, and you can* work.

He didn't have time to watch and find out. Dom's gun was soaked, So Micah went for the knife on his belt. Micah's fingers trembled as he struggled to unfold the blade. He couldn't focus his eyes.

Behind him, Slate stood with a growl.

Fifteen years on the force, and Chris Phillips had never seen anything like this.

The ground floor was bad enough.. The whole parking lot was filled with soaked lodge patrons.

There was a triage post set up on the front lawn, separating the indents from their well-to-do holders. For his part, Chris was trying to figure out what the hell had been going on in the basement.

They had found the stairs just as the door burst open, a dozen people rushing up at them. Most of them had indents in tow: beaten, starved things that had made Chris wince in sympathy. He didn't ask what they had been doing. He was more interested in getting them up and out of the building without crushing each other in their panic.

He was concerned by the variety of bite marks he was seeing on the panicked group. He caught an indent by the arm, gesturing to the bleeding wound. She just shook her head.

"Don't go down there."

Chris nodded and let her go. She hurried toward the main doors and he keyed his radio.

"We're gonna need creacon down here. Something's gotten loose." He paused. "Maybe several somethings."

Ges, he's dying. I can't feel him anymore. Ges, please, please, I need you. Don't let him die.

Micah's blade flicked open and he turned, brandishing it at Slate's approaching form. In the distance, he could hear screams and growling. He thought of the slaves who had stayed in their cells, waiting silently for their master's orders.

Slate eyed the blade, circling cautiously to Micah's side.

Micah turned his thoughts away from the dying. He couldn't help them now.

Slate grabbed for him, and Micah lashed out. He might have drawn blood. There was too much to tell now.

Darkness was spreading across Micah's vision. He stayed between Slate and Dominic, holding his ground.

Ges would come.

He reached for the angel again, but all he got back was a flash of grim determination. Resignation and regret.

It's too late.

Darkness.

Micah grit his teeth, keeping his eyes on Slate. The other man was inching closer. He knew Micah was faltering.

Even if I win this, I can't fight what's coming after, Micah pleaded. *I can't protect him.*

Slate lunged, and Micah rose to meet him. Slate hadn't anticipated a counterattack—his eyes widened as Micah's blade disappeared between two ribs. Micah grit his teeth again and *twisted*, feeling the scrape of bone as dark blood spurted over his hands.

Slate staggered back, gasping.

I'm sorry, Micah.

Claws dug into Ges's shoulders and then—

Micah's vision filled with a flash of violet, burning out the darkness, the hallway, the dying man in front of him. He couldn't breathe.

He dropped to his knees, gagging. His mouth tasted like blood. He was hit with a wave of vertigo and he pulled back, trying to understand what was happening to Ges.

Someone was screaming as pain flooded through the bond, fire scorching down to the marrow of Micah's bones.

Slate. Slate was screaming, the veins beneath his skin burning red and then black, a cascade of ash spilling from the wound in his chest.

Micah let himself collapse then, sliding back into the dirty water, landing on his back, too tired to care that he was soaked and shivering. Everything hurt, but that didn't matter now.

Ges's light had vanished, and as the darkness closed over him, Micah was alone.

CHAPTER TWENTY-TWO

Thirty-six minutes into the raid, the crowd outside went into an uproar as twenty-two people simultaneously clutched at their throats and collapsed. They were dead before they hit the ground, their veins burning a dull red in the morning gloom. Across the country, forty-seven more died under similar circumstances, plus at least sixteen overseas.

Gestalt had been right about the bond magic, not that anyone would ever really know the full story.

It took fourteen hours for creacon to clear the whole facility. Inside, the human body count totaled around thirty people, about half of them slaves that had stayed behind rather than run. The rest were owners, killed in the midst of a variety of activities that their heirs and estates would later vigorously deny. To the best of anyone's knowledge, none of the creatures ever made it out of the basement.

A consensus was never reached on how they'd been released. Slate had been responsible for at least a few, but on closer examination, many of the cages had been forced open. Maybe the slaves had freed them to cover their own escape, or maybe some of the creatures had stopped to help one another. Nobody ever found out.

Six hours after breaching the basement doors, a team of creature controllers found three bodies laid out in a hallway. The controllers moved them to the side, and were ready to leave them for the coroner, when one of them moved. He reached out and grabbed on to a controller's wrist, staring into his eyes with surprising determination.

"Help Dominic," he'd said, before dropping back into unconsciousness.

Or, at least, that was how Micah heard the story later. He didn't remember any of it.

He didn't remember the EMTs loading them onto gurneys or getting them outside. He didn't remember Ian identifying him, or Amanda rushing to his side to lay a healing poultice across the black skin of his abdomen.

They visited him later, with news. Updates.

Micah asked about the room Carol had directed him to, the room with the gate. He had to make several long phone calls on the topic, but in the end, he got the report from the controllers that had cleared it.

The room had been trashed and empty. No gate, no angel, no creatures, nothing. Just a lot of blood, some feathers, and five silver bangles, lying forgotten on the wet floor.

Micah thanked them and hung up.

He sunk back into the chair and listened to the beeping of the monitors and resisted the urge to hurl the phone into the wall.

Gestalt was gone.

That had been six days ago.

Dominic was not improving.

Micah knew it, the nurses who kept coming to check on him knew it, hell, even the other slaves knew it.

The whole wing was full of them, three or four to a room, while they recovered. There was semi-permanent emergency lodging set up nearby for anyone well enough to be discharged. The authorities couldn't figure out what to do with them. Their holders were mostly dead, and the estates of the deceased were doing everything possible to sweep them under various rugs as fast as possible. Many had been functionally seized as evidence in a boondoggle of interwoven civil cases, not the least of which was a class action suit filed by the New York Civil Liberty Union (with help from the local members of the Indent Autonomy movement) seeking to invalidate their indentured status. They'd petitioned the government to void their contracts on the grounds of negligence and gross violation of terms.

Micah wished them luck with that.

He listened when Carol came in to talk to him, and that was mostly what she talked about. They didn't talk about the place they had been, or what had happened there. Carol didn't ask him to get off the floor. She sat in the chair to Dominic's side and talked to Micah as though it were perfectly normal for him to be kneeling at the foot of the bed.

Keeping vigil, is how Micah thought of it. For when Dominic woke up.

It was very quiet inside his head.

He hadn't realized how acclimated he'd become to the others, until they were gone. He still reached for Dominic. He listened for Ges.

But it was all silence.

The nurses weren't sure what to do about Micah.

They came every few hours to change Dominic's IV or check the catheter or move Dominic around so he wouldn't get bedsores. They tried to check on Micah too, but he waved them off.

Before she'd gone home to Selina, Amanda had made a set of poultices and made Micah promise to use them. They'd helped his scars heal faster. The letters on his chest and back were now the puffy red of a year's healing, rather than a week. Even still, they couldn't heal him completely. The scars would always be there, fading more with each passing year but never gone.

Micah thought that was all right. He'd taken the jewelry out, but he thought maybe it was best if the words stayed.

If Dominic had seen them, all those months ago, maybe he'd have walked away.

He wouldn't be lying here now, surrounded by tubes and monitors.

"*Damaged goods*," he told Dominic. "Good for no one."

Dominic didn't respond.

The other slaves brought things. They didn't come in, didn't dare. But as rumors spread, gifts started appearing by the door. Drawings.

Bread rolls. Notes. Little cups of pudding or fruit. Pills, sometimes, until the nurses realized what was happening.

Micah collected them from the hallway and brought them to Dominic. He piled them into a makeshift shrine, covering the bedside table so Dominic would see them when he woke up.

Dominic did not wake up.

After eight days, someone came to talk to Micah about palliative care.

Dominic might not wake up for a long time, they said. He was unlikely to wake up at all. The doctors were doing what they could, but medicine and magic both had their limits.

Micah knelt silently by the foot of the bed, watching.

Micah didn't have power of attorney, they said. He had the opportunity to voice an opinion on what happened, but at the end of the day, Dominic couldn't stay where he was forever.

He wasn't really *living*, they said.

They left pamphlets, which Micah didn't look at. Whoever was making decisions for Dominic now, it shouldn't be him. *Anyone* was better than him.

Time passed inconsistently, fast then slow.

Micah thought he was probably sleeping more than he used to. He had new nightmares, where he was home again. Dominic and Ges were safe and whole but even looking at them he knew they were shadows of a reality where—

He woke to silence and the sound of monitors beeping.

One of the nurses bullied him back into his own bed. She was concerned that he'd reopened something, that he was bleeding into his abdominal cavity again. She made him sit still while she wrapped a complicated pattern of ikon tape around his torso.

When she left, he returned to the foot of Dominic's bed.

After ten days, they sent a grief counselor. She told Micah that loss was a natural part of life. She said that he needed to focus on moving forward. On returning to his normal life, without Dominic.

Micah was too tired to laugh.

Which normal life? The one where he was a pet, treasured by people who would trade him away without saying goodbye? Or the one where people told him he was worthy of love and then got killed for their mistake?

The counselor wanted to know when he'd eaten last. She sounded worried.

Micah hadn't thought about it.

Turkey sandwich, he decided at last. The taste had made him sick. He hadn't been hungry since then. He didn't tell the counselor this. He didn't want anyone coming in here to force food down his throat.

Dominic was getting his meals through an IV. Because of Micah.

I wish you'd never bought me, Micah told him. *They'd have sent me to a work camp and it would be me dying, not you.*

Dominic didn't answer. Eventually, the counselor went away.

On the twelfth night, Micah dreamed of light.

Hello, Micah.

Micah relaxed, letting himself smile. *Hey, Ges.*

He had this dream a lot. It was second only to the one where Dominic was awake again.

Where are you?

Still at the hospital, Micah answered. *Waiting for Dominic to wake up.*

The dream-Ges nodded. He looked bigger, in Micah's mind. More solid. His wings spread from his back in a wash of stygian purple.

Is this what you look like? Micah asked. *Back in your own world?*

Gestalt reached for Micah, drawing him close, stroking his hair back. Micah let his forehead rest against Ges's shoulder. He didn't trust himself to embrace the angel.

Dominic's dying, Micah said quietly. His throat felt tight. He hadn't said it out loud, not yet.

I know, Gestalt answered. His wings were warm, circling around Micah's shoulders. *I'm sorry.*

I can't help him.

No, Ges agreed, and Micah felt something break inside himself. He put his arms around Gestalt, his shoulders hitching as he started to cry.

What do I do, Ges?

Gestalt waited a moment, then pressed his lips to the top of Micah's head.

Wait for me.

It wasn't a dream, Micah insisted. He insisted to Carol, he insisted to the nurses, he insisted to the grief counselor when she came back.

It wasn't a dream.

Two days after that, the counselor returned with a pair of orderlies. She was worried about Micah's mental state and it had been decided that he would benefit from medical intervention.

Micah stood, forcing his weakened body into a defensive stance, and swore on his life that he was going nowhere. He was going to see this through to whatever end may come.

The counselor said she understood, that it was difficult to move on from a life in which someone else figured prominently. She said lots of people thought they couldn't cope, and many of them clung to the expectation that their loved one would be granted a miracle. It wasn't realistic, she told him, and one of the orderlies reached for Micah's arm.

Micah jerked back, raising his hands to protect his center. They were here for him, but he shifted slightly anyway, putting Dominic behind him.

"I'm not leaving him," he said flatly.

One of the orderlies rolled up his sleeves. Micah centered himself, ready for whatever came.

And that was when the doorframe exploded inward.

Thank the gods, Micah thought. For two weeks, he'd been holding his reality together with willpower alone, wondering whether his mind or body would collapse first, waiting for something to change. He'd hung his future on a dream that didn't feel like a dream. Now, one way or another, it was all over.

Ges stepped out of the nothing and into the room, shaking smoking wood chips from his messy hair.

Micah let go, falling to his knees like a puppet without strings. Distantly, he wondered if this was the dream again. If it was, he found himself without the energy to care.

The angel looked different, a little bit. The angle of his jaw, the set of his eyes. His skin was slightly darker, and his wings appeared as black etchings, wrapped around his shoulders and down his arms. Micah's mark was gone from his chest, and Dominic's from his arm.

He was also completely naked.

He smiled. "Hello, Micah."

Micah smiled back. "Hey, Ges."

The angel tilted his head. "You do not look well."

Micah laughed. It wasn't a good laugh. "That's what they tell me."

Ges crossed the room in silence, passing the counselor and the orderlies without acknowledgment. They gaped at him but didn't comment. He knelt in front of Micah, reaching out to stroke his fingers across the other man's cheek.

For a moment, the only sound was the beeping of the monitors and the crackling of the ruined doorframe.

"They've marked you again," Ges noted, indicating Micah's bandaged chest.

Micah blinked burning eyes. "It's a warning."

"Hmm," Ges answered. "May I take it away?"

Micah waved him off. "Don't bother with me. Dominic needs you."

"Dominic can sleep another few minutes." Gestalt looked up into Micah's eyes, pushing hair out of his face. "It hurt him terribly to see what they did to you."

"I know." Micah glanced toward the bed, wiping his eyes. "That's why I'm keeping them. They're an apology. So when he wakes up, he knows I'm sorry. That I've been punished for lying to him."

Ges nodded once. "Would he punish you that way? If he were awake?"

Micah paused, trying to rationalize, then shook his head.

"You must decide, then," Gestalt murmured, "whether you hate yourself more than he loves you."

"I need to pay for this," Micah protested, his throat going tight. Gestalt's light was filling his mind now, bright and ultraviolet, burning away the darkness that had followed Micah since he'd woken up here.

He couldn't explain it to Ges, the same way he couldn't explain to Amanda or Carol or the nurses. Couldn't make them understand that this whole mess was *someone's* burden. If he didn't shoulder it, someone else would have to. If he wasn't punished for failing, then *things could not get better.*

Ges pressed his lips to Micah's brow. "Micah, you have paid for a hundredfold more wrongs than you have ever committed. Dominic wasn't angry that you lied. He was angry that they'd hurt you. And he was devastated that he couldn't save you."

For the second time, Micah let his forehead rest on Ges's shoulder. His throat burned, and his cheeks were wet. When Micah reached out, he could feel the bond there, thrumming with life.

"If you care for my opinion," Gestalt told him, turning his head to whisper in Micah's ear, "I'd want to see you unmarred, your skin as perfect as your soul."

Micah choked on his protest, his body finally refusing to take it anymore. A violent sob wracked through him, and Ges's arms came up around him, encircling him almost hesitantly. The motion almost set Micah laughing, because here was this being, older than time and unsure how to hug, pressing warm and soft into his soul and telling him he was *loved.*

Micah exhaled, slowly, and gave himself permission to believe it.

"Take them away, then," he said quietly. "Just let him wake up."

Gestalt breathed, and Micah felt cold prickles radiating from the angel's fingers.

Dominic opened his eyes and was instantly alert.

The ceiling wasn't the ceiling he'd been staring at when he passed out. It was dry, for one thing.

He sat up, taking in the room. Three strangers were staring at him in barely disguised shock. Micah was by the foot of the bed, dressed in a plain T-shirt and looking significantly more haggard than usual.

And then there was Ges, standing with his fingers resting gently on Dominic's arm, utterly comfortable with the fact that he was naked.

Dominic blinked, shifting minutely in bed. "Uh . . . how long was I out?"

"Two weeks," Micah answered immediately. His voice was uncharacteristically rough.

Dominic reached for him through the bond, almost reflexively, trying to stem the waves of pain coming off his lover.

Micah smiled, dropping his eyes and waving him off.

"Not to be that guy," Dominic said, addressing the strangers, "but can somebody call me a nurse? Because I feel like I've got a tube in my dick, and it's way too early for that."

One of them stammered and backed out of the room, avoiding eye contact as he did. The other two followed after, mumbling sheepishly about giving them a moment.

"They didn't think you were coming back," Micah explained. He was grinning openly now, wiping at his eyes as he talked. "I kept telling them, but no one believed me."

Now it was Ges's turn to look down. "I apologize for that. My avatar was destroyed working Lilin's spell; the blood caught fire. It was rather unpleasant. I had to rebuild it from scratch."

"Oh!" Dominic said, sitting up fully now. "What happened? Everything after I got shot."

Ges frowned. "There was some kind of creature waiting by the gate. I don't know what it was; I do know that it didn't belong anywhere near humans. I think maybe the Hellfires were meddling in worlds other than mine. It very nearly stopped me from finishing the spell. I had to force it through the gateway to destroy it, but then I was trapped inside as well. I was able to release the suppression bands, but my avatar was immolated in the process."

"You don't need one on the other side, though, right?" Micah asked.

"I need it on this side," Gestalt answered simply.

Dominic frowned. "So then, what, you kept the gate from closing so you'd have time to rebuild your avatar?"

Gestalt fixed him with a stare. "The gate is closed," he said levelly. "I don't think it will be possible to reopen it from this side."

Dominic opened his mouth to protest, then closed it again. Gestalt was still staring at him, the implications of his words burning clear through the bond.

"You can't get home?" Micah asked, looking stricken. Dominic suddenly had a memory of Micah, standing in their kitchen. His hair was tied half-up, and he was saying something as the smell of cinnamon filled the air. He turned his head, breaking into a smile, and Dominic realized with a start that the memory wasn't his. He was *in* it, coming up behind Micah to press a kiss to his shoulder.

"You stayed to save my life," Dom said quietly. "Shit, Ges."

"I've grown fond of you," the daiyura said with a shrug. Something slipped through the bond that made Dominic think suddenly, inexplicably, of his father. Then it was gone. "And Micah likes you. If it makes you feel better, I didn't expect to survive at all."

"*What*?" Micah asked, taking Ges by the shoulder.

Dominic's response was interrupted by the arrival of the doctor. She came in very much surprised to see that her patient was not only conscious but actually speaking in full sentences.

There had been, Dominic gathered, quite a bit of brain damage.

Something about a massive amount of blood loss and blunt force trauma to the head, probably from when he fell.

Someone got Gestalt a hospital gown, which he stared at in distaste until they caved and brought him a pair of scrubs from somewhere. These he regarded with only slightly less contempt but was eventually persuaded to wear.

There were a deeply uncomfortable number of tubes to remove from Dominic's body. He tried to joke his way through it and not think too closely about how he'd nearly spent the rest of his life in that bed.

The doctor did a thorough physical, checking Dominic's vitals again and again, like she didn't believe what she was seeing. She tried to check the wound too, but when Dominic lifted up the gown, it was gone. Entry and exit both.

Like it had never happened.

It was four hours before Dominic could convince anyone he was ready to leave, and by that point, he was about ready to have Gestalt draw him a Door.

His car had been put in long-term parking at the hospital, courtesy of the Troy police department. Micah had already gone through Dominic's duffel and brought him a set of clean clothes.

"For when you woke up," Micah explained, and Dominic didn't like the hollow edge his voice took on when he said it.

The hallway was full of people—silent, wide-eyed people. Dominic froze in the doorway, looking out across the crowd with more than a little apprehension.

"Micah?"

"The other slaves," Micah explained. "They're glad you're awake."

Dominic nodded, silently, then gave them a little wave. "Hi," he said weakly. He wasn't used to being stared at.

Gestalt pushed past, out the door, and the crowd moved back as a unit, letting the daiyura pass. Some of them reached out to touch him as he walked by, their fingertips resting lightly against the black feather marks on his arms.

Dominic followed, keeping his head down. He was glad he had Micah at his back.

Someone began to hum, and the others must have known the song, because they picked it up quickly.

The three of them stepped into the elevator, and Dominic turned to look at the gathered crowd. They smiled back at him, and the doors slid shut on the sound of music.

EPILOGUE

∞

Eighteen months later

"Dude, come see this. The guy built a helicopter out of a taxidermied cat."

Micah scowled from his place at the kitchen table. "I'm trying to study. Anyway, I saw it."

"How does that even happen in someone's head?" Dominic mused, ignoring him. "Who looks at a dead cat and thinks, 'Man, this needs to fly'?"

"Maybe he's a case," Micah answered, not looking up from his textbook.

Dominic groaned, rolling off the couch and going to look over Micah's shoulder. "Give it a rest; you know that crap forward and backward. You're gonna strain something if you keep staring at it." He leaned down, pressing a kiss to the side of Micah's throat. "Let's do something fun."

"You're incorrigible," Micah muttered, but Dominic could hear the smile in his voice. He closed his eyes and focused, sending Micah images of massage oils and candles and this nifty nubby little back massager they'd gotten—

"The exam is in three days," Micah griped. "I'm never going to be a controller if I can't get the damn phylum straight."

"You're going to be a controller either way," Dominic assured him, kissing his way down Micah's shoulder. He sent an image of Micah, from behind, pulling his shirt over his head.

Micah sent Dom a picture of himself, locked in the woodshed.

Dominic laughed. "Stop worrying."

Micah rolled his eyes. "No."

They were interrupted by a crash. Ges stumbled across the living room floor, hitting the edge of the couch and almost going down.

Micah was on his feet in a second. "You okay?"

Gestalt shook his head, laughing. "Misjudged the difference in velocity. It was a large jump."

"And how is Australia this time of year?" Dominic asked, watching Micah check Ges over for damage.

"Hot," Ges answered simply. "Dry. Filled with things that bite. Very beautiful, though."

"This isn't healing, Ges," Micah interrupted.

Gestalt looked down, noting the tiny cut on his hand. "I think I'll survive, Micah."

"You need to stop going so long between transfers," Micah insisted. He sat down on the couch, pulling Ges on top of him so the daiyura was straddling his hips. Gestalt looked like he was going to protest, but Micah pulled him into a deep kiss before he could get the words out. Dominic could see the sparks of energy as their lips met. The cut on Ges's hand glowed with a pale amber light, and then vanished.

"Oh, sure, you'll quit studying for *him*," Dominic groused, but his heart wasn't in it. Even after all this time, there was something about seeing the two of them together that never failed to make him smile.

Ges pulled back, and Micah blinked sleepily up at him.

Dominic laughed. "C'mon, sleeping beauty, let's get you to bed before you pass out on the couch."

Dominic went to help him up, but Ges beat him to it, lifting the other man easily and carrying him into the bedroom.

"Romance isn't dead yet!" Dominic called after them. Micah grumbled something he didn't catch.

A few minutes later, Ges reappeared in the doorway. "He's asleep."

"He's right, you know," Dominic answered. "You need to stop going so long between transfers. You're cut off from your home world; all you've got is us now."

Gestalt shrugged, avoiding his eyes. "I forget. There is a lot to this world, and the experience of it is . . ." He held his hands out, turning them over as he contemplated them. "Different. In person."

Dominic didn't say anything. They'd been over this before.

Ges looked back at him. "I don't regret it, you know. Staying here with you."

Dominic nodded. He knew that too. Ges had never said it; he didn't need to. One of the great benefits of mind reading.

"Speaking of mind reading," Gestalt said casually, sidling up beside Dominic, "I believe you and Micah were saying something about massage oil, before I showed up?"

"You are the *worst* angel." Dominic laughed, leaning down to kiss him.

"But I'm yours," Ges answered, and Dominic had no argument with that.

Explore more of *The Powers That Be* series at:
riptidepublishing.com/collections/series-the-powers-that-be

Dear Reader,

Thank you for reading Hazel Domain's *Any Cost*!

We know your time is precious and you have many, many entertainment options, so it means a lot that you've chosen to spend your time reading. We really hope you enjoyed it.

We'd be honored if you'd consider posting a review—good or bad—on sites like **Amazon, Barnes & Noble, Kobo, Goodreads, Twitter, Facebook, Tumblr,** and your blog or website. We'd also be honored if you told your friends and family about this book. Word of mouth is a book's lifeblood!

For more information on upcoming releases, author interviews, blog tours, contests, giveaways, and more, please sign up for our weekly, spam-free newsletter and visit us around the web:

Newsletter: riptidepublishing.com/newsletter
Twitter: twitter.com/RiptideBooks
Facebook: facebook.com/RiptidePublishing
Goodreads: tinyurl.com/RiptideOnGoodreads
Tumblr: riptidepublishing.tumblr.com

Thank you so much for Reading the Rainbow!

RiptidePublishing.com

ALSO BY HAZEL DOMAIN

The Powers That Be
Any Price
Broken Contracts

ABOUT THE AUTHOR

∞

Hazel Domain is a cryptid who escaped Ohio and can now be found roaming the woods of eastern Maine. Hazel spends their time fixing computers, fiddling with databases, making renaissance faire costumes and, when all alternatives have been exhausted, writing.

Hazel has five Nanowrimo certificates, a doctorate in parapsychology, and a cat.

Tumblr: .tumblr.com/hazeldomain
Twitter: twitter.com/HazelDomain
TikTok: tiktok.com/@theehazeldomain

www.ingramcontent.com/pod-product-compliance
Lightning Source LLC
LaVergne TN
LVHW091121080826
845145LV00008B/2007